The High Priest of Hallelujah

by

Robert Nichols

Mountain Muse Publishing

ISBN: 978-0-9980910-1-3
Paperback Fiction
©1999 Robert Nichols
©2017 Robert Nichols
All rights reserved

ISBN: 978-0-9861050-0-5
 e-Book Edition
©2015 Robert Nichols
All rights reserved
BOD ISBN
Request for information should be addressed to:

Robert Nichols
Box 406
Lincoln City, OR 97367

MtMuse44@aol.com

Cover art and design, typesetting
sundry custodial / mechanical / technical toil—
and writing by Robert Nichols.

Dedication

To Carol and Kristin
whose love makes me real.

Table of Contents

Other Works by Robert Nichols

PART ONE

Sometimes I hear her laughter and yet I know nobody's around but me. I'm alone and the breath-close beauty of laughing love is right here with me, making me ache for the sweet sorrow of what never again can be.

That's the way it is with Lori and me.

When we first got married a buddy of mine said, "Jackson, she's such a great **looking** woman."

And it was true. She was a beautiful woman. But I've never really thought of her as a woman. That sounds so mature. But she wasn't a girl either. I think we need a new word for females of any age who are old enough to be called "women" but **light** enough of spirit to defy the serious status of earth-mother womanhood.

She was like that. A woman-girl. A lady-child. And, in any case, she was only twenty-three when she was killed. Pretty young for anyone to be terminally labeled an adult, don't you think?

And us…it **wasn't** as if we were mature for our ages or anything so dreadful as that. No, we were the best of young lovers— carefree enough to be childlike and just **lus**ty enough to make pleasure a grown-up game. Old enough to vote and drink whiskey and get into dirty movies if we were so inclined; but young enough so it was still all toys and dreams with us.

Sometimes I can see her so vividly. It's been years, but her image is etched into that fleeting realm of elusive recollection accessible only by an unsuspecting glance. Etched and deathly still she lingers there like a painting. I could tell you about the depth of her eyes and the way her dark blonde hair draped the nape of her neck. I could tell you the naked wonder of her and you, too, could know her like a work of art. But I won't.

Let it suffice that my friend was right. She was "a great **looking** woman."

I remember how I answered his compliment, and I wasn't being facetious. "Sure she's beautiful, but the best thing about her is she laughs at my jokes." And that's the best, and of course, the most painful part of her that I still possess. Her laughter is what haunts and blesses me. Such sweet cruelty, her laughter is yet alive. So clearly it speaks to me—the music of sensually-softened chimes ringing ever within me. How I cherish the agony of hearing it.

Brother Earl

In addition to pounding, punching, grinding, melting, fusing, cutting, polishing, and drilling machines; in factories there is a contraption that bends metal. Large sheets of material can be fed into its wide mouth and, with a growl and a puff of air, be bent into a "V" of predetermined angle. If one looks around at all of the bent pieces of metal in our world, the value of such a machine becomes obvious. There are various names used to designate this category of equipment, however, I always called the one I operated for eight to ten hours a day, six days a week, "You Son of a Bitch." My time card read, "Blake, Jackson W., Machine Operator—Brake Bar."

It was a huge plant and the Brake Bar Department was buried deep in the middle of the building in a region isolated from the physical or mental egress of windows or doors. While the energies of machines tirelessly fashioned integral components for the industrial complex, changing seasons could easily slip silently upon the earth-scape without notice. I felt trapped and escaped at every opportunity. In the ten-minute rest period given the Brake Bar Department each morning and again each afternoon, by jogging, and thus violating a basic tenet of occupational safety, I was able to zigzag through stacks of materials and around great, rumbling machinery, dash frantically down forklift freeways, and finally make my way to one of the fire doors on the perimeter of the factory; look through the dust-covered window or sometimes even dare to step outside a door for a furtive breath of the sky-roofed world; then reluctantly retrace my rapid route; and return to my machine just in time to begin work again.

What price too great for sanity?

It was after such a marathon that I stood before the vista-green and safety-yellow hulk of my machine, breathing heavily and cursing the two thousand three hundred forty-six pieces I had yet to bend on my current work order (before I would once again have the joy of setting up and starting another work order). Just as the hypnotic rhythm of production was lulling me into the drift of another afternoon, from the shadowed aisle that passed behind the machines, over the grumble and growl of the puffing progenitors of the American Gross National Product, I heard a voice that I will never forget. It was a whine of a voice straining over the roaring din.

"Why do y'all do that, boy?"

It startled me from daydreams. "Do what?" I asked.

"Take off a-runnin' ever time the break whistle goes off like some kinda rabbit with dogs on his tail. That's what." The man still had not appeared from behind the machine, but I recognized his voice as being that of one of the spot welder operators from the next section over. Earl was his name.

."So, what's it to you what I do with my break.

"Jus' tell me what 'ur up to, Boy, don't worry none about my reasons."

"Sure," I said. Life was still pretty innocent back then and who was I to complicate its mysteries by trying to understand them? So, in a voice shouted over the rumble of machinery, I answered his question. "I feel closed in here with no windows. I just like to go over to the outside wall to look and see if it's raining, or snowing, or if an early autumn front might have cooled the summer heat for a few hours or if, right across the highway, there might be hordes of naked women assembling armies for an assault on the Getzman Refrigerator Factory. You never know if you don't look."

There was a momentary pause. Just as I was entertaining the pleasing thought that my inquisitor might have left, the voice spoke up and said, "I think you're crazy, boy."

"You're not the first," I replied.

"Don't you worry none about what's a-goin' on outside, Mister. You jus' tend to your own business in here."

"Why?" I asked in genuine amazement that anybody would give a hoot about my break-time activities. "What's wrong with taking a little stroll—it's my time, isn't it?"

And with a voice expressing not the slightest touch of amicability or human compassion, much less humor, he said, "It ain't natural, what you been a-doin' durin' break. God-fearin' workin' men sit down and drink Pepsi-Cola pop when the whistle blows and don't waste their time buttin' into God's work outside a window.

With considerable self-control restraining an outburst of either laughter or anger, perhaps both, I retorted. "But I have loved ones out there."

"So you do, Boy. So you do," spoke the harsh whinny of a voice.

The guy was really starting to get to me. What right did he have to intrude in my business?

"What do you do, keep track of all the sinners for God?" I asked with indignation, though I was still on the verge of laughing at the ridiculous situation.

"'At's right, Boy," he said and then with a sudden, chilling shift in dialect, with words and intonation spoken from rote he said, "And if you persist in this irreverent activity then most certainly, you will burn in the eternal flames of Hell."

And the voice was gone.

I was twenty-four years old, going to night school to get a college education so as to better myself, being one hundred percent faithful to Lori, my beautiful bride of eight months, getting to work on time every day even though the monotony of the job was giving me an ulcer—all the ingredients for pure Americana—and I was already damned to Hell. And just for taking a glance out a factory window.

"A fella doesn't have a chance, You Son of a Bitch," I laughingly said to my machine.

Obviously, at that tender age, I had no concept of the scope and power of ignorance.

I was damned.

Damned.

You know, it's funny though. During all the years that had led me from the cradle to the Getzman Refrigerator Factory, I had quietly, unpretentiously assumed myself to be blessed. I had never been exceptional at any of my endeavors, but had always assumed whatever distraction that was currently enveloping my life—whether it be school, household chores, or a massive stack of metal in need of bending—was just that: a temporary detour from some profound path, predetermined by birth or the alignment of constellations and planets or just by immense good fortune, which would surely lead me to greatness.

So certain was I of this grand destiny, I had seldom made any overt attempts to seek it out. I figured the proper course would be blatantly obvious once the forces of fate had maneuvered me

5

into position. In the meantime I spent days in front of factory machinery, evenings attending night classes at a nearby university, and weekends studying dull books and basking in the pleasures of my young wife. It wasn't such a bad way to spend my time while waiting around for the real purpose of my life to magically emerge.

And then Earl came along and shipped me off to Hell.

"Well, rats," I said to the son of a bitch and all it said was "growl-puff, growl-puff."

My mother and sister had been the religious contingent of our family. Dad didn't have much to say about such matters—come to think of it, he might have been waiting around for his own call to destiny, just like me. But Mom was a seriously religious woman and the only thing she was waiting around for was the second coming of Christ so she could get on to Heaven where there wasn't so damned much housework. She wasn't waiting so much as she was "putting up with." However, we were a tolerant lot, seldom prone to the kinds of theological discussions that so often lead to familial schisms. Actually, the rites deemed precious to my sister and mother often proved advantageous to Dad and me. By the time they were just mumbling down to the last "Amen" of grace, we usually had our plates filled.

Throughout my childhood, though my mother never damned me—she loved me and wouldn't think of such a thing—she did fairly regularly find subtle means of instructing me about God's punishment for the wrongdoer. But there was one less-than-subtle occasion when Mother lowered the Judeo-Christian boom upon my young soul and, somehow, her lesson associating God's love with excruciating pain proved to be a precursor to the dreadful times forthcoming with Earl. Upon that fateful day at the Getzman Refrigerator Factory, I was no stranger to the threat of Divine Retribution.

I recall a time from my childhood in Missouri. The humidity and heat had formed their annual alliance producing a level of discomfort that was almost unbearable. I was at the difficult developmental plateau known as early adolescence and, true to the dictates of this chemically and mentally disoriented stage, prided myself in entertaining those who shared my small world by accomplishing feats of unequalled bad taste. My mid-adolescent sister and early middle-aged parents were sitting around the kitchen table trying to consume the evening's repast with as little heat-producing movement as possible. Shirtless and sweaty, I came rushing in from a stimulating afternoon of spitting at grasshoppers in the backyard of my best friend, Chester Jennings, III.

To the pubescently twisted perception of my mind, the situation was ideal for performing a new trick of my own creation perfected that very morning. The whole family was assembled, the tension of physical discomfort emanating from the table could only enhance the effectiveness of my depraved attempt at humor, the stifling heat would likely lessen the possibility of violent physical reaction on the part of my father: no better stage could have been set for my mad performance.

Naked to the waist, in a rush I dashed into the kitchen with such flourish I immediately commanded the listless attention of my beloved family. Taking a short bow, I then deftly flopped upon my back in the middle of the floor. With the bodily control of a yogi, by moving my shoulders and pelvis and utilizing the sealing effects of the moisture that drenched my bare flesh, I created in the pocket formed between the linoleum floor and the curvature of my spine, a vacuum.

"What foolishness are you up to now?" my mother asked in the monotone of her summer apathy.

"Oh, Mother Dear, I fear I am becoming ill," I quavered. Then, in one great, swelling upheaval, I arched my back, thus allowing the damp warm air to be sucked noisily along the whole contour of my body from shoulder blades to waistline—creating a fart-like sound of enormous proportion.

With demonic grin upon my lean face, I forestalled the howling laughter crowding the confines of my diaphragm so as to observe the reactions of my family. Father actually was unable to suppress a smile and had to turn away to avoid bestowing the unthinkable reward of laughing at me. Sister rolled her eyes in disgust and said, "God help us, Mother, does he have to live here?" And Mother, exercising a supreme degree of personal restraint, sternly said, "That will be quite enough, Jackson!"

But, remember, I was an early adolescent—by no earthly reach of the imagination was it "quite enough." Immediately I began rapidly undulating on the floor, producing a veritable storm of rattling obnoxiousness accentuated by the nasal rasping of my thirteen-year-old hysteria.

Then I managed to suck a vertebra out of alignment and, with a gasp, grew silent in semi-paralytic throes of incredible pain. My mother looked up toward Heaven as if to say, "Take me now, Lord, take me now." Then, after muttering a few words of prayer, the look of bewilderment slid from her face and with a smile that knew the Source of eternal justice, she stared into my wretched eyes and pronounced, without the least hint of malice and in tones of a loving and responsible parent, His holy judgement.

She said, "See."

So it was that the events of the days following the threat of Earl, the spot welder, were not without precedent in my personal history. A couple of days had passed since his first appearance and I was hard at work bending metal. "You Son of a Bitch!" I raged at my machine. "Do you realize we've got three hours to go yet?"

And the machine said, "Growl-puff, growl-puff, growl-puff."

Sometimes it seemed that the entire momentum of my young life was forever stalled with three more hours left to the workday afternoon. It had all the symptoms of another abysmally dull day when from out of the shadows appeared the face and form of the bearer of the voice of my condemnation. In an ambivalent Ozark-mountain-East-Texas-Oklahoma whine, he said, "Hi! My name's Brother Earl. Does y'all like country music?"

He was less than five and a half feet tall, stout, bordering on being fat. And, glaring from their notch above the ruddy swell of his cheeks and beaming smile, was the coldest set of eyes I had ever seen.

I had just recommenced the manufacturing process following my afternoon break. Two days had passed since my first encounter with Holy Earl. I had not made my ten-minute dash for the daylight due to a recent lesson I had received which updated my appreciation of the might of Divine Retribution. Within an hour of my initial encounter with the strange voice of *Godfearin'* folk, while waiting in line for a sandwich at lunch, a machine operator from the spot welding section had accidentally dropped a fifty-five pound tool box on my right foot. Not only had it hurt a great deal, and not only had there been no indication of the slightest trace of regret on the part of the conveniently clumsy

8

spot welder, but also, when in great pain, I limped back from the clinic and began working again, there was a familiar country voice from behind The Son of a Bitch that said, "See."

He had asked the question, "Does y'all like country music?"

My foot was hurting, my spirit daunted by the reality of three more hours of bending steel before another four hours of the near-insuperable tedium of night school, and I knew that in some way the beady-eyed bastard standing in front of me had arranged for the flattening of my favorite foot—but I thought, forget it, I'll tell the fool what he wants to hear.

"Yeah," I lied, "I'm crazy about country music."

Normally, I can say I'm a very honest person. That is, honest except in certain situations where diplomacy and survival are at stake. Working in factories there were occasions that necessitated a lessening of the truth just for the sake of human relations. If I had ever honestly expressed my opinion of possum huntin' to the hillbillies, drag racin' to the city guys, or the rise and fall of the Roman Empire to John Bonkowsky, the Polish machinist/world historian, I would have been ostracized for being a jerk. But, rarely had I been blatantly dishonest and usually then only with some justification—say, in matters of life and death or honor. Such had been the case months earlier when I lied to the scariest guy at the factory.

The fiercest, most frightening man who worked at the Getzman Refrigerator Factory was a big black forklift operator named Zed. Zed had devil eyes and huge muscles. He roared around the aisles of the plant on a lift truck that smoked and popped and spat fire. In the wake of his intermittent passing there were not only choking clouds of carbon monoxide but, also, whispered tales of the horrible things he had done with knives and bare hands. Even the foreman of the material handlers, Tony, the Italian Tyrant, would never dare to address Zed in any but the most guarded tones. The shop superintendent, Nervous Charlie, was visibly terrified at the very presence of the man.

It was late on a Friday afternoon in December—almost quitting time. Lori and I had decided, since night school was out for Christmas break and Friday was payday and her mother was on the verge of noticing I was sharing an apartment with her daughter, that we would get married when I got home from work. Though we had made our decision a week or so earlier, I had attempted to forego the verbal jostling associated with such occasions by concealing the event from co-workers. However, one of my fellow factory guys had talked to Lori when she was waiting for me in the parking lot the night before and, by ten o'clock Friday morning, everyone in my department was making fun of me.

"Jackson's gonna get some, Jackson's gonna get some," they said. "College Boy's gonna get laid."

"Let them have their childish fun, you Son of a Bitch," I said to my machine.

Men were starting to gather inconspicuously in corners and nooks near time clocks in anticipation of the afternoon whistle. There was muffled laughter and a general salivation at the nearing prospect of happy-hour beers in various roadside taverns and neighborhood bars.

Then, suddenly, with charging engine and squealing tires, Zed, the forklift-man, burst into the scene and screeched to a stop. All became quiet. A sinister cloud of exhaust vapor filled the area.

"Hey," he barked in a deep, gruff voice, "I want to talk to you."

In the focus of his scathing attention I felt the heat of his terrible eyes.

"Yeah, you. Come on over here. I got something to say to you, Blake."

"Oh, Jesus, he even knows my name" I said to myself as I stumbled obediently toward the menacing figure on the idling forklift. It seemed so unfair that my short life should end on the very threshold of entering into a respectable relationship with the girl I loved.

Feeling small and weak, I stood before the evil machine. From high up on the seat, the man leaned his huge, muscular frame threateningly toward me and said, "I hear you're getting married tonight. That right?"

"Yes, Mr. Zed, I'm supposed to get married this evening. That is, if I am fortunate enough to live so long."

There was a pause as he contemplated my answer. Then he asked, "This girl, she nice lookin'?"

"Yes, Sir, I think she's beautiful," I replied cautiously.

Another pause—his eyes staring off into the smoky gloom beyond me and then refocusing on mine. "You ever screw her yet?"

And without a flinch, I opted for Lori's honor over my own male pride, "No, Sir," I lied. "Not yet."

No one within earshot had taken an audible breath since his arrival. Slowly and pensively he scratched his head with his massive left hand.

Finally, he spoke. Revving the motor to a rattling snarl, he shouted, "Well, then maybe you'd better rub her boobies a little bit first!" and, with a roar and the blackest billow of smoke ever belched from the innards of an internal combustion engine, he was gone.

Lies.

What the heck, I thought if I can lie to Zed I can easily lie to this squatty-assed bastard from spot welding.

"Yeah, I like country music," I said. "If it weren't for my complete collection of Buck Owens albums, I don't know how me and the missus could ever get through a Saturday night."

I had fallen right into his trap.

"You're lyin' ta me, Boy," said the man with cold eyes squinting from the pressure of his smile which had shifted from that of pseudo-friendliness to smug self-righteousness. "Y'all don't like country music at all."

"I don't like country music?"

"No sir. You can't lie to me, Boy. I see right through it all. I know you're lyin' because I know the Truth and the Truth has set me free! Praise the Lord! I know the lies of heathens."

"How do I get into these situations, You Son of a Bitch?" I said to my machine.

"Go ahead, Sinner. You can call me names, you can blaspheme, profane, and defame 'til you turn blue—but you just as well admit it here and now, Boy: Y'all don't like country music. I see it right there in your lyin' face."

"My foot hurts! Who are you anyway?"

"My name is Brother Earl and I know the Ways of the Serpent."

"I'm sure you do, Earl."

"I know the Truth and it has set me free. Now you tell Brother Earl the truth—you're lyin', aint you?"

I just shook my head and said, "Well, Earl, since you obviously can look right into core of my deceitful soul, I've got to fess up. You've caught me here in the middle of a blatant act of deception. You've got me dead to rights, Earl. To tell the truth, I think country music is a mournful, maudlin, self-pitying, sleazy bunch of noise—I can't stand it. Yes, I lied. Country music is crap, Earl. Do you hear me? Crap!"

"Amen!" he shouted. "Now you're talkin', Boy. You tell old Earl the truth and he'll help you out of this heathen mess you're in. We're gonna put a stop to this irreverent behavior everywhere, ya hear."

"What a relief this is to me. I mean, it's about time that someone put an end to all the evil ways of man. And what a privilege it is for me to be blessed by the good fortune of actually meeting, face to face, The Messiah returned right here at the Getzman Refrigerator Factory. I didn't even have to follow a star to find you."

"Don't you get smarty-mouthed around me, Boy. I know the reward for those who don't fear the Lord. I know just what happens to sinners. You'd better listen to Brother Earl—you don't want to get me too riled up. I know the terrible power of righteousness against the blasphemy of the Devil."

"Tell me, Earl, just how does it feel to walk on water?"

"You're tryin' me, Son. Now I've been watchin' your devilish ways and you've been warned about bein' irreverent and you've had your foot stomped flat by the *Will* of God. Don't press me no more. I know the power of the Lord and you'd better believe me, Brother Earl will use it to educate the sinner, to bring sinners of the world to the righteous path. I know the Ways of the Serpent."

Something of inordinate proportion was happening. A man was going into a full-scale evangelistic rage at me for refusing to drink soft drinks and sit around talking about huntin' and fishin'. I had become the prime target for the wrath of his holy madness and, in my youth, had no better sense than to further provoke the fool.

"You turn Pepsi-Cola into wine and maybe I'll start listening to you."

And slowly, with heat he pronounced his doom upon me. "That done it, Boy," he said as he turned away, looking back over his shoulder as he moved into the shadows, smiling like a pious demon. "Brother Earl has warned you and now you shall know his wrath, sinner." And he was gone.

I laughed so loudly that the man at the next work station heard me over the "growl-puff, growl-puff" of his machine and stopped to gaze in my direction as if I were crazy.

2 Tracks

A seer once told me about the Spirit Guides who accompany invisible levels of our consciousness—tracking the movements of our own existences. Sometimes they hover behind and take account of the impressions we have made upon the paths we follow. Sometimes they scout the trails ahead and, if we are willing to hear their wisdom, hazards of the journey can be averted. But in the rapid pace of this world, often it is all they can do to rush along as, in hot pursuit, our awareness shadows the events of our own lives.

At times the trails follow solid ground; at times they lead us over the edge of seemingly bottomless abysses.

It was raining. A radio was playing sadly in a distant corner of my apartment. Lori—my bride, my laughter, my ambition, my heart—was dead.

Then, later, it was snowing outside a classroom window. Dr. Byron M. Fintin, Professor of English, was mumbling in the distant background, and my precious Lori was dead.

Much later, on a bright Saturday morning with bird-sounds and lilac smells, a warm sun shone through the window of the bedroom and the stirrings of yet another blessed spring were all about me but Lori, my love, was dead.

Finally, it was June. Lori had been dead for nine months. Long before she was murdered I had promised her I would finish my college degree and, because of that promise made to a living person, I quit my job. It happened, her murder that is, on a Sunday afternoon two days after my second encounter with Brother Earl— and I never went back to the factory. I didn't return to pick up my tools, my quart jar of Kosher dill pickles, my paycheck—I never entered the Getzman Refrigerator Factory again. Instead, I withdrew most of what Lori and I had ironically referred to as our life savings and enrolled as a full-time student at the university so as to finish in two semesters what would have taken three or four in night classes.

It was June and I was standing outside a college auditorium

13

sweltering beneath the ludicrous anachronism of a thick, black, medieval gown after having participated in a ritual marking the completion of the task I had promised— terminating any obligation on my part to exist.

"I suppose congratulations are in order, Mr. Blake. I must admit, I never thought of you as one who would finish his degree." Professor Fintin was a tall, thin man who almost looked dignified, but not quite. If he had been a judge or a doctor or a Roto-Rooter Man he might have carried it off, but there is some inherent weakness in many English professors that subtly diminishes their stature and forces them to the desperation of intellectual arrogance.

Fintin had been the most prominent aggravation vexing my tragic commitment to finish an education and, as such, had unwittingly extended my lifespan by grueling months. A promise is one thing; survival is another. In his overwhelmingly pedantic style of instruction, there were elements so exasperating to me that, of all the potentially effective stimuli I had experienced in those lifeless hours and weeks following her death, he alone had generated enough ire in me to penetrate the otherwise benumbed core of my being. I had hated the haughty prick— and stayed alive.

There were weekends—weekends were the worst—when, after I had exhausted my ability to persevere in studies of the trivial and complex and had run out of beer and, due to blatantly masochistic tendencies, had directly confronted the specter of death that dwelled with me in the mockery of our apartment (sleeping in our bed, eating at our table), sometimes the only thing that saved me from the alluring pits of oblivion was focusing all of my self-destructive energies on the thought of how much I detested the pompous ass.

"Thank you, Dr. Fintin." I said. "I would have never made it without you."

"Oh, really. I didn't realize I had that much influence on you, Blake. It does this old pedagogue good to hear that his insight and conviction might have served as an inspiration to a student."

"Believe me, reflections on your teaching got me through some rather precarious times."

"Strange. It never occurred to me that you were the kind of individual who reflected much about anything, much less the lofty lessons of the bards. You were always so subdued in my classes. I simply assumed your silence was a result of a profound lack of knowledge."

"Times have been a bit strained for me recently, Professor."

"Yes, I understand, Blake, terrible thing about your wife, terrible… uh… er…. tell me, what are your plans now that you have completed your baccalaureate degree?"

"Oh, they're very simple, Dr. Fintin. There is no complexity to my future at all."

"I see. Then you've got matters pretty well mapped out, do you?"

"Yes, indeed. I have absolutely no question about the direction of my life."

"Such confidence," he said and laughed the same disdainful laugh that had echoed countless times off the stilted walls of his classroom. "Such naïveté. Young man, nobody knows exactly what is going to happen in the next minute, much less the next day or, as you seem to believe, in his whole lifetime. Surely, this is not what you're asserting: that you have a soothsayer's vision of your own destiny. Bosh. For a moment there I thought you might have really learned something from the literature and my lectures."

"God help you if you ever begin to know half of what I've learned in this life, Professor. And, yes, I do claim to know exactly the course of my lifetime."

"Come now, Blake," he said, ignoring the intent of my words. "You're not serious. I can't believe anyone as old as you and as well-educated would be foolish enough to actually stand here before me and say he knows precisely what he is going to do with the rest of his entire life."

"Believe it. It's all very simple."

"Well, pray tell, Mr. Blake, enlighten me. What is this absolute plan you are going to initiate tomorrow?" He was irked at the assurance of my answers but he deserved to be irked at the exaggerated confidence of another human being in matters of a subjective nature. Damn the hours I had spent listening to his static interpretations of the vitality and moment of literature.

"I can tell you exactly what I'm going to do with my life, Sir. At 2:17 tomorrow morning I'm going to end it."

I had finally forced the professor to react to something he hadn't said himself. He was momentarily shocked and then, construing my statement to be sarcasm, angered.

"You certainly don't take the future very seriously, do you, Blake?"

There was perceptible element of disgust in his voice—I relished it.

"To the contrary, Professor, I probably take the future more seriously than anyone you've ever met. I take it so seriously that, in fact, I am going to eliminate its potential for dabbling into my affairs any further. The future is but a terrible place where more bad times are waiting to happen to all of us, even college professors. And, theologically speaking, I can assure you any intellectual analysis of reality which doubts the existence of an all-powerful force determining the course of the universe is erroneous. There is a Force that has the ability to manipulate the future of our planet and of each of us who individually stumble across its surface. And here's the best part, Dr. Fintin—the undeniable truth that makes the concept of the future such a ludicrous notion—the Force that runs this game of stars and oceans, pretty girls and professors is absolutely malevolent."

"'Malevolent,' you say?" There was something missing from his voice. He suddenly sounded much less uppity-British, much more human.

"You've got that right, Professor," I was on a roll. There was no cause for restraint. "A vicious, evil force controls every drop of rain or blowing mote of dust and curses every hopeless, life-dashed second of existence."

"My God, Blake... Jackson is it?"

"Jackson."

"Jackson, I believe you actually intend on taking your own life."

"Now we're getting somewhere, Doctor. We are finally establishing communication on a level you used to say only existed between poets and people with Ph.Ds. in English literature. We're beginning to speak an absolute truth aren't we?"

"Calm down, Young Man. I understand." Again, there was a human touch to his voice that had never once entered the sanctimonious realm of his classroom. There was almost a hesitation in the flow of his words as if something was shaking within him. "This is all because of your wife's death, isn't it? You lost your wife and now you want to die."

I couldn't let it go. I couldn't just appreciate his first shot at humanity and return to the awful seclusion of my inner self.

"You put that so well, so tactfully, Dr. Fintin—'lost my wife'— it sounds as if she might have wandered off into the moonlit marsh of some mythical sea or was taken by the mist of an early morning or just plain misplaced somewhere out there in the clutter of it all. I lost her all right." And then, in sing-song-y madness I sang, "'I lost my wife and I'll **lose** my life, said Barnacle Bill the sailor." I was clearly losing it. "How pleasant. Lost their mittens, lost those damned mittens again, naughty fucking kittens."

"Allow me to rephrase… "

"No, no. You said it right. Lost. Do you want to hear how she was lost?"

"I read about it in the paper. An appalling accident—dreadful. Unfortunate."

"Dreadful indeed. I'll tell you exactly how she was lost. She was alive—laughing, loving, soft-fleshed and music-voiced—and then in an instant she was struck stiff and stone-eyed, dead and black like bad toast. Charred and, oh, so very dead."

All of those months of simmering silence and then I boiled my heart empty to a dried-up old windbag of a teacher.

After a moment to allow me to regain my composure, Dr. Fintin asked, "Perhaps this is a foolish question, but how on earth did you determine the exact moment of your impending suicide to be, what was it, 2:17 a.m.?"

"That's the exact time a sixty-mile-per-hour freight train passes behind Izzy's Highway Hamburger Haven."

"Izzy's Hamburger Haven?"

"Yes—delightful place to eat. You'll have to take an evening's repast there sometime. I highly recommend the 'Burger *a la* cheese and onion.'"

"There must be some sentimental reason for Izzy's and the 2:17 train."

"Indeed there is, Sir.

"I see."

Bullshit. He couldn't see. I was the only survivor in the land of the living to *see*. Once there were two of us in the entire world who understood the significance of the intersection of a train, a hamburger joint, and love. Now there was but one.

We, Lori and I, had only gone out together a few times. She was a beautiful and delicate young lady, full of the stirrings which motivate life but none of the weighty experiences that make it real. I was a year older, a man of travel and experience, and she had allowed herself to be dazzled by my distances and seduced by the laughter I had given her.

The lights at Izzy's were just being turned off when we pulled into the parking lot. It didn't matter, our appetites had little to do with hamburgers. I parked the car in the back of the deserted lot and we sat so close. We were laughing at irrelevant matters as we circled closer and closer to the good feelings that were happening in our closeness. The last dishwasher at Izzy's finally left and we were alone in the quiet.

It was a fresh warm night and she said, "Let's get out of the car."

There was a board fence along the back of the lot. We walked around it and into the blue-edged darkness cast by the mercury vapor lights burning eternally over the drive-in. We walked down across a wide gully lined with soft grass and up the other side to the railroad track. Standing on the gravel roadbed, I kissed her and in a smooth, heated rush of expectation exalting in discovery, I felt her warm lips and then her arms and then the press of her body tight against me, and forever the lush excitement of her whole being enmeshed with my mortal essence. There was no need to speak of love. The only sounds were of breathing and the rustle of our clothing as we clasped each other in a bond existing from that moment until she had no more moments.

With a startling blast of air horn, dreadful rumble, and the glare of brilliant headlight, the night train tore upon us. We held our ground and our embrace tightened in the terror and excitement of the mass of energy and noise and danger roaring upon us and past us only a few feet from our fragile bodies.

And in the mad peak of that love and exhilaration and the terrifying sound and motion she said, "Make love to me, Jackson. Take me right now. Make me yours."

And, hence, the 2:17 rendezvous with a deadly train. Just a final touch of sentiment and I would be finished with the sorrow that had become my life. In one final and definitive encounter, I would once again know the horrendous and wonderful power that had drawn us into sexual and emotional unity, and say to that part of night which is death, "Take me right now. Make me yours."

"Jackson," the professor said with a tone of voice which was less aloof than any I had ever heard him utter, "it is terrible to lose a loved one, I beg your pardon, to have someone we love die. Five years ago my wife became ill and died, and, believe me, after having twenty-five years of loving companionship, the emptiness I encountered was almost more than I felt I could bear. But, I survived, and in time I became glad I was still alive. My life will never be the same, but it is a life with some trace of pleasure, some substance yet—a life worth continuing."

"I'm sorry your wife is dead, Dr. Fintin. And I appreciate what you are saying, but, I don't think you understand the magnitude of my Lori's death. You had your loving years together; we did not. Your wife was the victim of a terrible disease; my wife was brutally murdered. In an indelible, eternal moment, all the wonders of a life to be were struck to never. There is a difference."

"Yes, of course," he said. "The shock would be more profound from the suddenness of her demise. And she was so very young." And then, almost as an aside, he said, "Sometimes it is most difficult to communicate what is most important to say. But, Jackson," he continued, "perhaps I am mistaken. Correct me if I am wrong. It is my recollection that your wife died as a result of an accident."

"No. She was murdered."

Dr. Fintin was normally pale of complexion, but, as he spoke he took on a starker shade of white. "Wasn't she struck by lightning?"

"Yes. That is correct."

3 More Tracks

I had honestly believed my decision "not to be" was as unchangeable as the events leading to it. But I was wrong. In my obsessive resolve, my Spirit Guide was to have rushed upon a spot where my tracks ceased on the edge of a void so absolute as to preclude even the most subtle trace of a trail. I wonder about this invisible companion of my awareness. Upon my suicide, would he have pitched forward over the abyss, following me beyond the disappearance of my tracks into nonexistence? Or, worse, would my self-destruction have cursed him to an eternal fate of wandering the brink of death, hopelessly seeking the lost trail, ever frustrated in quest of a future?

What a lousy thing to do to a faithful spirit.

"'To be or not to be' really is the question, isn't it, Blake?" asked Dr. Fintin, obviously pleased to have finally found a real situation upon which to apply a literary allusion.

Several hours had elapsed since departing our conversation at commencement. Immediately after I had given sufficient credibility to my plan for exiting this earthly plane and had clarified my belief that my beloved Lori had been murdered by God, a drastic change came over Dr. Fintin. His normal pale complexion going to ghastly white. "You're not just being cynical or iconoclastic are you?" he had asked.

"No, Sir, I am not. I would never deny a wealth of bitterness concerning the whole matter; but, now I can also speak of it with a strange, chilling objectivity. No matter what my emotional bias may be, over the past nine months, whenever I wasn't distracted by writing inane research papers for you and your colleagues, I expended considerable effort collecting a body of, though somewhat circumstantial, rather conclusive evidence proving the bolt of lightning that struck down my wife was not a blind and impersonal discharge of energy due to a natural process. It was certainly the malicious and premeditated weapon used in a killing perpetrated by none other than God: The Cosmic Murderer!"

There was a sudden glint in his eyes and he said, "Now I

remember who you are, Blake. You're the bloody fool who wrote those verbose monstrosities in lieu of producing the fruit of honest research for term papers. Yes, you're the one who created eleven thousand words of gibberish about Hamlet's aversion to taking definitive action being a result of Lady Gerturde's, as you put it, ' … piss-poor job of potty training little Ham.' I should have flunked you. I would have if it were not for a perverse sense of admiration for the sheer gall demonstrated by such reams of pure rubbish. And so sloppily produced on an elite typewriter and, as the coup de grâce, singly spaced."

"Yep," I grinned. "That was me, all right. I believe I detect a hint of appreciation for my quiet little rebellion against esoteric drivel. It was all somewhat therapeutic, you know. You'd be surprised how delving into petty matters can distract one from head-on confrontation with full-fledged reality."

"You might be surprised yourself, Jackson. The creation of volumes of malarkey is something I can appreciate more than I am normally willing to admit. I've produced several books which now sit in dusty abandonment on forgotten shelves of literate niches about the illiterate world. But, I can't believe even the most maniacal or fanatic of purposes could have driven you to single space that rubbish. There has to have been more to it than mere idealism or revolt."

"Well," I said sheepishly, "to tell the truth, it was my apartment. I just didn't think there was room in that tiny, haunted cell for anything as expansive as double spacing."

The scholar shook his head slowly and just stared at me.

"Don't worry, Dr. Fintin," I consoled. "It doesn't matter if I'm a bit mad. I'll be dead in a few hours anyway."

"Yes, Blake, I suppose we needn't worry too much about your mental state at this point."

"Not really."

"Say, Blake," he said as he reached down (he was several inches taller than I) and firmly clasped my left shoulder, "perchance, are you a drinking man?"

"Why, strange you should ask, Professor, on fairly frequent occasions I have been known to nip."

"Excellent," he said. "You've got hours to kill, pardon the pun. Why don't you abandon your graduation frock and we can continue this conversation over a couple of cold ones out at Sassy Sally's

Blue Bird Cafe and Lounge on Skintz Bottom Road? What do you say?"

It was incredible that the renowned pedant, Mr. Pomposity in the flesh, Doctor Byron (as in Lord Byron) M. (Milton) Fintin had even heard of a tavern of such bucolic distinction as Sally's Blue Bird. That he recommended we go there was baffling to the point of fascination. And, he was right, I had hours before it was time to throw myself under a freight train. I thought to myself that there was more to the professor than had heretofore met the eye.

"You'll listen to my theories about the murder of my wife?"

"Of course."

"Then I shall be glad to join you at Sassy Sally's. However, there is one problem."

"A tad short of funds, Blake?"

"A bit. But, that's not the problem I was talking about. The fact is I can't take off this graduation robe."

"Why not?"

"I'm naked under here. A week ago I sold all my earthly possessions and gave the money away. This morning I pitched the clothes I was wearing and put on this robe. I own nothing; I wear nothing."

"You have to turn in that robe. It's the final requirement for receiving your degree. The fake-leather folder they presented to you in the ceremony is empty. In addition to an extensive background in the humanities, competence in two foreign languages, a dabble of science, and years of concentrated study in your major area, the receipt of your liberal arts degree from this university finally hinges upon the return of that rented nightgown you are wearing."

"I never intended to pick up my degree—what good are credentials to a corpse?"

"Point well taken, Blake. Now tell the truth, not even a pair of skivvies?"

"Bare to the buff."

Standing before the learned professor was a naked man beneath a medieval frock.

Not to be flustered, he pressed on. "Very well, then. I'm going home and change clothes myself. Can you meet me at the tavern in about an hour and a half?"

"I'll be there, Dr. Fintin," I said.

"Fine, fine, fine... " he muttered—I think, "bare to the buff" had almost done him in. He dipped into the folds of one of his massive black sleeves and pulled out a five-dollar bill which he handed to me. "Buy yourself a drink and I'll meet you at the bar," he said, and with a nod he was gone.

"He doesn't really think I'm going to kill myself tomorrow in the early a.m., does he?" I said to no one. And then, with a dizzying sense of lightness, I asked, "I wonder if he might be right?"

(An explanation of why I went to the trouble of converting all of my material goods into cash: I didn't capitalize my couch, coats, and car so as to enhance the coffers of my family. My parents are sufficiently flush in their distant lives and my sister is married to a prominent West Coast architect. Therefore, there were no real demands upon my fortune which might have justified the need for generosity in my departure—actually, the sum I amassed in cashing in all of my chips would have been small change to any of them. The fact is, I turned all of my belongings into bucks so as to make a contribution to the Milton J. Larbletter Research Foudation of Bunn, North Carolina. Milton J. Larbletter, the founder and, as far as I knew, only human participant in the research project, was in the process of attempting to prove his theory that God is a huge energy field floating about the vastness of the universe affecting the movements of minute organisms like human beings by zapping them with energy waves so subtle no man other than himself had ever detected their existence. Though he had extensive theoretical documentation, his only physical evidence in support of the idea was produced by a machine of his invention with which, solely relying upon the radiation of these "Apocalyptic Rays" as he referred to them, he swore he could bake a potato in less than two minutes.

Why not? Perhaps he was right. In any case I decided to chip in—what the heck, maybe he would come up with a better God than the one I had turned up. At least the Cosmos is far enough removed that you can't feel the son of a bitch breathing down the back of your neck.

4 Beneath the Water

Gleeful graduates ambled the sidewalks of campus thinking, "Wahoo! I'm finally through with all this crap," but saying, "Thank you, Mom, thank you, Dad, thank you federally-subsidized education loan."

I ambled right along with my momentary peers—though I was the only one still wearing my graduation attire. So I suppose, in fact, I had already departed the dubious security of a peer group when they had exchanged silk for sheepskin and I had simply pitched my fake leather folder into a trash barrel. But, I did wander with them along the tree-arched paths of learning toward the parking lot at the edge of the campus, though it was only for lack of a more meaningful direction to travel—a week earlier I had sold my fifteen-year-old automobile along with my socks and electric skillet. (An entrepreneur of second-hand treasures had given me $125 for the car and another $50 for everything we could stuff inside it, or tie on top of it, or suspend from its sides by rope, wire, and faith-in-defiance-of-gravity. He bought everything I owned except for the clothes on my back. When he drove off, the old beast literally sagged from the weight the mattress and springs and couch and kitchen dinette and God knows what else upon its roof. As it passed I saw the bathroom scale go by—crammed against the back window with its bubble dial and grim numbers looking like the face of a lost soul.)

Any freshness that the morning might have possessed had been banished by the combination of heat, humidity, and the belabored profundity of the ceremony I had endured as a final, symbolic act of fidelity. Beneath the thickness of the heavy, black robe, I was perspiring miserably. Then I queried the apathetic solitude surrounding me, "Why should I be hot and uncomfortable on the last day of my life?" It didn't make sense. So, without altering my stately, baccalaureate gait, or changing the stoic expression on my face, I departed the smiling scores of scattering graduates proudly marching off with friends and loved ones to join the

24

exciting world of college-graduate America and walked into the duck pond.

One Sunday, years earlier, when I was really a kid—not a twenty-five-year-old widower with a death wish—I read a comic strip "featuring" Buzz Sawyer's pal, Roscoe Sweeney. In it, Roscoe accomplished an amazing feat. He was taking a hike and, when he came to a small lake, he just continued walking—right along the bottom, with the surface of the water well above his head. I loved the concept projected by the Sunday-color, cartoon image of him calmly meandering along the depths, as if the water had no effect upon his body. It was imagination's open contradiction of physics' laws of buoyancy. It was clearly spirit's supremacy over the immutable decrees of drab science, and I was immediately convinced that, with proper sense of determination, I, too, could defy the rote restrictions of textbooks.

The next afternoon, accompanied by my friend, Chester Jennings, III, rather than going directly home from the bus stop, I headed for the largest body of water in the neighborhood—a small ravine filled with water due to a chronically-clogged storm drain—where I fully intended to replicate what I had designated "The Sweeney Technique."

"It will never work," Chester had said—Chester the skeptic.

"Yeah it will," I assured him enthusiastically, "All I have to do is think real hard about staying on the bottom and, sure enough, that's where I'll be, just taking a stroll—BENEATH THE WATER!"

"Like poop, Jackson. Like poop!" said Chester. "You'll just float up to the surface and all you'll be is wet and in trouble with your mom and she'll send you to your room cuz you got your clothes wet and it's October and you'll probably catch a cold and get pneumonia and maybe even die or flunk fifth grade or worse and… "

"And what?" I asked—I knew my buddy Chester pretty well.

"And if you do it, I'll probably try it, too, and I'll get wet and my mom will get mad and…"

"Chester, Chester," I interrupted. "We'd all still be riding around on bicycles and watching the birds fly by if weren't for the Wright brothers having the courage to believe in an idea. Right?"

"Maybe."

"Sometimes you just have to take a chance—it's worth risking getting into a little trouble when you're out there advancing the progress of mankind. Right?"

25

"Jackson, you're full of poop."

"All right, Chester. Stand upon the shore as I walk into the future."

"Aw, heck. At least I'm going to take off my school shoes before I make a fool of myself." •

"That's the attitude, Chester. I tell you it'll work. Just think of what a wonderful discovery this will be for the world. We can teach the Sweeney Technique to the Army. We'll be heroes—just think of all the time and money the Infantry will save on bridges when the troops just take a deep breath, concentrate, and march right on into the water and, bingo, they'll be on the other side. All we have to do is show them, Chester. Trust me."

And then, two hours later, hungry for the dinner of which I had been deprived, bored by the narrow dimensions of my bedroom in which I was being confined, guilty about the trouble into which I had gotten my best friend, Chester Jennings, III, and bitter about the lesson I had learned of the limitations of even the most determined of human efforts— I was thinking about how easy it was for someone to draw a line and call it the surface of a pond and, then, with the flick of an artist's pencil, put a Roscoe Sweeney way down on the bottom where only a rock could walk without swirling arms and exhausting undulation of the entire body regardless of faith or willpower to the contrary.

But, all that occurred before I had bestowed upon myself the blessings of advanced study. Who can say the dreams of childhood cannot become reality through the benefits of a college education? On graduation day, by God, I walked right along the bottom of the University Duck Pond just like Roscoe Sweeney. If I had not spent vital years of my young life in laborious pursuit of obscure knowledge, then I would have never earned the right to wear a heavy black robe which, having absorbed a weighty quantity of duck-water, gave my body the added ballast needed to enable me to walk with normal motion and movement: BENEATH THE WATER!

Nobody paid much attention to me when I first headed for the pond. Perhaps a few might have momentarily escaped their own revelry and thought, "Look. How sentimental. A fellow graduate walking over to the water's brim for one last communion with the gently feathered beasts before heading out into the big world with the rest of us in quest of fame, fortune, and semi-annual debauches in Las Vegas."

But, of course, I heard no such thoughts. Thoughts make no sound—in each of our minds they are trapped until freed by expression. Regardless of intent, unless somehow told, they remain as secrets. It occurred to me, as I neared the edge of the brown pond, that I had never told Lori how much I admired her teeth. I wasn't being facetious either. It was very important that Lori knew as many of my thousands of good thoughts about her as possible, and it was too late to tell her about the admiration I had for her perfect white teeth. I had told her about her beautiful eyes, her soft lips, her funny nose, her just-right boobs, the cute little smiles that were formed where her bottom curved under to meet the insides of her thighs, the dazzling dangle of her earlobes—I even told her about each of her wonderful toes. Damn the mute, irrelevance of thoughts too late to be spoken—she would never know how much I had loved her teeth as they glowed through her smile at me.

I had taken several steps into the water before I heard the first shouts. "Hey, that crazy bastard is walking right into the duck pond!"

Ignoring the general alarm, I kept walking and getting wetter and heavier, my step normal except that my stride was slightly hindered by my shoes getting bogged down in duck-murk. Deeper and deeper I went, and, just as my head was about to disappear beneath the surface I shouted, "Roscoe Sweeney, eat your heart out!" Then, taking a giant breath, I marched on and under, completely submerging myself from the sight of my aghast, former schoolmates.

"Where did he go?" I'm sure that they asked one another, for I had to hike a fair distance before the pond bottom began sloping upward again.

"There he is!" someone shouted as I resurfaced on the far side of the pond from the sidewalk.

I stopped with my chin just clearing the water. I don't know whether it was the shock of my presence or the hypnotic effect of the tassel which swung like a tiny little mop from the corner of my mortarboard graduation cap, but not more than eight inches from my nose floated a totally transfixed duck.

The other waterfowl scurried, quarreling, from the pond and took refuge in the bushes along the shore. The surface of the lake became still and mirror-like. To an observer on the sidewalk, there was only a head wearing a ridiculous hat and, facing it, almost nose to bill, a large, white duck.

"You are in my power," I said.

"Quack," said the duck.

"I am God of all the suffering world and you, an innocent creature of the Earth, are unmercifully subject to my whims, my wills, and the wrath of my judgment."

"Quack," agreed the duck.

"I detest you, Duck! You obese, feather-covered dung barge!" I roared in a terrible raging voice. "Wipe that smirk off your bill, Duck. You are fat from Lori's bread crumbs, Lori's potato chips, Lori's beloved oyster crackers." It had been some other age, some mystical time pre-dating any semblance of the sorrows of the present when she and I had spent precious Sundays in the University Library while I compiled data from ancient and worthless texts in compliance with the requirements of ancient and worthless classes. Lori's job was to nudge me whenever I would fall asleep and begin drooling on the old pages. "Just trying to settle the dust," I would say. And after hours of toil dedicated to such rich and rewarding tasks as translating passages of the Kentish dialect of Middle English into modern terms, for the sake of sanity, we would escape to the pond and feed the ducks.

Lori loved ducks.

Lori was dead.

Yet, the fat duck lived!

"I am the lightning and you are the innocence and beauty of the Earth," I proclaimed as I grabbed the creature's big orange feet and disappeared, duck and all, BENEATH THE WATER.

"Quack, bubble," said the duck.

5 Hi Ho Silver

I was angry enough to drown the poor thing, but not cruel enough to play God and actually go through with it.

After a few frantic and somewhat sobering instants sensing the unfortunate creature flailing about at the ends of my arms, I was overcome with a wave of understanding that banished from my heart the depths of despair that were to be expended in my meeting with the 2:17 train: even when you are perfectly justified in the outlet of your rage and possess sufficient means for enacting your infinite wrath, it's not easy to be God.

In an instant, submerged in the murky brown depths of a duck pond, I began a process of reckoning with the Absolute Force that dwells within the Great Swirling Energy Field of the Universe and started seeking more local sources of Divine Maliciousness.

Only the most petty vengeance could drown a portly duck for the heinous crime of eating bread crumbs. And besides, while grasping the profound nature of the encounter, the feathered deliverer of my revelation was pecking the hell out of my nose.

So, freed of the immense burden of despising the Universe and with a hopeful glimpse of a life beyond 2:17 the next morning breaking the gloom of my former vision like a streak of morning sunlight beaming through a hole in a window shade, I released the duck and he popped to the surface like a cork (in addition to being waterproof, they're amazingly buoyant) and, with great fluidity of motion, I emerged back on the sidewalk side of the duck pond.

I was grinning. I was going to live.

The crowd that had gathered to witness the spectacle of my survival was considerably less exuberant than I at the marvel of redemption from the depths. One massive lady, tugging at the arm of her son, the college graduate, proclaimed, "You see, Irving? You see how the value of your hard-earned college education can be ruined by allowing crazies and dope fiends to graduate? Do you see?"

And for the most part, the mumble of the crowd concurred with her assessment of the situation. Except, of course, several of the crazies and dope fiends who bellowed in hazy retort, "Far out, man. Far out!"

I hardly noticed the people. I just kept walking on up the sidewalk, only stopping once to glance back at the pond where my hapless companion was indignantly attempting to put his feathers back into some semblance of order. "Thank you, Mr. Duck. You've been a real pal!" I shouted, and then turned away from the college, the graduates, and the stagnant toxin of dreamless days. I could feel in that moment, pressing me with ever-increasing momentum, the impetus of all the days of my life streaming like a train behind me, and I knew I was at the absolute head of that procession of years and movement and incident. With the exhilaration of the winds at the forefront of my existence parting upon my face, I moved toward life for the first time since Lori had died.

Just then I noticed, rushing right along beside me with powerful stride was the visible form of my Spirit Guide whose kindly eyes were watching me and noticing each of my steps as they made fresh tracks beneath my feet—for at that incredible instant, awareness and incident were fused into one.

"You're an Indian," I said.

"No kidding, Jackson," he said with a good-natured laugh. "This damned feather gives me away every time."

"I'm going to try to keep us out of death for a while," I said.

"Good!" he answered.

"But stay close, old friend. Stay close."

"No problem, Kemo Sabe," he said with a grin and returned to the invisible realm.

And I sang:
Zip-a-dee doo-dah, Zip-a-dee ay...
(There was no denying she was dead. I still loved her. I would always love her and always miss her. I would ever wonder at the world she might have known with me.)

But... *zip-a-dee doo-dah*... (I had hated her death even more than I had hated my own life after her death.) ... *zip-a-dee ay. Wonderful feeling...*
(Christ, how I missed her.)

6 Sassy Sally's

Walking and hitchhiking, it took me over an hour to journey out to Sassy Sally's Blue Bird Cafe and Lounge. It was located a couple of miles out of town on Skintz Bottom Road. The "Bottom" of Skintz Bottom Road referred to the fact that the road, once it had traversed miles of urban clutter and complexity, dropped down to follow the wide and flat floodplain of the Missouri River. In stark contrast to the sprawl of the city, due to the river's tendency to inundate the entire area every three or four years, there were very few houses or businesses beyond the point where the road fell to the bottom for which it was partially named. The "Skintz" part of the road's designation was based upon a late nineteenth century inhabitant of the flood plain, Andre Ezekiel Skintz, Weasel Baron of the Mud Flats. Through a lifetime dedicated to matching cunning and persistence with weasels, he succeeded in accumulating enough wealth to assume ownership of over ten thousand acres of mud, gravel, and weeds surrounding the modern location of the thoroughfare upon which Sassy Sally's Cafe was located. Sally, whose full given name was Sassy Sally Skintz, was a direct descendant of the Baron himself and had financed the creation of her infamous roadhouse by selling off sections of the estate to sand and gravel companies. Even to the most casual passerby, the message of the large sign mounted on the roof of the bar left a lasting impression. It read:

SASSY SALLY'S
BLUE BIRD CAFE AND LOUNGE
country music, country hospitality,
and all the weasel y'all can eat!

Sally and her establishment had weathered numerous seasons upon the mud flat. The tavern, unlike other structures built upon the bottom, was situated upon the only solid parcel of raised ground for miles around and, hence, had survived decades of periodic incursions by the great river. When the floods would come, as always they would, the Blue Bird rode high above the rebellious currents, and, like the tidal monastery of Mont St. Michel in France, would stay the wash, becoming an island fortress—standing firm and aloof from the ravages of a languid, mud-brown sea.

Months prior to the rendezvous with Dr. Fintin for which I was bound on the day of my graduation, the Blue Bird, Sassy Sally, and several of her more hard-core clients had become the focus of national attention. Unseasonable winter rains had fallen upon the Great Plains upriver and with exceptional speed had spilled across the frozen earth of the river flats, stranding a crowd of late night drunken souls in the bar. A news correspondent and a cameraman from a national network were aboard one of the boats when a rescue team arrived early the next morning and the whole country became witness to what became widely known as a "Holy Wonder."

I mention it here because my old buddy from the refrigerator factory, Brother Earl, the spot-welding evangelist, was at the crux of the miracle. Of the people trapped by the flood and the fiery preacher, all but one emerged from the night-long ordeal in the drunkard's den pronouncing the conversion of their souls and the salvation of their spirits by the blessings of belief, and the dedication of their hearts to the spiritual guidance of the aforementioned, self-proclaimed holy man.

I heard about it the next day on Brother Earl's daily devotional radio broadcast (paid for solely by the donations of his ever-growing flock of faithful contributors). That a sawed-off, bilge-sputtering wacko from the spot welding department of the Getzman Refrigerator Factory had his own religious radio program hadn't come as any great surprise to me in those days. Nor would it now. I had listened to it regularly, compulsively since Lori's death as part of my ongoing research and also, because in those dark days, the energy of rage was often the only thing that propelled me.

With exuberance he had broadcasted news of his triumph.

"Yes, brothers and sisters, the Devil and his tool, the lure of sin, had driven them into the evil place; but, God, riding the crest of mighty flood waters had drawn them out."

Whenever I would hear his ignorant whine, I could clearly see his cold eyes and the deception of his smile.

He continued:

"It was late into the black night and I was returnin' from a mission of salvation across the river at Willow City. My heart

32

was full of the power of conversion and the love of righteousness when the Lord grabbed the wheel of the Brother Earl Evangelistic Van right away from me and steered me into the parking lot of the temple of the Devil—the Sassy Sally Blue Bird Cafe and Lounge. For a second there my whole body quaked and I shuddered and I shook and I said in a voice full of the pitiful frailty of man alone, 'Oh, Lord, give me strength in the face of such wretched enemies as drink and solicitous women!' And He spoke within me sayin', 'Go on in there, Earl, you got faith that's stronger than anything the Devil can put in a bottle or spray with perfume.' So, praise the Lord, I climbed up those concrete stairs and walked right in amongst the sinners. Oh, David in the lion's den, I know it so well. But a man who knows the Ways of the Serpent, brothers and sisters, who knows the Truth as revealed by the Prophets, who knows the blessings of salvation and the wages of sin, who knows the depravity of the flesh and the judgment of the soul, hallelujah, who knows the power of the Light in the presence of the Darkness, who knows the Path of Righteousness through the mazes of desperation, who knows the way, brothers and sisters, who knows the way. He who had joined the fight against irreverent behavior, who had enlisted in His Army as a soldier in the war against evil, hallelujah, the man who knows the Truth shall have no fear of the sinner.

"So, with the shield of the Lord protecting me, I entered the place of evil. I drank their poisoned liquor and never lost my mind, I let their whoring women touch me but this flesh was like stone to their excitation—I heard the Devil singin' country music on the jukebox, beloved, but I never tapped a toe.

"Now listen to old Brother Earl, dear ones. I nearly weep as I speak of the fearful risk of it all—the terrible lure of cheap whiskey and wild women, the pagan drumming of the music, the wiles of the wicked pulling me down. But, wait! Don't despair. I did not enter that palace of Satan unarmed. Brother Earl carries a concealed weapon wherever he goes, and he's got a permit for it, too. He carries the magnum pistol of Faith, brothers and sisters, licensed by the Absolute Authority of Holy Writ. As I moved about the barroom, midst the bottles and the painted faces and the tight jeans, jokin' and laughin' and talkin' dirty to the despicable creatures, playing the part of a secret agent for the Lord, I was carrying the heavy artillery of Belief, hallelujah, and I was wearing the bulletproof vest of Salvation to protect me from assault of the Devil.

"Once they thought I was a good-old boy, I knew all I needed was to get their attention and I'd convert all but the worst of them. Just a sign from God. I prayed. Just a hint of the power and they'd all be mine—I knew I could steal their souls from the Prince of Darkness and give them to the King of the Holy Light.

"So I started preachin'. A man is a never a fool if he's speaking for the Lord. I told them, 'Listen up, you sinners, ya hear. I'm a Christian in disguise and I'm about to show you the light!'

"Oh, how the drunkards laughed, the harlots shrieked, brothers and sisters. I can still hear their howls and catcalls. Oh, how they mocked me when I first began to speak the Truth. But I didn't slow down a syllable for all their slobberin' insults. Not a breath of hesitation did I breathe in the face of their sinful furor because I knew the Lord would show them. I knew his wrath was on the way. 'Laugh sinners, laugh!' I cried. 'Hoot and holler all you can, fools. I'm tellin' ya the Power is a-comin' to destroy you all if you don't change your ways. It's a-comin'!' I shouted and right then, hallelujah. Right then at that very moment my prayers for a sign were answered; the flood waters rose and, praise the Lord, the sinners fell to their knees!"

****

At least Sassy Sally showed the strength of character in the face of such overwhelming circumstance to survive the ordeal with most of her indecency intact.

7 Mad Mike and the Thunder

I spent memorable moments in the barroom before Professor Fintin appeared and had me join his private table in a small room accessible through a closed door in back of the place. It had probably only been a few minutes but seemed much longer due to the awkwardness I felt wearing graduation togs in a room filled with genuine or wanna-be good-ole-persons. But my anxiety was for the most part ill-founded. Aside from a bit of a strange grin on the face of the lady bartender as she said, "What's ya drinkin', Professor?" I almost succeeded in avoiding much notice during my sojourn in the establishment.

Almost.

I was passing, in the eyes of most of the men and women in the bar, as just another dope fiend who had wandered in for an alcohol hit on his way back to town after a shopping trip to the Willow City Truth Center. Local rumor had determined beyond a doubt that the Truth Center was home for any number of notorious drug dealers. I was doing just fine blending right in with preconceived notions and stereotypical expectations, when, with terrible clapping rage, the menacing sky broke forth with the dreaded, death-speaking fury of a storm. With flashes of lightning etching their brilliance into every corner of the dingy tavern, and with explosion and roar rattling through the bones of every man and woman there assembled, the tempest mercilessly cast me into the hellish grasp of a waking nightmare. Seized by the thunder-triggered vision of a persistent and tragic memory, with a terrified cry of "Ahhhh!" I executed what must have appeared to the astonished patrons of the Blue Bird as a near-perfect swan dive and all but disappeared beneath one of the large empty tables that cluttered the center of the room.

Time has no measurable dimension when the mind is in flight. Besieged by the horror of memory and the distortion of fear, I can't say how long it was before I was able to fight off the terrible images and begin to regain composure. It wasn't the first time nor, I was certain, would it be the last, but the embarrassment of returning to

35

the reality of Sassy Sally's Saturday afternoon *brew ha-ha* seemed exceedingly undesirable. It occurred to me that two hours earlier such an example of life's penchant for humiliation would have had no effect upon me. Hadn't I proven that at the duck pond?

"It could be worse," I said, trying to allay some of the moments' mortification.

"How?" barked a voice not a foot away from me. With a start I opened my eyes for the first glimpse of light since the storm had hit and realized I was not alone beneath the table. At an angle indicating a flight path originating a few stools up the bar from where I had been quietly sipping a beer, was man who, like myself, lay with his arms tightly clasped about his head and his eyes most cautiously squinting open.

A moment passed as we just lay there glaring at each other. Then, almost at the same instant we both spoke.

"The war?" I asked, trying to determine why anyone other than Jackson Blake, ex-brake-bar operator, former student, current widower and arch-coward could be so deranged as to have reacted in such a bizarre manner to the explosive sounds of a storm.

"Masquerade party?" he asked.

"No. I'm a college graduate—can't you tell?"

With a voice not half so mellifluous as that of a ratchet wrench he snapped, "On second thought, it was a stupid question—where's the rest of your fucking class?"

I liked this guy right away. He was ugly, sarcastic, obviously nuts, and likely dangerous, but I liked him.

"So what's your excuse?" I asked, attempting to match the swagger of his voice. "Did you get blown up in the war?"

"Hell no. I just look like I've been blown up. Actually my problem started when I was still in the womb—my mother had terrible gas. And how the hell's it any of your business anyway?"

"Just trying to make conversation," I replied. "It's not like we just ran into each other waiting for a bus. This is somewhat of an awkward encounter, you have to admit."

"Awkward! Awkward you say. Just how much could a kid like you know about awkward?" His face was a compilation of angles and wrinkles setting off a steady set of wildly sparkling eyes. His head was a sun-browned dome surrounded by erratic tufts of white hair. "I'll tell you about awkward, Kid. One time I was in a bar downtown near the Convention Center when the damned weather hit. I misjudged my dive and skidded under a table of delegates attending the annual convention of the National Association of Bumpkins. Before I could get my mind back and get the hell out of there one of the bastards shouted, 'Whee-doggies, boys! It's one of them big city preverts! Let's all stomp him into the floor.' Jesus, you should have seen all those sharp-pointed cowboy boots start to kick. Now that's awkward, Kid. Really awkward."

"Sounds really awkward." I said.

"Yeah. So, what are you going to do now?"

"I don't know. I suppose I'll crawl back out from under this table and sheepishly go back over to the bar and try to finish my beer."

"No kidding? I thought you were going to stay down here for the evening. I'm not talking about 'now,' Kid. I'm talking about 'now that you've graduated.' Nobody gives a damn if you go over there and finish that beer or not—especially me. I've never yet been to a bar, and trust me I've been to a few, that wasn't filled with ninety percent fools and ten percent philosophers. The fools are too wrapped up in their own beer tears to ever notice there might be a few others of us sharing the frigging planet with them, and the philosophers think they know everything before it happens anyway. Nobody up there gives a squat about a couple of Willow City crazies doing a little body surfing across the beer-sloshed planks, believe me."

"That's reassuring," I said.

"I'll try again. What are you going to do now that you have documented the dismal persistence of your mind to the ink-blinded mentors of some university? If you think you're some level-headed, future-secure, junior pillar of the community, you'd better check out where your ass is sitting, or should I say 'lying' right now."

"I am belly-down under a barroom table wearing a graduation gown and square cap with a tassel, aren't I?" I conceded.

"Well, from this perspective, if you were an idealist you'd be hard pressed for clouds to lose your head in—from here at best I'd have to tell you to get your head down out of the old chewing gum."

"The man's a genius," I said blankly to the forest of wooden legs and the meadowland of scuff-marked floor.

"Well. Spit it out. Are you going to talk or go right back out and join the fools?"

"Let me warn you. It might sound ridiculous," I muttered.

"Damn it, speak up! I can hardly hear you over the jukebox," he said. "And besides, considering the situation, I wouldn't worry too much about shocking me with a ridiculous idea—I'm prepared for the worst."

"Remember you were warned," I cautioned him. "My plan for months now has been to kill myself at 2:17 the morning after graduation. But today I had a talk with a duck and decided I would stay alive for a while longer so I hitchhiked out here to meet, as you put it, the biggest ink-blinded mentor of them all to tell him maybe God was misinformed or confused or maybe not even in town when the Heavens killed my wife... Shall I go on?"

"I had to ask, didn't I? Maybe someday it'll quit raining altogether and I won't have to worry about running into nuts like you."

"Then how the heck you gonna wash your dirty neck if it ain't gonna rain no more?"

"You're a real comedian, Kid."

"Thanks."

"Sure."

"So, how'd you get out the mess you were in beneath that table with all the shit-kicking cowboy boots?" I asked, involuntarily mimicking his infectious verbal irascibility.

"It wasn't easy... "

"Tell me. I might be in a similar predicament someday myself."

"Well, let me put it this way, why the hell do you think I look like I've been through a war?"

"Oh," I said.

And the jukebox said:

> *Leavin's gonna be awful,*
> *but stayin's got to be worse—*
> *our song is long past singin',*
> *this goodbye is the final verse.*

"Glad to meet you, Blake. My name is Mike."

"Likewise, but how do you know my name?"

"You're the one Fintin, the CIA man, sent me out here to find. You might know he'd be recruiting the biggest wacko in the joint."

"Dr. Fintin works for the government?" I asked in disbelief. "He's a 'Company' man," I bellowed with unrestrained laughter.

"Well," interrupted a hushed, extremely dry, and painfully familiar voice from above, "if you two keep broadcasting the nature of my clandestine vocation to the crowd here, you'll endanger the success of an undertaking vital to national security."

I looked up and was shocked by what I saw. I recognized Dr. Fintin's face, but the rest of him was thoroughly cloaked in disguise. From the Stetson hat sitting at a cocky angle on the top of his head, to the red bandanna tied neatly about his neck, past the brilliant turquoise cow-shirt embroidered with lariat loops, to the wagon wheel belt buckle and boot-cut blue jeans, and finally, to the spit-polished cowboy boots with silver-tipped toes—aside from his chalk-pale cheeks and studious eyes, there was no discernible portion of the professor I had known and detested throughout the epoch of my college education.

"Dr. Fintin!" I said.

"Blake," he said in a sharp whisper of admonishment. "My name here is Elmer Hooker and I must insist that you refer to me by that name only."

"Sure thing, ELMER," I emphasized as my new friend and I returned to the realm of the upright.

"And, as for you," he said to Mike in a much restrained voice. "You damned fool, someday your honesty will get us both killed!"

And then, in a voice that was quite public, he said, "Now, why don't you-all boys come on back to my table and have a nip of old Elmer's whiskey to help ya get over your flitters from this here little old storm?"

"We-all thank ya," we-all replied.

8 The Committee

"Mr. Blake, allow me to introduce you to the members of The Committee."

"Please do."

"First, let me emphasize that this is a highly secretive organization. You must never speak of this encounter to anyone nor identify any of the gentlemen to whom you are about to be introduced. It is imperative that beyond this meeting room the names and positions held by these individuals remain absolutely confidential. Is that understood?"

"Sure."

"Very well. Based upon my assurances to the effect that you might possibly shed some relevant light upon the work of our group, we have agreed to take you into our confidence in hopes of establishing communication of mutual benefit to you and ourselves. Our mission, as I shall explain in greater detail shortly, involves the penetration of some of the most basic levels of society, the Sassy Sally crowd for example, and, thus, necessitates taking extreme measures to obfuscate the identities of our members. Hence, certain affectations of dialect and modification of taste, particularly in dress, were in order."

"It would seem so," I said. There were four members sitting around a larger version of the kind of table from under which Mike and I had been recently retrieved. "Do all of you always wear identical western outfits and place your Stetsons cocked at exactly the same angle?" I asked.

A small round man with glasses and a sharp pointed pencil in his hand spoke up. "I'm Jenkins W. Jenkins, Professor of Economics. It is my function on The Committee to lend economic expertise to the operation of the project. As we are established on a somewhat nebulous fiscal basis, I deemed it prudent to implant a seed of austerity in the spending policies we adopted. Therefore, keeping with this spirit of frugality, the membership agreed with my judgment that we should acquiesce to the dictates of economic reality and, by abandoning our individual inclination for unique attire, reap the benefit of mass purchasing power— a 10% discount from Uncle Tubb's Western Duds, Inc."

"And a sound move it was indeed, Jenks," interjected Dr. Fintin, alias Elmer.

"Let me introduce the other members of The Committee, or, perhaps I'll just let each introduce himself and give a succinct explanation of his role in the proceedings. Is that agreeable, gentlemen?"

"Yes, very," they responded in unison.

"Why don't you start, Philbrick?"

"Oh, yes, yes, of course, Dr. Fintin, I'll start. I've never been one to hesitate when given the call. 'Into the fray' is my motto. I come from generations of starters, not a laggard in the group, not one. Starters all, to a man, woman, and child. Now, tell me, Dr. Fintin, er, just what was it that you wanted me to start?"

"Phineas, please pay attention," chided Dr. Fintin. "Tell Mr. Blake who you are and what your function is on The Committee."

"Yes, of course. Sorry, old man. Thinking you know—much on the mind, much on the mind. Some may dawdle and daydream—not me, sir. My mind is ever-reaching further and further into streams of knowledge which flow from the thousands of books soundly imbedded in my memory. No idle drifting will likely cause my attention to stray. No trifle can distract this perceptual center from purposes profound. It is only the manipulation and analysis of the greatest collected thoughts known to man that will justify the temporary severing of my rapt attention upon the activities of this august body of intellectually refined individuals making up this consortium of which I feel quite privileged to be a charter member."

"Phineas!"

"Very well, Dr. Fintin, very well. I'll save these thoughts for some other, more appropriate occasion. Mr... er... what was this fellow's name, Fintin. It seems to have momentarily eluded me. No wait, don't tell me. Was it Burke?"

"Blake," I corrected.

"Yes, Blake. I see. He and Burke were contemporaries, you know. One a great political writer, the other the mystical poet and engraver. Did you know that Blake was an engraver—a good one at that?"

"Yes. Dr. Fintin mentioned that William Blake was a noted engraver," I answered, wondering   if I was ever to be able to terminate my encounter with The Committee and get on with breathing the new breath of life I had granted myself.

"I can see you're a college man, Blake. Good for you. Yes indeed, a college man. You and I speak the same language, Burke... I mean Blake. I am Dr. Phineas Philbrick, Professor of Esoteric Proliferation. It is my duty as a member of this forum to code, so to speak, any communications we send out into the world so they cannot be readily interpreted by the layman. It's all legitimate speech, you know, but speech cloaked in erudition—best code in world: educated verbiage. I use seldom-quoted Latin phrases, literary allusions, metaphorical language, extensive vocabulary— any device that raises the message to a level of comprehension higher than the common person has the background or intelligence to grasp. For example, if I were to ask you to give me eight one-dollar bills, I would say, 'Sir, I wish to requisition a quantity of lucre equal to twice the number of basic physical elements acknowledged by medieval philosophers, and please denominate it in like forms bearing a representation of our nation's progenitor as portrayed by modern practitioners of Blake's craft upon contemporary products evolved from what was the primary export of the ancient city of Byblos. Do you see what I mean, Burke, I mean Blake?"

"Yes, I do. But don't you have a hell of a time ordering a beer out there in the real world?"

"No matter. The rustics who run this inn don't carry my brand of mead anyway."

"Somehow I'm not surprised," I said with strained joviality. "Dr. Fintin, we're not getting anywhere," I pleaded.

"Patience, Blake," said Dr. Fintin. "You'll understand everything momentarily. Could the rest of you attempt to be briefer in your introductions?"

"I certainly will be," said a tall, morose looking man with dark-framed glasses peering out from under the rakish brim of his hat. "I'm Dr. Tann. Psychology is my area and the only contribution I make to this project is an attempt to keep the rest of these bastards from going insane. Tell me, Mr. Blake, do you feel comfortable in that graduation robe? Perhaps did your mother dress you in long nightgowns when you were a toddler? Or did she wear a full-length black dress when she toilet trained you?"

"I can't give you a definite answer about back in the days when I was house-broken, but I can assure you beneath this gown I probably feel less restrained than most of you."

"Did Mother come to see you graduate?"

"No, I didn't invite her."

"Hmmm. I see," said Dr. Tann and then he said no more.

"I'm David Barker, Mr. Blake, and I'm very glad to meet you," said a pale younger man who stood up with an outstretched hand and a smile that appeared disarmingly genuine. As I shook his unexpectedly firm grip, he said, "My area is history and it is my task here to keep a written record of the proceedings so that at some future date when the country is more ready to deal with our findings, an appropriate document might be prepared for circulation beyond the confines of this small room. Just think of it, Mr. Blake," he said as he theatrically spread his arms. "All that you've done is walk into a room and nod your head at a group of strangers and already you are a part of a record of great historical significance. Isn't it exciting to think of the potential each of us possesses, when combined with the right circumstances—moments, human elements, catastrophic or fortuitous physical phenomena, the presence of extreme evil or extreme good—to become part of, to share in the relative immortality of written history? Oh, think of it..." he said, almost whispering, his eyes rolled heavenward, his head tilted back to gaze into the realm of the vast and invisible conceptual cloud apparently hovering somewhere between the tops of his colleagues' heads and the ceiling of Sassy Sally's poker room. Then, with the force of monumental revelation bearing upon him, his burning eyes returned from Cosmic distances to sweep the group and finally fix themselves upon me, and in a voice deep and throbbing with ill-constrained emotion he said, "You know, we are all history. Every one of us. Every breath we take."

The weight of Dr. Barker's remarks brought silence to the room. After a rather long pause, he spoke up in a voice that was obviously drained, "You must excuse me, Mr. Blake, I have to write this down immediately."

"Certainly," I said as he began furiously attacking a spiral notebook with a pen.

"Mr. Blake is going to be history much sooner than any of you would have imagined," said Dr. Fintin. "2:17 is it, Blake?"

I nodded my head in agreement, "2:17," I said.

"We are all very fortunate to have the opportunity to hear Mr. Blake's story this evening, gentlemen, because tomorrow morning at 2:17 he is going to throw himself under a fast-moving locomotive."

The group was momentarily taken aback and then, one by one, the members reacted.

Jenkins W. Jenkins said, "Rather a waste of an expensive education, don't you think?"

Phineas Philbrick said, "Tolstoy died alone in a Russian railroad station."

Dr. Tann said nothing but he did flash a weak smile and began confidently nodding his head up and down and humming.

David Barker asked, "Are you certain this is the most opportune moment for you to depart?"

"Dr. Fintin," I spoke up. "I've been thinking about this decision of mine."

"I see," he said, leaning his crane-like frame toward me. "Then (as was quoted earlier), 'to be or not to be,' is the question, isn't it, Blake?"

"It was the question, but there is no question anymore. I've decided to live. I've decided that there would be no purpose served by dying at 2:17 tomorrow morning. Perhaps some other time I'll jump under a train, but right now I'm going to live and the best thing I can do is get right out there and start doing it. There's a world to travel, people to meet. Maybe death won't have to be on my mind every lucid moment of my conscious existence."

"Then I did have some influence upon you in our little chat earlier this afternoon."

"Well, honestly, it wasn't so much your influence as that of a duck, but I do appreciate your effort."

"A duck? You're still somewhat unhinged, aren't you, Blake?"

"Unhinged!" shouted Mike, speaking for the first time since the meeting began. "You bastards are fine ones to talk about other people being nuts." His coarse, metallic voice cut across the stifling intellectual atmosphere like a ripsaw. "I've never heard such a concentrated bunch of crap since I decided to get a real education and said to hell with college over thirty years ago. You should hear yourselves. One of you pinches the money, one of you muddles the proceedings, one of you gives cockeyed analysis of the participants, one of you puts down the bullshit for posterity to step in, and Fintin, hell, all he does is buy cowboy suits with taxpayers' money. Don't you realize that not a damn one of you really does anything real or important? All you people do is freeload off reality. You hang around out on the periphery of the world, a worthless cluster of self-proclaimed significance dwelling upon, feeding upon the very heart of meaningful existence—parasites tolerated out of some mysterious sense of obligation on the part of the functioning members of the species who actually see to it that the miserable planet gets spun around every day. If it were up to intellectuals like you, Fintin, and your goddamned committees, it would be one thirty in the dull-fucking afternoon forever!"

The group seemed totally unaffected by what I considered to be a painfully accurate assessment of its worth. Dr. Fintin just sighed and said, "Blake, don't pay any attention to Mike. He goes through some variation of the same tirade every time we meet."

I looked at Mike and he shrugged his shoulders. "He's right, Kid. Everything is bullshit when nobody's listening. I just add to the hot air along with the rest of the fools."

"I can tell you're a rebel. You're not even wearing a cowboy uniform."

"A man's got to draw the line somewhere."

"You sure it wasn't the war?" I repeated.

"Hell no! Goddamn it, I told you it was gas."

"Gentlemen," said Dr. Fintin with the practiced sternness of a teacher, "May we go on?"

Mike and I nodded.

"We use Mike as an operative in this project. His earthiness enables him to more readily communicate with some of the less refined individuals whom we need to contact in our investigations. We've found him to be quite valuable though a bit volatile at times."

The professors chuckled in unison.

"The company ain't much," said Mike. "But the pay is fantastic."

"Now," Fintin continued, "Phineas will begin a discussion of the purpose of The Committee. Perhaps we can quell some of your curiosity as to our intentions in having you join us here this afternoon."

Silence.

"Phineas, Will you please start?"

"What? Oh, yes, Dr.Fintin, of course I'll start. I've never been one to procrastinate. I…"

"Stop!" I shouted. "I've got to get out of here. You guys are driving me nuts. I've just given my life upon the face of this world a wonderful extension and you people are getting in my way. You're delaying the incredible urgency of existence. I've got miles to experience, people to hear, seasons to know, oceans to wrap me in their chilling rage and crash me upon their many shores. For the past nine months, under the guidance of learned men and women I have been progressing laboriously—a word, a phrase, a line, a paragraph at a time—toward death. And now I need to reverse my direction and return to hope and life. Damn the mire of death, gentlemen, I'm going to laugh again!"

"Yes!" shouted Mike. "Nice little speech, Blake."

"Thanks," I said.

"So, if you have business with me, get on with it. I can't afford to waste the very precious moments of my life here."

"Very well then, Blake, I'll briefly explain what I had hoped my colleagues could reveal in greater detail. The Company and I are investigating, with the assistance of this panel, the possibility that there exists among members of a certain fringe of fanatic clerics a dangerous religious conspiracy, and, specifically, the likelihood these alleged conspirators might have at their disposal dire means of enforcing their narrow beliefs. Hence, when I attempted to have polite conversation with you following graduation this afternoon and you erupted into a diatribe against God, saying you had collected evidence relating to your wife's death that established a connection between 'The Cosmic Killer' and the malicious expression of a natural phenomenon, I thought perhaps, though you were and apparently still are somewhat crazed, you might be able to shed some light on our investigations.

"I have but one question I wish to ask you, Jackson. During the days immediately prior to your wife's death, did you have a hostile encounter with a religious extremist?"

"That's it!" I cried rising from my chair. "That's my evidence. I've read all of his hateful publications, scrupulously listened to his ranting on the radio, sat in the shadows outside of his traveling tent show as he spread his pious venom. It was that crazy preacher Brother Earl."

"Brother Earl?" asked Dr. Fintin. "You're sure."

"Yes. You've heard of him?"

"Perhaps—do go on."

"I was right. wasn't I? Earl told God I was irreverent at the factory and God killed my pretty Lori with his 'terrible swift sword.' Earl to God, God to the wrathful clouds, and lightning to the delicate flesh of my love. I hear the bastard laughing now. 'See,' says God to me as I kneel beside the smoking corpse. 'See!'"

As I looked about the room at the assembled committeemen the realization occurred to me that it was probably better to have been mad than to have been correct in such bizarre speculation. "You know what I'm talking about, don't you?"

They all nodded in agreement and I settled wearily back into my chair.

"There have been several such zealots," said Dr. Fintin solemnly.

"Then I was right," I said.

"Apparently so. To a degree you were correct in your speculation—at least in considering that a mad cleric might have had some complicity in the death of your wife. We're not absolutely certain about any of this yet. We haven't really gotten this committee rolling as well as we had hoped to by now. But, we are making steady progress, I'll assure you. It just takes time to identify specific areas to be examined. We endeavor to seek the terrible truth here, fearlessly, but, I must admit, not without experiencing some pain in the process." In that moment I sensed, in the uncharacteristic hesitance of his voice and the weakening of his gaze, a deep and striking presence of sadness in Dr. Fintin. It had been easier to despise the son of a bitch than to pity him.

The room was suddenly filled with ghosts—Lori's included.

"You and I, all of us assembled here, share a common ground of experience. To a man in this room, all of us have had wives who met violent and vicious deaths. The fate of your wife seems to fit a definite pattern which we have identified with such consistency as to eliminate the likelihood of mere coincidence sufficing as an explanation. Without exception, their deaths have occurred following our contact with one of these maniacal zealots. I told you my wife had died of an illness. Actually, she died as a result of an injury that befell her while she was in a hospital waiting to die from cancer. The morning of her death, a supposed holy man, whom I later identified as one of the cult leaders named Dr. Hazzard, accosted me on a street corner outside the hospital and told me that for a 'love contribution' of two hundred dollars he would cast out the Devil and heal my wife's disease. In my desperate fury, I told him Hell wasn't full of fire and brimstone. It was full of the echoes of greedy preachers. A few hours later a sudden and terrible gust of wind snapped a huge oak tree next to the solarium where my beloved bride of thirty-five years had been left in a wheelchair. She was crushed and died instantly. In the minuscule mention it garnered in the local newspaper, the authorities referred to the incident as an unfortunate and tragic accident.

"There have been several of such 'accidents.' Jenkin's wife was drowned in a flash flood; Philbrick's wife was killed in her car when she was caught in a rock slide; Dr. Tann has never revealed to us the actual circumstance of his wife's death but assures us it was violent and a result of an uncanny twist of nature; Brandon's wife was smothered by an avalanche while she was skiing; Mike's wife was struck down by a giant hailstone—and in every case the 'accident' occurred shortly after we outspoken fools dared to counter the will of one of these 'holy' conspirators.

"For a time now we have been formulating a course of action to address and hopefully confront and defeat the band of murderers. We have much work to do in preparation for such a battle, of course. Research and the like, you know. Sometimes it seems that we are all too close, too personally involved to effectively approach the situation. But, who else but a victim would believe such a ridiculous theory? If not us, then who else?"

I looked about the table. "All of your wives, too?" I asked in plaintive wonder. "Just like mine?"

And with a solemn nod, each man concurred.

"How about the CIA, Dr. Fintin? Somebody at the Central Intelligence Agency must consider your conspiracy idea a valid enough concern to justify funding your research."

"Well," said Dr. Fintin tentatively, "it is a rather large organization. Worldwide, you know. And considering the scope and diversity of so many clandestine and complex theaters of operation I'm sure our little project is of little note in the grand scheme of things."

Mike started laughing.

"You find this amusing?" asked Dr. Fintin.

"Come on, secret agent man, tell the truth."

"Pray tell, how have I misrepresented our situation?"

"You neglected to mention an important detail, Fintin—the fact that you haven't been contacted by the organization since you were hired five years ago. You see, Blake, it's true that he is a CIA agent. They send him a large check every month and cover every expense voucher he sends them. Shall I tell him about your distinguished career in cloak and dagger, Byron?"

"By all means, Michael. You seem to be quite the authority on the subject."

"What he means is, he has as little to say as I do. It started five years ago when Mrs. Fintin was killed. As a man who craved death but felt it would be immoral just to curl up his toes and die of loneliness, he decided to abandon the academic world and become a spy. His vision was of the quick and quietly heroic demise of a secret agent in some distant and exotic setting replete with half empty glasses of cognac, a dark-eyed woman who loved like the devil but never cried, and a sense of urgency and importance in a mission. It didn't matter if he lived or died."

"When did I tell you all of this?"

"Remember the night that Jenks and his damned calculator couldn't make the meeting and we ran up a bar tab that Sassy Sally still smiles about?"

"Well, some of the details are vague."

"Let me refresh your memory. You told me all about your trip to Virginia, and how you were hired for an assignment that was considerably short of the foreign intrigue you had fantasized."

"I may never imbibe again," said Fintin with a hint of humor.

"They made him a spy all right. But it wasn't in Algiers or Moscow or even in the ranks of trash collectors in Washington, D.C. It was right up the road at good old Dipshit University observing the international implications of activities of campus dissidents. Fintin's a CIA narc. They pay him a pile of bucks every month to keep an eye on junior subversives. The only time he had direct contact with the agency was when they hired him. They probably haven't cut him off or questioned any of the expense of this committee because he might blow the whistle on the fact that his activities are illegal within the United States."

"A narc, Dr. Fintin?"

"I prefer to think of myself as a domestic spy."

"Then, they, the CIA, the spymasters of the planet don't know any specifics about The Committee other than the cost of a few rounds from a tavern out here on Skintz Bottom Road every month or so and that they had to pay for five matching cowboy suits."

"That's right," said Mike.

I looked at Dr. Fintin and he shrugged and in a mysterious manner said, "Believe whatever you wish."

A deep sadness settled upon me. It was not the kind of sorrow that brings tears or muffled sobs. It was a remorse that shuddered through me like the damp cold of Midwestern winter. There was an aura of impotence saturating the moment of the small men gathered in that room—the helpless cluster of little men in their disguises, surrounded first by the specter of their dead wives, and beyond, in a larger sense, surrounded by a force either created of their own projected anxieties or of some real and external source, that was of such an overwhelming magnitude there was nothing in the shuffling of their papers or in the precedence of their logic even having a hint of the power necessary to overcome it. Much less, even vex it. They were, in the full cry of the distracted state of their fear and rage and emptiness, as single grains of sand in the shoe of a giant—incapable of even causing him to limp, much less fall.

I knew at that moment that there existed forces much larger and even more malevolent than Brother Earl.

9 An Invitation Declined

"I'm not certain, but I believe Uncle Tubb's Western Duds might extend our volume discount for the purchase of one more *Complete Ensemble* if we order promptly," said Jenkins W. Jenkins.

The Committee leaned toward me in anticipation.

With formal voice nearly breaking in the suffocating hopelessness of the moment, I said, "Gentlemen, I am afraid I must decline. Though I am deeply honored by your offer, at this time I am compelled to move on. I hope you understand. And, please, let me encourage all of you to keep up the effort. I'm sure that with your perseverance, something will come of this. Keep up the good work."

"Don't worry about that , Blake. We'll get this project moving in good time. Any day now."

"I'm sure you will," I said and then, with a sober nod and accompanied by my new friend Mike, I left the room.

As we made our way through Sassy Sally's stuporous crowd, Mike said, "Let's get the hell out of this place—I hate the smell of fried weasel."

And the jukebox said:

> When I saw you wink at the milkman,
> you said you just wanted a drink.
> Then I caught you wakin' up the Maytag Man
> and I really began to think.
>
> But the last straw was in the bedroom
> where I was greeted by a pair of stares,
> and you said, "This here's the Serta Man—
> we was just tryin' out his wares."

10 Whispering Hope

Just a little drunk and absolutely alone for the first time in remembrance, I existed in the momentary vacuum that either follows significant events or precedes them, or, in this case, both.

A Cosmic hesitation.

Alone upon the temporal measure of the planet. Mike, with gruff and good-natured adieu, had let me off in front of my apartment building, saying we would meet again sometime later when I was older and hopefully less ignorant.

Alone in stark and chilling awareness of the soul's isolation from all the other souls of existence, I sat down on my front steps.

I was still very young then. But even so, I was beginning to sense that life has a pace that must be recognized and respected. Time is generally irrelevant, an arbitrary instrument of regimentation insensitive to the natural movement of energies and entities. There are times to dash about and times to feign procrastination, but there is no more substance to minutes and hours than there is to the lines of longitudes and latitude scribed upon the mock reality of a globe.

I had escaped the meeting with Fintin's committee, rushing into the fresh promise of evening. Guzzling the wild foolishness of rowdy-bar beer, shouting oaths of life to the quavering forms of shadow-hidden fears; I had laughed mad raging truth to the blood-draining death of sorrow's grasp.

And then alone, I sat down upon the front steps of an apartment where ancient history had been enacted and textures of the past coursed through the fibers of my memory.

I ceased the reckless pattern of the night, not in contemplation of either past or future, but rather, to sense the pace of life's movements and to let settle about me the silent sentinels of my being.

"Are you here, my friend?" I asked the vacant street.

And the stillness told me that to be alone was not to be without Spirit.

It was a June night in the Midwest and muggy with the weight of warmth and dampness. What stars that were not distracted to invisibility by the glare of the city were dim and indistinct glimmers in the haze of smog and humidity.

It was 2:17a.m. and there was neither the mind-piercing swath of blinding headlight, nor the rumbling roar and might of a raging locomotive, nor was there the fervent clasp of an excited and willing virgin about my heart and flesh. Past and present balanced in a null and delicate suspension upon the moment of my non-death. Life was a recently compacted resolution pending only the whim and wonder of limitless fortune, death was simply an option not chosen.

I heard the whisper and it startled me.

A familiar voice whispered, "Alive!"

"What?" I spoke into the weary, street-lighted night.

No answer.

There was no waking soul upon the block. As my eyes scanned the darkness between rain-puddle pools of colored light reflected from parked cars up and down the street, I realized the whisper had come from my own lips.

Death had almost been my only truth. Now my truth was to be the challenge of life and its solitude.

It was time to go inside. Though I had vacated my small dwelling earlier in preparation for death, I still had three weeks of rent paid up on the lease. I went down to the basement where the storage bins were located and found the keys Lori and I had hidden there in case we misplaced our others. How very prudent we had been to have anticipated such an eventuality. I checked the mailbox. The envelope I addressed to Milton J. Larbletter had been returned with the words stamped across it, *No longer at this address. No forwarding address*. I guessed old Milton had already headed out for the Cosmos. I opened the envelope and pulled out the wad of cash I had sent. "Maybe I'll buy myself some clothes tomorrow, Milton," I said.

The hall and stairway were dimly lit by "landlord special" twenty-five watt light bulbs. "Cheap sons of bitches," I mumbled as I reached the door to my apartment. I scratched around with the key. My heart was pounding.

For months I had dwelled alone in this haunted cell, but they were months committed to the certainty of death. I would honor my promise to my wife and then I would be dead. Nowhere in that scenario had I confronted the depth of emptiness that awaited me beyond such a familiar door on this night when a train had been missed and a life had recommenced. Life without Lori had never occurred to me. Now it scared the hell out of me.

When I was a Boy Scout (and believe me I was a lousy Boy Scout—I never mastered my knots or learned to love the perverse camaraderie of adolescent guys out on a weekend's venture into nature) one of the Scout leaders led us on an exploration of Fisher Cave in the hill country of Missouri. We all had flashlights and a couple of the adults carried Coleman lanterns. A great time was being had by all until, somewhere deep inside the damp and crusty bowels of the earth, our leaders commanded us to turn off our lights. "Now, you're going to find out what darkness is really about," said our guide. We clicked off our flashlights, they shut down the valves on the gas lanterns, and, with a quick sputter all light was extinguished. Boy, was it dark. Dark like there wasn't even air for us to breathe in that emptiness. Nobody said anything. We were all hushed by the choking closeness of nothing. Then, thank God, somebody farted and we all were able to laugh away our fears. That's how it was when I pushed the door open and walked through the entryway and into the living room. Boy, was it dark in there. So empty. And there was no laughter in my entire soul to dispel the pall of such abandonment.

So, gathering my black robe about me like a cocoon, I fell asleep in a corner of the room, awaiting dawn.

11 Laughter

She awoke me with her laughter.

I had known Lori's ghost to be near, but never had it blessed me with more than a sense of subtle energies I had sadly dismissed as the desperate imaginings of a lonely man.

But on that first full morning of the rest of my life, she stirred me from bad sleep with the clear and lovely sound of her laughing within my soul.

It was not the sound of hilarity I felt that morning. It was the gentle sweetness of a lover's intimate joy, the playful prodding of a heart-touching friend that resounded throughout me.

I was not alone.

PART TWO

I recall now in dreamlike consciousness, we wandered the gray-green paths in silent awe—listening to every whisper and call of the moist forest. The subtle mists moved about the giant trees and arching ferns, touching us, making us wet—chilling us. The ever-gray sky steadily stirred the leaves with a quiet, thorough rain and, standing upon the damp floor of the rain forest, I clasped her hand in reassurance and knew we stood together before the entire Universe.

Or, was I alone?

Clasping my own hands as if to pray.

1 Recollection of the Years: So Many Tracks

Two years traveling: gathering.

Three years teaching junior high school English to the hormonally eerie. Two years repairing refrigerators and extracting mildewed panties from the bind of washing machine pumps.

One year picking banjo with a mad band of bluegrass troubadours.

One year driving massive diesel trucks about the oil patches of the Great Plains where fields were summer sun-scorched, autumn rain-muddied, and winter scattered with snow-steaming cow dung.

Another year's traveling: gathering.

Ten years of circling the surface of existence in replication of a shallow experiment of action, reaction, momentary pleasures, tearless grief, and passing people—ever skirting the grasp of sweet-reaching hearts and hearths of warmth and comfort.

A decade of hiding. Hiding from the allure and incredible risk of love, but, mostly, hiding from God.

> ("What the hell are you doin' back here, Son? Ain't you seen enough of these God-forsaken rocks?"
>
> And looking about me at the desolate, sun-white and night-black rock—Earth ripped open exposing its jagged bowels, barren of vegetation, I said, "There's always something new and exciting to do at Craters of the Moon National Monument."
>
> The old maintenance man just wandered away shaking his head and mumbling curses about dope fiends and crazies.)

A decade when love was so distant as to seem safe from sorrow, when security was but the transient insulation of a bedroll or a run of steady work. When God was yet death, and all the heart and spirit of mankind but the creation of a cruel and elaborate illusion.

Written on a bathroom wall in Cincinnati, Ohio: Imperative to human survival is the development of an ability to withstand the effects of repetitious activity and its consequent boredom.

Written on a bathroom wall in Port Orford, Oregon: Life is such a trip—every time I take a piss it's like a brand-new experience.

A decade of a few laughs, a few truths, and plenty of miles.

2   The Old Man

(or... The Day I Cussed and Hit the Dust)

Though at the time it was difficult to see in such a positive light, I had been very lucky.

When they ejected me from the car it could have been much worse than merely painful. If it were not for the cushioning effect of the dust and the fact that four-wheel-drive Ford pickup trucks have exceptional ground clearance, I probably would have ended up entirely too dead to have continued on quest of another day's set of deep breaths and heartbeats.

I am a lucky man—just listen to the air sounds of my lungs. Right?

We had been rolling along at over eighty miles per hour with the radio blaring the ripsaw harmony of a fiddle-wild country duet singing:

It might have been the music,
it might have been the gin;
but in the long run, Baby,
it was the flesh that did me in.

For over an hour we had been laughing and telling jokes and lies and listening to country music on the radin and then I had to go and commit an unpardonable faux pas. With the rhythm of their harsh hearts pounding in the swollen arteries of the men's blood-colored necks, and waves of indignant rage emanating from the jungles of peroxided cowgirl curls surrounding the bitter, pouting faces of the ladies; and with no discernible decrease in rate of speed they had swung through the parking lot and in a violent commotion of sharp pointed cowboy boots, hard fists protruding from pearl-buttoned sleeves, and flailing fingernails painted bright red, they had abruptly departed my company.

And all I did was say "fuck."

They had picked me up in front of a highway junkyard where, due to the inevitable happenstance of malfunction, I had abandoned the security and corresponding burden of an automobile. The "salvage-master" had generously given me one hundred dollars cash and a six pack of rot-gut brew in payment for the remains. I was sitting on a convenient roadside rick sipping my second beer when they pulled over in their big Cadillac and offered me a ride.

There were five of them—three Texas cowboys wearing big hats riding in the front seat of the car, and two Texas cowgirls wearing tight blouses with big puffy sleeves in the back seat—a carload of cowpersons traversing the Great Southwestern Desert. "Just jump on in back there with the gals." shouted the driver over the blast of the radio and the roar of the wind. "We're a car full of Texans headin' for Las Vegas, Nevada, to make a bunch of money playin' them gamblin machines."

"Sounds fine to me," I said and jumped on in the back with the gals.

There were five shiny sets of cowboy boots, two sky-bound, bra-launched sets of boobs, countless bony elbows, and an ice chest packed with Lone Star Beer.

We drank, we laughed, we got bawdy as hell, and I was loving it.

"Three cowboys and two cowgirls," I said. "Someone's going to be lonesome tonight."

"Not if I can help it, Sugar," said Jenny Sue who was sitting on my lap. Oh, how we laughed.

"Stop the car! Stop the car!" shouted Tammie Arlene. "Dang it all, I've gotta take a piss."

Screeching tires, a cloud of dust, and with mock crossness in her voice, "Now, you-all don't peek," she shrieked as she squatted on the side of the highway.

"Damned earthy," I said, laughing.

We sang songs along with the radio, told jokes about whorehouses and making love to sheep, and by all it was agreed—for a damned Yankee, I was a pretty good old boy.

Then I had to go and say the "F" word.

It just kind of slipped out between the "galdangs" and the "sum-bitches" like it so often does in modern, sophisticated conversation.

It became suddenly silent. Jenny Sue's syrupy smile turned to an icy frown and she thrust herself from my lap. None of the cowboy trio in the front looked at me but I could feel the intensity of their anger.

"Oh, Jesus," I said. "You guys don't say 'fuck' around women yet, do you?" I said as I grabbed the handle of my canvas suitcase.

What happened next, I have already described.

As I rolled across the choking carpet of dust, beneath the tall Ford pickup truck, and finally came to rest against a gas pump, I said to myself, "This all seems rather arbitrary."

It was early in the autumn of my thirty-sixth year and, unlike the average, upwardly-mobile college graduates of my generation, instead of just beginning to see the principal of the mortgage on my suburban palace diminishing in the onslaught of a hundred or so hearty monthly payments, I was just able to see the sand-dust dominated scene of a desert filling station/trading post through wind-gust clouds and the disheveled state of my dazed perception.

Lori had been dead for eleven years and this was the point to which my life had evolved through a decade of wandering, working, studying the fates of man and beast, experiencing wind-known direction of place and time, and enduring the gnawing persistence of death.

And, as I said, it could have been worse. Sometimes we are in the adoring arms of love, sometimes in the rapture of holy Truth, sometimes in the stupor of inebriation. For that matter, sometimes we're on the toilet—whether our lives have followed the culturally-blessed spiral toward riches and mediocrity, or have sputtered along like an ailing airplane in rises, plummets, and ever-falling altitude—all moments lead to a single moment and mine happened to be occurring in a dirt parking lot.

The wind-wrapped dust clouds had long dimmed the sun to a yellow-brown hue. In rising and falling currents, the adobe buildings and bleak landscape blended in and out of near-invisibility.

I considered the option of getting up, but there seemed little reason to justify the effort. So, I chose to dwell forever in the shelter of dirt.

"If you are not dead I think it would be prudent for you to get up before you get run over. People have actually been known to pull into this outpost when in desperate need of either gasoline or a bathroom."

I was startled by the powerful voice.

"What?" I asked.

"Why don't you shake the dirt out of your ears so you can

listen?"

I couldn't find the source of the words though they seemed to be coming from a pile of garbage stacked in the back of a truck parked about twenty feet from where I lay.

As I slowly rose to my feet, checking for broken parts, the voice said, "Oh good, you can move. I'm glad you've survived."

"Thank you," I said as I glanced about trying to locate where the words were coming from. "So am I. I guess."

"If you wish to see me, you must come closer. Not only am I well camouflaged by this trash, but, also my people have been living in this country so long that we are the color of its wind."

A hot dry gust swirled about me as I stepped toward the old pickup truck. In back there were two open oil drums overflowing with trash, a scattering of cans, a dead dog, some oil-stained rags, a hammer with a broken handle, and a faded red and gray blanket crammed between the oil drums against the cab.

"I am here," said the blanket.

Peering into the wrinkled mass of wool, I encountered an ancient, bloodless face.

"My God!" I said, amazed at the decrepit appearance of the origin of such a strong and energetic voice. "Are you all right?"

"Oh, yes," he said with laughter. "You'll have to forgive the condition of my body. It is very old and hasn't been given the best of care over these many years on the desert. And besides, I am supposed be dead."

"Well, you sure look the part," I said. "If you hadn't spoken you could have fooled me."

"Excellent. It is imperative that I look extremely dead."

"Don't worry. You're doing a fine imitation of a corpse. Nothing short of ghastly."

"It takes a great deal of concentration to remain this still—especially for an active individual like myself. Until this morning when I decided it was time to play dead, it was not uncommon for my dog and me to walk ten or fifteen miles a day across the arid reaches and bluffs of this land."

Outside, there was no one else around. In the wind and distance from the trading post, no one was within earshot.

I sat down on the opened tailgate of the truck. My travels over the previous decade had taught me most people don't mind being asked personal questions by strangers—either to allow themselves the opportunity to verbalize hidden memories or thoughts to someone who doesn't directly affect their lives, or to give themselves a clear shot at telling someone to mind his own business. In any case, as demonstrated by my recent roll through the parking lot, I was certainly someone who could survive the effects of being told where to get off.

So, without any apology for the bluntness of my inquiry, I said, "Why are you wrapped up in an old blanket in the back of a truck full of garbage, no offense, playing dead?"

His answer was as direct as my question. "I am attempting to escape from a prison."

"A real prison with walls and guards?" I asked.

"No, Son. A real prison of narrow traditions, old age, and the suffocating love or, more honestly, obligations of well-meaning relatives."

"You're doing such a fine job of being dead—aren't you afraid they'll bury you?"

"It is possible. There is risk to any great undertaking. But if we are to be rich we must risk being poor, if we are to be alive we must risk being dead."

I knew very little. Perhaps even less and less as miles and years took their toll through the erosion of belief. But, with rare exception, I knew more than the people I met. And, yet it was obvious in the tenor of his voice and the gentle power of his eyes that his wisdom was far beyond my own.

"Tell me your plan, Old Man."

"The first thing I am going to do is kick your ass if you call me an old man again. Time and wrinkles do not have a damned thing to do with old age."

"I'm sorry, sir. I meant no insult."

"I know it. Just be careful when you designate a person feeble and alive beyond having any worth."

"Sure thing."

"My plan started early this morning. Just after the family breakfast, my dog and I were found lying 'lifeless' in front of the small house which my younger relatives provide me. I had assumed correctly that the mysterious coincidence of an affliction leading to the simultaneous demise of both a man and his dog without any notable indications of cause would generate enough fear of an epidemic to justify the inconvenience and expense of hauling our corpses to a medical examiner in the city."

"Didn't anyone check your pulse or listen for a heartbeat? Wasn't a doctor called?"

"My people have little money. Doctors are a luxury reserved for the preservation of life when it is young and fresh. When it has not yet had an opportunity to grow. The death of, as you put it, an old man like myself is accepted and no vigorous attempts are made to forestall its arrival. As to my disguising the gross signs of life which are routinely checked, I have mastered a meditative technique that all but eliminates the sound of the heart or the perceptible presence of breathing. And, in any case, I am a very old person and my ways are not always in agreement with the values of younger generations of my relatives. Tradition forced them to consult with me in making important decisions. I often disagreed with their wishes and their needs. I had become a grumbling old pain in the ass with an old dog that farted too much and kept them awake at nights barking at ghosts. When they found us they were not seeking signs of life, and consequently, found none."

"They really believe you are dead, don't they?"

"Of course."

"And your dog?"

"He does what I tell him."

"I see. Then what are your people waiting for. Hadn't they better hurry and get you to the city before you start to rot?"

"This climate is dry. They have sufficient time to raise the money it will take to make the journey. It will be several more hours before they come up with the necessary funds."

"Are you a Native American?"

"Indian!" he corrected. I am much too old to be a 'Native American.'"

"Sorry. Are you an Indian?"

"Not entirely. Generally, they take better care of their dead. I am a mixture of many elements and all of them misplaced. I am a blue-eyed Indian, a whiskey-drinking Mormon, a hunter who reveres the life of all creatures, a philosopher who reads rocks and shadows more than books. My clan was built from the refuge of any culture stupid enough to try to exist in this country."

"Doesn't it bother you that your relatives are glad you're dead?"

"Oh, they are not glad I am dead—only relieved."

"Couldn't you have just left?"

"No. I told you I am escaping a prison. Obligation is a form of self-inflicted internment. I'm leaving for good today and am much too obligated to these people to leave them with the cruelty of expecting my return. I love my people. They will suffer less from my death than from my departure."

"You're not afraid of confronting anything, are you?"

"Only of the failure of my greatest dream, Jackson. It is time for us to leave."

"Did you call me 'Jackson?'"

"Perhaps."

You travel a long time and when it begins to happen you can either run like hell or stay with it. I had been thrown from a speeding car that day and had lived with but a few scratches, a little pain, and a set of inordinately dirty elbows.

What the heck.

"Where are your people now?"

"They are in the back room of the trading post sitting around and waiting for more relatives to show up with money."

"Will they take eighty dollars for this truck if I promise to deliver you to a big-city coroner?"

"I am certain they will—but do not be stupid."

"You mean I'm not supposed to take you to the city?"

"Of course you are supposed to get me out of here. Just do not be stupid. You can get this old heap for seventy bucks."

"All right," I said with some indignation. "I'll try not to be stupid if you try not to be a grumbling old man!"

With a laugh as familiar and yet as distant as some childhood memory, he said, "That is a deal."

As I stood up, the lifeless hulk of dead dog stirred momentarily, looked up at me, and wagged its tail one time.

3 Connections

There are roads across the desert seldom traveled by tourists or truckers—tracks upon the rock and sand through the wind-sculpted canyons beyond the insipid course of four-laned security.

The old man knew such roads. At a dusty and rough-rutted crawl we progressed toward the city to the south in the garbage-heap pickup truck. The old man had been right, his grieving family members were blatant in their sense of relief at the prospect of me taking possession of the truck and its resident corpse. (Just to spite the old man I had argued them down to $60.) I had driven several miles before stopping. I pulled off the main road and down into a shallow ravine so as to avoid being seen by any of the assembled nieces and nephews who might have finished their mourning and headed home to their various dwellings on the desert.

"I think it's all clear now," I said as I climbed out of the truck and walked around to the back.

There was no answer.

I reached over the side of the truck and gently pulled on the blanket. "Are you all right? You haven't really died on me, have you?"

Still no answer.

I climbed into the bed of the truck and removed the blanket from his face. He wore time-faded blue jeans, a red flannel shirt. On a chain about his neck there hung a silver amulet—an ankh.

"I am quite all right," he said in a serene voice. The color was already returning to his flesh and he hardly looked dead at all. "I have just been gathering force before joining you up front."

"Sorry to interrupt," I said. It was amazing how his appearance had improved in the short time since I had met him.

"Oh, you have not interrupted me. The process goes on and on regardless of the world about me. I have been preparing for this journey for some time and have gathered a great deal of energy. To be honest, I was probably not absorbing force so much as I was bidding an old friend adieu. Sometimes a physical environment becomes as personal a part of an existence as human contact.

Inanimate elements—rock and shadow, texture of sand, the warm touch of the air—can be transformed by human contemplation into the comforting strength and familiarity of a companion. So much of what we identify as being Truth or Beauty or Love is in fact a product of reflection upon natural phenomena rather than the direct or immediate result of an interaction."

"What?" I said to the man wedged between the garbage cans who had suddenly waxed philosophical.

"I will give you an example. Non-Platonic love is basically motivated by a desire to have sexual intercourse. Once all the ritualistic dances have been performed and mutual consent has allowed the act to be completed, love could easily be forgotten—at least until passions rise again—if it were not for a reflective definition of love. Reflection allows a man to realize that his willingness to commit the resources of the remainder of his life to one sweet young girl is based on higher consideration than the fact that she causes a recurrent lump to appear in his shorts. Do you understand? Reality is nothing without the reflective manipulation of the mind. Love is nothing more than a roll in the sack, home is nothing more than a pile of stone, and this planet no more than the blind electrical interaction of chemicals, It is all momentary and insignificant if not embellished by the spirit. I am departing a world created from decades of contemplation of the chaos of raw, random data. It is time for me to free myself from the specifics of air and earth that constitute this "home" in which I have dwelled for these many years. It is time to head for the city, Jackson, we have brief business there."

I really had little idea what this "corpse" was rambling on about—especially the part about "we." But who was I to question the madness of that day?

"Are you certain you're ready to leave? I don't want to rush you—there's no place where I have to be."

"Oh, yes there is." Shaking his shoulders to adjust the leather pack strapped to his back, as he rose from the refuse and stretched his sturdy frame, he said, "Let's get going, but not on the interstate highways—at least not until we run out of my roads."

"Okay," I said. "It seems you know more about my direction than I do."

"Perhaps I do."

So I followed his roads and said little. I listened and, as he spoke, a larger presence than that of a time-crusted eccentric emerged in the poetry of his words.

"I will tell you about the connectedness of things, the circle of existence that, slightly altered, becomes the spiral of the spirit. And, in doing so, I will explain why I might look like an old desert rat, I might smell like an old desert rat, but, by damn, I do not talk like an old desert rat." He paused, breathing deeply and evenly, and, in a fixed and powerful state, and, in a voice strong, personal, and yet detached, he began to speak.

There is an early time each morning when dreams and visions succumb to light and sleep transcends to dawn. A time when, in precise balance, a moment may hover between the fantastic realm of night and the fresh and vivid nourishment of day. A moment born of two worlds, a part of neither—reclusive, ephemeral, perceived as shadow and then ever past.

It was at such a moment over thirty years ago when I was a young man just into my fifties that I sensed a glimpse of the vision I seek today. Sleep had been fitful as I was cast by desperate images about the restless sea of my subconscious, only settling into deep pools of rest in the final fading hour of darkness. When light spoke morning through the eastern window of my hut and stirred me from sleep, the magic instant was filled with glowing tones of color and brilliant sounds and exhilarating, vibrating, invisible sensations of the soul and then was gone, and I knew upon that day I was to commence the final journey of my human trek.

Outside my window raged the wonderful promise of a terrible wind.

I dressed quickly and, grabbing my pack and walking staff, I rushed into the storm to feel its howling currents of violent air and stinging sand. Wrapping my blanket about me, I dared the dangers of the arid tempest in order to seek its mysteries. In a glimpse of the infinite, my rambling life had found direction.

Like you, I had spent years in random abandon, wandering the aimless paths of watercourse earth down sloping ravines of time—marveling at the enlightening happenstance of rare moments, despairing at the cumbersome emptiness of the surrounding months and years, No time blessed with awareness is time wasted—there is use for all things gathered. But without direction, we can expire—gasping our last breaths while yet in search of reason for gasping our first.

I had spent my life listening to the voice of the storm. Touching the elements of its power. Sensing the sporadic might of its uncharted course. I had meditated often on the insubstantial nature of the land upon which I lived—that it would rise into the sky at the slightest movement of the wind, restless as my own spirit, incessantly shifting between the realm of the planet and the realm of the air. But on the day my journey commenced, I began realize the unity of air and earth and man within the matrix of the storm. The wind was so strong that, though my feet could feel the ground beneath me, my vision could not differentiate between what was the earth and what was the dirt vapor of the earth and air. Like some Chinese mountain mystic dwelling in the clouds, I sensed the transient nature of the physical world.

I carefully followed the familiar feel of the path from my home toward the highway intending to make my way to the very trading post where you purchased my body and this pickup truck today. However, along the way, I came upon a partially buried car that had run off the road. The passengers were not injured but were stunned by the hopelessness of their situation. Their car was tilted and stuck, the highway was invisible, and they were in the middle of some god-forsaken desert a million miles from home.

I rescued them by forming a human chain with myself as the first link, followed by the wife, then the two children, and finally the husband. Hand in hand, I simply led them up the side of a steep slope to an altitude above the ground storm. We sat down on rocks and watched the earth boiling beneath us. The children absently played with stones, the husband stared blankly forward and the wife sat close to me—continuing to hold my hand.

I took them to a nearby wind cave I had stocked as a meditative retreat. There was water and the overhanging rock gave shelter from the elements. I told them they would be safe there until the storm had subsided and then I would help them free their car and be on their way.

The children found a stone that glittered and gave it to me as their gift. It was their gift.

The husband and the children reclined in the cool depths of the shelter and became deeply engulfed in slumber. The wife, who had sat patiently until the others fell asleep, then quietly left the cave, motioning for me to follow her. She led me some distance away and in the shadow of a large rock she expressed her gratitude to me.

When we returned to the cave she smiled at me and then joined her family in sleep. I sat down and...

Slamming on the brakes of the old pickup truck right in the middle of the dirt road, I had to interrupt the old man's mystic tale. "Hold on here a minute! I followed you from dreams to light, from sleep to enlightenment, into a raging dust storm, up a damned cliff and now you just skim right over the best part! Just how the hell did the lady express her appreciation in the seclusion of the great boulder?"

"Use your imagination, Jackson."

"Why should I when you're capable of so eloquently expressing yourself."

"Some things are corrupted by their telling."

"Aha!" I said. "She did you didn't she? Come on tell the truth."

He elevated himself in feigned annoyance and said, "May I go on with my story? It is more important than your crude fixation."

"Right out there in the wind-swept desert she did you in the dirt. Wow!"

"'Wow,'" he said with mock contempt. "Remind me never to trust your imagination again. Your filthy frustrations belie

71

such fears. To be graphic, Jackson, the fine lady only kissed me and it was no solicitous, slobbering act of salacious lust as I am sure you would envision."

"She just kissed you?"

"Yes. She reached up to me and placed her arms about my neck, her eyes became misted, her smile became soft, and she drew me to her and kissed me with lips that spoke neither of passion's promise nor of obligatory ritual. Her kiss was a split-instant of immeasurable love and then, with a school-girl blush, she parted and with light and fleeting stride returned to her family."

"And left you out there with your staff sticking in the sand, right?"

"Yes," he laughed. "Just me and my old staff sticking in the sand."

"I like my version better," I said.

"You would have to have been there, Jackson. It was a beautiful gift. The children gave me a stone, the mother gave me a light-second's touch of love—but, let me go on. It was the father's gift that I most want to explain to you."

"Well, if you let him give you a kiss, I'm turning around and selling your old bones back to your nephews."

"May I go on?" Again, shifting into that special tone of his, he continued.

The storm had long abated before they awoke. I watched as it weakened and gave increasing clarity to the land below.

We returned to their car and I let some air out of the rear tires for better traction and was able to push them free of the sand and back up onto the pavement.

The man had said so little, I feared he might have felt slighted by my actions and was silent in resentment. But soon my apprehension seemed ill-founded, for as we were parting it was he who shook my hand most fervently and in a sudden shift expressed the most ardent appreciation to me. It was not until the car was road worthy and his family safe within it that the burden of the situation was lifted and the flow of his heart was clear.

He, too, had a gift for me.

His gift was a book.

As he dug through an old briefcase that had been wedged behind the spare tire in the trunk of the car, he told me he had found the book years earlier in an antique store somewhere back East. He had been studying its cryptic messages ever since. He told me its words were as holy as any revealed to prophets by ancient gods. I protested that no gift was necessary, particularly one of such personal attachment. But, as he proudly retrieved it from the trunk and blew the dust from its cracked leather cover, he insisted, "I want you to have my book. I know its words, perhaps you will understand their meaning."

As he handed me the book he hesitated and said, "But, first, you must promise you will read every single word of it. You will overlook no part of it. You'll read it all."

"I promise," I said, nearly trembling in anticipation of its wisdom.

He released his grip on the book and climbed into the car. With arms waving and voices shouting farewell, they departed down the storm-ravaged highway.

The book was entitled *One Hundred Coordinates for the Cosmos.* I sensed it to be a key to vast knowledge and understanding.

I placed the stone of the children in my pocket, the kiss of the woman in my heart, and the book in my pack and climbed back up to the wind cave.

There were still some hours left of the magical first day of my spiritual journey—borne of early light, charged by raging storm, blessed by human touch.

I was seeking a path of human access to the marvel of spiritual energy that is Universe, to the power that spins the stars and planets in arching exaltation through the wondrous vastness of the void. The happenstance of the storm, the stranded family, and the book upon the day of my cosmic embarkation surely portended great discovery.

I settled into a corner shaded from the late afternoon sun, and for a moment, I just held the small book in my hands. "I'm ready," I said aloud as I turned to the first page of text.

I can recite Chapter One for you in its entirety. It was only four words long. It read: Beers rhymes with tears.

"What!" I shouted to the barren reach of the storm-stilled air.

"Chapter Two: Hi, Mom!"

"WHAT?" I repeated with a voice of stunned rage.

"Chapter Three: Everybody do-dos."

I jumped to my feet and reared back to cast the stupid tome to the sands. "I should have fucked your old lady when I had a chance!" I yelled to the southern brim of my stone-petty world where I was certain the son of a bitch was likely to careen into another sand wash from the swerving hilarity of his joke.

I had to interrupt again. "This book of universal wisdom just said 'Everybody do-dos'? This is the cosmic connection? The universe unfolded for all to view—everyone, I mean everyone do-dos."

"Everyone," the old man assured me with a nod of his head.

"Well, I can't argue with that. This absolute truth stuff is hard to refute."

"You can imagine how I felt—seeking the infinite and discovering the most mundane. I damned near near threw the book to the winds, but then recalled the promise I had made and decided to play the complete fool and read the whole thing before trashing it. If I was to be straight man for the bastard's joke, at least I would be an honest straight man."

"Surely, it got better."

"No. Of course not. It could not have gotten better. Jackson, over the decades since encountering the book I have sampled the world's finest expressions—its literature, its art, its music. I have read the philosophy of the Greeks and the Western Europeans and wisdom of the Orient. I devoured the small library in the town near my home and from there accessed the resources of the whole state. I have studied religion and culture and science and economics, sociology and psychology. I have listened to the great symphonies broadcast from distant cities. I have sensed the interrelationship of color, form, and texture that is visual art. Through volumes of color plates and occasional encounters with original paintings and sculptures that passed through my homeland as part of traveling art exhibits, I have known the masters. For a man whose world has been restricted to a few hundred square miles of moonscape, I have known much of what mankind has surmised from existence.

"And, aside from the joy of experiencing man's sporadic glimpses of the Gods expressed in the words, sounds, and shapes of his art, the fact was, through all of my reading and listening and viewing it seemed I was never to find a truth more profound than 'Beers rhymes with tears.'"

"Everybody do-dos." I said.

"Hi, Mom," he said.

We rode along in silence for a distance and then he spoke again.

There was more:

My search for "cosmic coordinates" seems to have borne fruit. By my delving into such diverse subjects as the harmony of Baroque chamber music, the incredibly precise timing of Mickey Mantle's micro-second impact with a baseball, and the grounding properties of electricity; I have made certain connections of a less earthbound, and hence, less mundane nature than those of the crude book from which I started.

There are, accessible to each of us, truths of the pedestrian paths of mortality and also, truths of the celestial flights of the unfettered soul—dangerous truths in the realm of jealous Gods. You see, there is a warning that prefaces all this. I must tell you about the hermit.

All of my life I had heard of him living in solitude in the rock mountains west of my homeland—a haunted form scurrying into crevices at the approach of any human being. A soulless specter of living death cursed by the Gods. Legend said his lonely cry was the voice of canyon winds.

I had dismissed the tales of the hermit as being part of the mythology of fear that dominates most of the beliefs of mankind. But then I met him and knew the tales of his damnation were true.

I was drawn to a desolate mountain and found him there waiting for me.

He had no name. He wore clothes made of entangled skins. He was so thin as to have little more form than that defined by the very edge of his bones. When I approached him he was not startled and without facing me motioned for me to sit across from him on a large rock overlooking a complex of canyons reaching to the horizon. In a voice as dry and jagged as his mountains, he spoke to me.

"It is at great risk that I speak with you but I must. Man, I must warn you of the Dark Spirits."

"I have known the Dark Spirits," I told him.

"That is true. You have known them. They have injured you, and even so, you survive. The Dark Ones have not finished with you. I must warn you their powers are vast and they are terrible."

"Tell me what I do not already know of these terrible Spirits." I said.

"They live upon the Mountain of Three Days. In the arrogance of my youth I insulted them and in the ignorant rage of their powers they condemned me to dwell forever in the emptiness of this hostile land—touching no human being, taking nourishment from no earthly riches, never to know again the joy of my own identity. You have traveled too far into the realm of their hateful secrets. It is only by the vast distance you have travelled that I may speak to you now. The Fiends cast me into this hell of rock and loneliness as easily as one would swat the annoyance of a fly. You, however, they clearly hate.

"Your only hope is to find your way to the Mountain, perform the Rites of Access, and pray that you may summon sufficient powers to address them. Or else, you will know a hell ten-fold worse than that of the eternal labyrinth of these canyons."

I looked out across the tormented vista of rock and shadow. With the hermit's voice yet trembling within me, I was truly afraid.

I turned back to the hermit and he was gone.

"I don't understand," I said. The old man had become silent and the rattle of the old truck punctuated my disorientation. "Why do you tell me about hermits and Cosmic coordinates?"

"Because, my friend, a truth untried is no better than a lie. You and I are heading for the Mountain of Three Days." he answered with a tone of assurance that made me feel like I was not in the least in control of my own destiny.

4 "Chapter Twenty-six"
From *One Hundred Coordinates for the Cosmos*

Ham and Eggs.

5 The Road to the City

"What's your name?"

"My name is Glory Hallelujah."

I laughed and said, "Well, praise the Lord."

"No." He was my father."

There is a place where the rugged high plateau country of the Southwest ceases abruptly and the land falls away a thousand feet to the hot dry sands of the lower desert. For me it has always seemed the edge of inhabitable land—a promontory overlooking the stifling, single-seasoned monotony of bland and blue-skied boredom. But others would disagree with me and view it as a point of departure down into a promised land where, gathered in RV clusters at every road juncture, they huddle beneath the sparse shade of patio covers—leather-skinned and listless immigrants from the harsh Northland—and in voices strained against the torment of the scorching wind, daily praise the one-hundred degree January sun and call the winterless wilds paradise.

"Look at that," he said as we stood by the truck and looked over at the expanse of heat and haze stretching a hundred miles to the edge of the planet. "No wonder I never left home."

"You senior citizen types are all supposed to love it down there where it never shivers your old bones."

"It looks like a staging area for people preparing for Hell. Personally, I will risk a bit of octogenarian chill for the touch of a wind with some character to it. And, not only do we leave any semblance of my homeland here, this is the end of my back roads. Here we must leave the earth and roll upon the pavement."

"And, hopefully, find a gas station."

"That, too," he agreed. "But we don't want to spend too much on fuel. I am surprised at how little money you've amassed over your years."

"Hey, I wouldn't be quite so destitute if I hadn't relinquished sixty percent of my net worth in the acquisition of an ungrateful corpse."

"Is your mother living?"

"Yes."

"She must worry a great deal."

"Well, bless Mother Hallelujah, wherever she may dwell, her fine son doesn't seem to have dazzled the financial community either."

"I might surprise you."

"Does this mean you're going to buy the gas?"

"What do you think?"

"I think my $40 is going to be $30 very soon."

"You might be more clever than I thought, Jackson," said Glory with a laugh. But you are mistaken about one thing."

"What's that?"

"This old corpse is grateful."

We were about to get back into the truck and continue on when I asked, "Shouldn't we give your dog some water or something? It's going to be pretty hot down there."

"Oh, do not worry about old Jeremiah. The sooner he dies the better. Right, Boy?"

And the damned dog looked up, panted a dizzy smile, and wagged its tail in agreement.

We twisted down the serpentine shelf of divided highway and out upon the flatland. "Isn't Glory Hallelujah kind of a strange name for a parent to give a kid?"

"I'd say. I grew up with kids who called themselves Bear Claw and Eagle Feather. It wasn't easy. But my mother was not to blame. She was a soft, gentle and beautiful Indian woman. My father was an insane, excommunicated, mixed-blooded Mormon who, in his zeal, had renamed himself Praise-the-Lord Hallelujah. When he was running about the country raving at heathens in one of his religious frenzies, my mother had an Indian name for me which she spoke in a kind, loving voice. She is the only person who ever uttered it to me. I translate it roughly as 'Strong-flower.'"

"'Strong-flower'," I repeated. "That says much."

"True. My mother said very little but probably taught me more about communication than many learn who spend years at universities."

"I don't doubt that. And, by the way, speaking of names, how did you know I'm called Jackson? It's about time I start to figure some of this out."

"I cannot say. I just know you are to accompany me on this

journey. It would seem we have some invisible elements in common."

"Not by chance, a native sort of a fellow wearing a feather?"

"Perhaps."

"My spirit guide," I said. "I haven't seen my mysterious Indian buddy for a while, but I've always known he was around somewhere. That he'd be there whenever I needed him."

"The Spirit is always close."

"I've probably been searching for you for all these years, haven't I?"

"Possibly."

"Too bad I didn't get pitched into your parking lot a decade ago—it would have saved me a lot of miles and shoe leather."

"Impossible," he said. "Ten years ago neither of us would have been ready."

"There are so many questions I need to ask you. Questions about evil and power and Gods and pettiness, hope and the burnt remains of love, desperate momentum through an empty existence... "

"Answers will come, my friend. But be patient. First you must get us to the city where we can find one of those topless bars I have heard my nephews talking about."

6 Kitty's Titties

Most of the guys didn't seem to notice that the women were naked. They just played pool or sat around telling lies about how they had put bosses or wives or highway patrolmen in their places. "So, I sez to that fuckin' cop, I sez, 'Well, you can just take your fuckin' job and shove it if you think I can't stay out nights drinking with my buddies and driving drunk." And, meanwhile, while the jerks stood there chalking up their pool cues, not a yard away would stand lovely young ladies, revealing their most intimate contours and patiently waiting for someone to notice that they had delivered another round of Coors.

"Just look at those fools. It costs five bucks to walk into the place, they charge double for the beers, and, except for the half dozen creep-os who drool around the dancers and stuff five dollar bills into G-strings, most of these losers could just as well be sipping tea in their grandmothers' parlors."

"Do not be too harsh on them," Glory said. "They purchased their masculinity at the front door and now, obviously, they are afraid of it."

"It's a hell of a waste of pretty ladies, isn't it?"

"Not completely," he said as he looked up and smiled at the waitress who had come to our table.

"My name is Kitty," she said. "What may I get for you?"

And, with unabashed honesty and appreciation, without taking his eyes from the beautiful woman who stood before him, Glory Hallelujah said to me, "My God, Jackson, just look at Kitty's titties."

It would have been difficult to have done anything else *but* look at Kitty's titties—not only were they the size and apparent firmness of full-grown grapefruits, not only were they magnificently smooth and uplifted, not only were they extensions of the chest of a girl bearing a most lovely and disarming smile, but, also, they were located less than six inches from the end of my eager little nose.

"Glory," I said with tears of thankfulness blurring my vision and the quaver of heartfelt sincerity in my voice, "I think I've fallen in love."

"Do not waste your time, Jackson" he said with a firm yet friendly voice as he took her hand and looked beyond her breast and into her eyes, and from there into her heart. "Kitty will be my love."

"Oh...,"I said. And apparently love is not nearly as complicated as soap operas and marriage counselors would have us believe, for in that instant with a blush unbecoming a topless queen and a rather unprofessional hardening of her nipples, Kitty became Katherine and Glory became her man.

An amazing transformation had occurred in my companion since I resurrected him from his death blanket only hours earlier. He had steadily become both larger and younger. While we rode along and I had listened to his stories and his wisdom, a metamorphosis commenced that transformed him from being an aged desert recluse with sunken frame and time-dulled eyes, to the mesmerizing Valentino who had so easily stolen my darling Kitty from me. He was a man of age, but not defeat. A man whose years had produced not only wisdom, but, also, the strength to live and share that wisdom rather than being crushed by its massive burden.

Earlier that afternoon, right in the middle of a sentence, he had stopped and said, "You really listen to me, don't you?"

"Sure," I said in genuine amazement. "Doesn't everyone listen to you?"

To that he replied only with a quiet chuckle and went on with his story.

Kitty walked to the bar to get us a couple of beers. I watched as she walked away. "My, God," I proclaimed, "she has an ass on her, too!"

"And a damned good thing it is," said Glory. "Someday she might decide to sit down."

"You know what I mean. Look at her. She not only a beautiful face and unbelievable boobs, she's got a bottom on her that Michelangelo couldn't have sculpted from the finest marble. She's the perfect woman."

Glory turned to me and with a sudden shift to seriousness said, "And that is all it takes."

"Well, it doesn't hurt," I answered defensively.

"Jackson, you are as afraid of love as those assholes at the pool table are afraid of sex."

That stunned me. With one devastating verbal punch he had temporarily knocked the facetiousness right out me. "I didn't used to be afraid of love, it hasn't been easy."

"I know."

Kitty was heading back across the large barroom as both of us sat awe-struck by her wonderful body. I gained my composure. "So what did you fall in love with? Her mind?"

He laughed and answered, "There are many levels emanating from the human spirit. The careful observer can sense much more than that of the shallow surface."

"Yeah, I can see she has lovely right level and a lovely left level and both of them are jiggling like Jello."

"You can say that again," said Glory as she arrived at the table.

"Sit down Katherine," he said. "Take a break with me. You can drink Jackson's beer. He's going to spend fifteen minutes up at the bar trying to fall in love again."

"I am?"

"Yes," he said.

7 Focus

"Yes, Glory, my wife was murdered by lightning eleven years ago. It was in a beautiful city park—acres of rolling green lawn and I was chasing her in the rain because lovers are never too old to play. We were running up a hill. She turned to laugh a breathless loving laugh with me when lightning tore from the awful sky and the Gods destroyed her."

We were waiting in the old pick-up truck drinking from a six pack we had purchased with the last of my money. It was very late and the bar was quieting and the final straggling drunks were staggering to their cars. The choice of that particular topless bar, The Naked Rose, had not been ours. We had run out of gas and rolled to a stop across the street from it hours earlier. Now we were broke and marooned but it didn't matter because we were waiting for the lights to shut down and for Kitty and a friend to join us.

We weren't drunk. I'm not certain why, but clearly, we were not overwhelmed by the alcohol we had consumed. Especially Glory. He was fine. I'll have to admit I had experienced several attacks of momentary giddiness throughout the evening, but it was late, quiet out along the street, and I was feeling more melancholic than inebriated. I was also dreading the awkwardness of meeting the friend Kitty had imposed upon to join us.

It had been quite an evening. We, or rather, Glory had become the center of attention for at least a dozen, beautiful, topless waitresses/dancers. Though Kitty had clearly staked her claim, there had been a steady flow of lovely ladies and giggling conversation throughout the night. Glory later told me it was not unusual for him to attract young women. He said it enhanced their vanity to sense they were capable of stirring the virility of a man in his eighties. Whatever the reason, I believed the results—I saw them in action. Women would come to the table and sit with us, Glory would tell them they were beautiful, and they would leave—glowing as if they had been blessed by a priest. During a lull in the procession I said, "You've got magic, don't you? I mean

I've never seen anything like the way Kitty fell for you. And these other girls—they all love you. It's magic isn't it. You don't just talk to hell-crazed old hermits, you've been cavorting with desert nymphs, haven't you?"

"I don't know if you would consider some of the spirits I've known to be nymphs, but, yes, I have discovered some of the magic that vibrates through the aura of my humanity. To one degree or another, all of us possess magic."

"Some to a much lesser degree, I'll assure you."

"It's there for the using, Jackson. You'll learn."

"Well start teaching, Merlin. These ladies are driving me crazy."

"Merlin? Not likely. Some would say I'm just a horny old man."

"Bullshit," I said. "Horny old men make young girls itch. You make these ladies feel like taking their clothes off—if they had any on in the first place. And, by the way, have you noticed that not one of them has shown the slightest interest in me?"

"Yes, I've noticed," he said with a laugh that was only a hair short of malicious. "Don't worry, My Son. Be patient. Someday you, too, might become an old stud just like me." And then with more laughter he turned to continue the blessing of the fleet. And, oh, what ships did sail.

The word "lightning" had visibly jarred my companion. He had pressed me to tell my story as we waited in the pickup truck and it had spilled forth from its prominent position in my memory. I stared out the window as I slowly spoke, reconstructing in mind and word the details, the sensations, the horrendous sorrow that surrounded Lori's death. For over a decade I had fought to preserve vivid recollection of the murder so as to continually shake my existence with the terror and ache of it as if it had just happened. I was determined my love for her and my loathing for her death would never be eroded from me by time's curative processes. Neither she nor her death would ever become as faded pictures viewed carefully and then returned to the pages of an old and dreadful album.

Glory said a strange thing. "It's good your rage is yet strong. We'll need it."

An occasional car would pass, the pounding bass beat of the jukebox ceased, and the last of the Rose's voyeurs and pool sharks were shown the door.

"Lightning," Glory repeated. "Much of our thinking is clouded by a haze of seemingly disassociated detail—an amorphous mass of moments, experiences, sensations, and thoughts with no clear relevance to anything—their only commonality being that they are part of the single collection that is our individual memory. Then—at the tolling of a single bell, a sight, an aroma, a touch of sunshine, a shadow cast by the moon, the utterance of a single word—certain of these myriad specks of our lives shimmer into crisp focus for an instant giving us a flash of the integral connectedness of all matter and ideas.

"You spoke the word 'lightning' and, in an instant, sixty years of diverse sensations were crystallized within me. With ages and worlds separating us, we sit on this sleazy back street with no gasoline or money and with the mention of a single word are united in a bond of experience and knowledge far beyond the temporal matters of our beings.

"I, too, well know of the wrath of the Gods and their deadly wielding of bolts of lightning."

8 Pearl Buttons

Stillness was broken by the sound of light conversation and the scrape of high heels on the gravel parking lot. The ladies were on their way out.

"Over here, Katherine," said Glory as he climbed out of the truck and held the door open. I sat behind the wheel hoping I would suddenly reverse the night's trend and become charming and irresistibly attractive to whomever it was Kitty had dragged along.

"Please get in," said Glory.

With dancers' grace the two of them glided into the narrow confines of the old pickup.

Glory squeezed in and closed the door. The four of us—a virile old man on the passenger's side, two voluptuous strangers in the middle, and me hanging halfway out the driver's window thinking of how much I wished I were in the back of the truck with the dying dog, Jeremiah—were sitting on a side street waiting for the next breath.

"Jackson," said Kitty, "this is Carrie. She's my roommate."

I recognized her as being one of the bartender ladies I had been buying beers from her off and on all evening. "Hi, Carrie," I said, smiling and trying to be clever. "You're the bartender lady."

"Hi, Jackson," she said. "You're the customer guy."

"Sure am."

We sat there and it seemed like it was getting pretty damned hot and Glory was no help to me because he was locked into love's selfish gaze with Kitty so I tried to be clever again. "So… "

"Yes?"

"Carrie sure is a pretty name."

"Thank you."

So, have you always worked in a topless bar?"

"No. Actually, I started out in kindergarten playing in a topless sandbox."

What a funny thing to say, I thought, and then I laughed too much.

"I'm sorry. I didn't mean it that way. I meant. Hell, I didn't mean anything. I was just saying stuff. I mean I don't know you except that you smile at guys when you serve them beers and I like that. But, you don't know me and I know this wasn't your idea. I mean you didn't pull Kitty aside and say how much you'd like to meet the guy sitting at the table with Glory. You just got stuck with me because Kitty asked you to do her a favor. Right?"

"You're shy."

"Not really."

"Sure you are. Most of the jerks Kitty introduces me to would have tried to chew the buttons off my blouse by now."

"I'm not shy, Carrie. At least not in the sense of being intimidated. I'm not afraid of you. You're beautiful and I'd love to eat your clothes, but I'd feel kind of stupid just saying hello and then filling my mouth with mother-of-pearl buttons. Men are really that forward with you?"

"Only once. Then they have a hard time telling the buttons from their own teeth."

"That's really funny," I said I laughed louder than I should have again, but what the heck. "You know," I said as it became obvious I had better stop laughing, "I think the worst part is the silence. Not knowing what to say is bad enough, but when we aren't talking we can hear those two panting at each other. God, I hope they don't start kissing. You ever listen to people kissing? It sounds disgusting if you aren't in the middle of it yourself."

"I've never really paid that much attention to the sound of kissers."

"You're lucky you've never noticed. It can drive you crazy, believe me."

"No doubt."

Silence.

"It sure can get quiet, can't it?"

"It sure can."

"But don't worry. I've thought of something else to say. Fear no silence, Jackson is here. I was in Paris once and in Paris or maybe even all of France or Europe even, people make a lot more noise when they kiss than we do here in the United States of America. I really could hardly stand to be around Parisians when they were kissing because of the sounds they made. I may not ever go back there because of those kissing sounds and it seems like they're always kissing. I was sitting on a bench in Luxembourg Gardens one morning eating a peanut butter sandwich and a couple on the next bench over was making such a racket I lost my appetite. I mean, they sounded like cartoon mice when they stick their lips together and stretch them apart about a yard or two and then pop them loose with an elastic snap that spins their goddamn little rodent heads around six or eight times making ropes out of their necks. I think Minnie's a slut anyway—no nice looking mouse like her is going to fall for a squeaky voiced little wimp like Mickey. It's obvious she's fucking—I mean screwing him for his money. Sorry, I don't mean to talk dirty and sometimes it gets me into trouble, but have you ever noticed how Disney characters aren't married—they've got girlfriends and, ha, nephews. Sure the little bastards are nephews. Huey, Dewey, and Louie Duck—all nephews. Come on, everyone knows Donald is a bachelor and was an only duckling. He doesn't have any nephews. Daisy was too much of a birdbrain to remember to take her birth control pills—that's what happened. So why don't we get out of this truck and go somewhere, Carrie, it's out of gas anyway. Want a cup of coffee or something?"

She was laughing. There was laughter about her and a comforting weariness.

"I'll make us some coffee—our apartment is right here."

I opened the door and we slid out my side.

"Your truck is really out of gas?" she asked as we walked along the sidewalk.

"Yeah. I had some gas money earlier today but I spent it all buying four-dollar beers and two-bit rejection at your bar."

"Rejection?"

"Yeah. That's what I call it. Rejection—you know, exclusion from acceptance: the self-inflicted sorrows and bruises to esteem resulting from the risking of the heart."

"Your heart. Come on."

"Well, at least my ego."

"What do you expect? A thousand male egos crawl in and out of the Naked Rose every week, and, believe me, most of them are about belly high to a snake, and do you men expect us to be dazzled by your baby blue eyes and Wrangler-shrink-to-fit butts?"

"Oh, not me. I've never thought of myself a being much of

a dazzler. Actually, I spent the last of my mortal fortune on high-priced beers in order to find focus for a lifelong quest of humility."

"Don't tell me you went to the Naked Rose looking for love."

"No. According to Glory, my new-found friend and spiritual confessor, I'm afraid of love anyway. But, I'll tell you, Carrie, lust is a pretty good substitute sometimes."

"Tell me about it." she said with an honest face. "But, Jackson, you don't ever want to confuse your heart with your hard-on—it will always get you into trouble."

And I laughed and said, "I'll try to remember that."

We climbed up the stairs to the apartment and I hoped that she liked me because I already thought she was fantastic.

She unlocked the door and we went inside. There was a light already on. "We always leave a light burning. Come on in the kitchen and sit down. I'll start the coffee."

Their apartment was small and tidy, somewhat cluttered with knickknacks, ruffled drapes and furniture—it had an old-fashioned touch to it more reminiscent of a cookie-jar aunt than what I would have expected of the love den of a pair of go-go queens.

"I like your place," I said as I pulled a high-backed chair up to the kitchen table."

"Thanks. It's a little corny, but after a night in the flesh market, it sure is nice to come home to a decent place."

"You hate your job, don't you?"

Her makeup had faded with the hours and her face was soft and suddenly fragile. She folded her arms across her chest and, withdrawing into herself, replied starkly, "Well, let's just say the uniform I wear gets a little chilly sometimes."

I met her eyes for an instant and then, not letting seriousness carry the night, I said, "Sure, but think of the money you save on dry cleaning."

"Oh, that really helps a lot." she laughed and turned back to the coffee pot and the cupboard and its fine coffee cups and white china saucers. We heard the front door open and Kitty and Glory entered and headed directly to a bedroom.

"Sweet dreams!" I said. "Now, how do you explain that? Glory wasn't lost in a sea of denim-coated snake-egos. He took his crusty old heart to the barroom and didn't get it kicked."

"I can't begin to explain what happened with them. I've known

Kitty for years and through a dozen romances and have never seen her as happy or excited as she's been tonight."

"It's not fair. He used magic on her."

"You're just jealous," she said. "I don't care if it's magic or chemistry or whatever, it's beautiful."

"He told me we all have magic in us. We just have to find it." I said as I stood up and with a light touch on her arm turned her to me. Staring deeply into her eyes I chanted, "Hocus-pocus, dom-in-oakkus..."

She laughed and playfully shoved me away, saying, "Just keep your rabbit in your hat, Fella, the coffee's almost ready."

And she moved lightly around the kitchen and as I sat down and watched her I realized she was very lovely and I was very tired. She poured us coffee and, without asking, sweetened both cups with honey.

"Decaf," she said. "It won't keep you awake."

She sat across from me and we sipped the hot brew and quite comfortably said little.

"I'll make the hide-a-bed for you," she said, putting to rest any remnant of my wild speculation.

I went back down to the truck to retrieve my bag. The night was close and silent and, as I sat on the tailgate scratching Jeremiah on his moribund head I thought of the great distances a single day could travel. When I returned to the apartment she had showered away all traces of mascara and lipstick and rouge and was wearing a simple nightgown that made me crazy. She handed me a towel and washcloth and said, "Jackson, are you always this dusty?"

"Only when I want to impress a beautiful lady," I said.

"I see," she said.

I watched as she crossed the room, entered her bedroom, and closed the door. An instant later, the door reopened and her sweet face peered out at me. "By the way," she said, "I haven't rejected you."

"You haven't?" I asked with exuberance.

"Well, not yet, anyway," she said, smiling as once again she closed the door.

9 Morning

Hide-a-bed mornings are awkward.

Though hardly conventional, my lifestyle had not become so alien to the Puritan Work Ethic that I could guiltlessly slumber away entire mornings. I would normally awake without the annoyance of an alarm clock at a decent though somewhat less than zealous hour. Even so, regardless of my resolve the night before, the morning found me sprawled out, stage-center in the middle of a near-stranger's living room, obviously the last to rise and, consequently, considerably ill at ease. We were adults and God knows I had already seen a major portion of Carrie's lovely flesh at the bar the previous night. But, with her right there in the adjoining kitchen making Henrietta Homemaker noises in the bright light of the most wholesome morning since Betty Crocker made her first cupcake, I was embarrassed to get out from under the covers and retrieve my pants.

I lay motionless.

"Good morning, Jackson," she sang. How could she know I was awake?

"Good morning, Carrie," I returned. "Don't look, I'm going to get dressed."

"Don't worry. I'll focus all my attention on not burning the bacon."

"I'll just be a minute."

"I was right, wasn't I?" she said with playful smugness as she poked at the sizzling skillet before her.

"About what?" I said, rapidly pulling up my pants.

She turned and faced me as I clumsily tucked and zipped and buckled. "You are shy."

I laughed and growled, "Just let me at those buttons—they'll taste good with bacon and eggs."

"You don't fool me, Jackson," she said. "How many eggs to you take?"

"Two, please."

Glory was gone. Somehow I knew that he and Kitty had left.

There was a small clock on a shelf in the bathroom. I was amazed that it was already past ten o'clock. I hadn't fallen asleep right away. After a long shower, I lay there listening to the incessant chattering of my unquiet mind and to the symphony of love sounds and laugh sounds and serious conversational sounds coming from Kitty's bedroom. They must have talked and loved and laughed and cried throughout the night. I finally pulled the pillow over my head and went to sleep when they started singing "Row, Row, Row Your Boat."

The door to Kitty's bedroom was open. The bed was made and the lace curtains opened wide. The room was full of light.

"Where did Glory and Kitty go?" I asked as I walked into the kitchen after swinging the hide-a-bed shut.

"They went to the courthouse to buy a marriage license, but they said for us to go ahead and have breakfast without them."

"Oh," I said. "Marriage license. Okay, I see."

"You do?" she asked incredulously and then we both laughed. She was wearing a pair of cutoff jeans and a tee shirt that read, "Blow your bubbles before the flavor is gone."

"Glory was saying something about a place called Three Days. Do you know anything about it, Jackson?"

"It's a holy mountain and I think he plans on going there for holy reasons."

"He's an unusual man."

"Not too strange to get laid last night," I said. "Maybe I need to spend a few more decades wandering around the desert talking to spirits and rocks myself."

"Maybe you should," she said and there was something wonderfully serene and playful about her that sunny morning— as if the night had not only dispelled her weariness but also had reinvigorated her tavern-dulled spirit. The previous night had been beer and boobs and the marvelous insanity of blithely trailing along in amazement behind the enactment of my own destiny. The morning was a different time. I awoke in the realm of a home. It was a place where there could be profound depth and repercussion to interaction with the very pretty lady who was artfully preparing our feast.

It scared the hell out of me, but I didn't run.

10 Breakfast

Upon the oak table, Carrie set before me the most beautiful pair of poached eggs I had ever seen—smooth, firm circles of flawless white upon a Delft-blue plate accoutered with light, white potatoes browned to God-golden perfection, four strips of bacon, and two pieces of broiled buttered toast.

The coffee smelled of all the magical, heart-touched, loving kitchens known to the blessed world.

I told her I probably was in love with her and she agreed she had cooked a damned fine breakfast.

11 RIP

There was an abrupt knocking at the door.

It was the police.

Rats. I had known passionate love's embrace that possessed less intimacy than what had been the moment of Carrie and the absolute breakfast.

Knocking at the door. A vision shattered.

"Do you happen to know who owns that piece-of-junk pickup truck parked in front of this building?"

"Yeah, I guess it's my truck."

""I hate to tell you this, Sir, but your dog is dead."

"Oh, no, officer," I laughed. "He's not really dead. He's just playing dead."

"Well, if he's acting, anybody downwind of the son of a bitch would nominate him for an Academy Award."

"Oh... " I said.

And the policeman was gone and the breakfast reduced to artless smears of remnant egg-yellow and a half piece of toast with a bite munched out of it.

The morning was no longer ours. "I'm sorry about your dog, Jackson."

"He isn't my dog. His name was Jeremiah. He just kind of came along with Glory. It's too bad he's dead. I talked to him last night when I went back out to the truck. He wasn't the liveliest pooch I'd ever petted, but he did wag his tail a couple of times."

"I'm sorry," she said.

"It is a damned shame he's dead."

I helped her with the dishes. She washed and I took the plates and saucers from her hands and dried them. We didn't speak but upon a silent signal of our hearts she turned and placed her wet hands about my neck and I pulled her close to me and we quietly embraced.

12 Three Days—The Beginning of an Explanation

I tried to be sensitive. I took Glory aside and spoke careful words about the demise of his long-time companion, Jeremiah the Dog. Matters were beginning to build and, as one senses the invisible precursors of a storm, the energy of the coming days was clearly swirling about us.

I gently informed Glory that his faithful fellow wanderer of the sacred wastelands had fled his earthly burden and was aromatically wending his way along the paths of decomposition back to the essence of dust.

"Jeremiah is dead?"

"Yes."

"Are you sure, Jackson. He could be meditating."

"I'm surprised you didn't notice on the way in."

"We came in from the back. Pretty strong?"

"I haven't reconnoitered the area personally, but the cops assured me word of his departure is clearly in the air."

"Jeremiah is dead."

"It seems so."

And then with a whoop and a leap the crazy bastard shouted with joy, "The mangy old cuss is finally dead! Pack your toothbrushes, ladies. It's time to go to Three Days!"

Glory and I were walking along a street near the apartment. I was laboring with a five gallon can filled with gasoline and Glory was struggling to contain an obvious desire to start skipping or spinning about in some imaginary game of hopscotch. He was exuberant. "Jackson, years, hell, we've spent lifetimes in anticipation of these next days."

I sat the can down, took a breath, and picked it up with my other hand. "Didn't you like your dog?" I asked, more as an expression of my bewilderment than a real question.

"Years," he said. "Don't worry about Jeremiah, he wasn't a dog anyway. He was a spirit trapped in a four-legged home for ambient fleas. His repentant soul is now free."

97

We walked on. He was silent though his eyes, his walk, the motions of his body were dashing about in excitement. He was thinking, planning.

"Is that gas can getting heavy?"

"A bit."

He stopped and considered me for a moment. Concentrating all the wild madness of the day upon me he said, "You've had the miles, the distances; you've traveled far, my friend. It's time that you begin to learn the Powers. The Powers are all around us, Jackson. Some, as you and I well know, would destroy us. They are invisible in the earthly realm of this city, but, believe me, they will take manifest form in the region of our destination. But there are other Powers—potent energies that counter weakness and evil. While we may not see them here, we can breathe them. The Powers don't dwell in the air, but the air is their symbol and we may use it to gain access to them. With strong heart, Jackson, seek the good Powers. Breathe the swirling airs deeply through the senses of your being. Breathe deeply.

"How?" I asked. The man was obviously nuts, but what the heck.

"Start with your lungs and your heart. Breathe the might of the airs through the center of your soul, breathe through your feet and the reach of your arms. Breathe through your eyes, Jackson, that you might breathe through your mind. Let the airs enter your spirit through the breathing of your skin."

And there I stood in the middle of the sidewalk breathing for all my worth and amazingly I began feeling the Powers. "Now what?" I cried, feeling the exhilaration and disorientation of the wonderful airs.

"The damned gas can," he said. "Breathe the Powers through the gas can."

He walked on ahead and I took deep, magical breaths of the Powers through my lungs and heart, my arms and legs, through my eyes and mind, and, finally, through the damned gas can and, to my utter amazement, I followed him with forty pounds of sloshing petrol and a big red can dangling as freely from my arm as an empty lunch box.

I caught up with him. I was laughing. "It works," I said. "The weight is gone from the can."

"That's part of it," he said laughing with me. "But, mostly, the

98

weakness is gone from your arm."

We rounded a corner and the stench of Jeremiah was even funny. "The old Grim Reaper breathes with a foul breath this morning," said Glory.

"Mighty foul," I heartedly agreed."

I poured the gasoline into the tank and then climbed into the passenger's seat. Glory got behind the wheel. "We've got to get rid of this corpse and get this truck to a carwash," he said. "But first let's go to a supermarket and get a vegetable bag in which to keep the heart."

"Good idea. That sounds reasonable to me—pretty messy business, those hearts, that is without a plastic bag from the produce department." And I mumbled, "Apples, oranges, a head of lettuce, the heart of a dog." The madness was accelerating. In just over a day I had been thrown from a car, captured by the allure of an escaping mystic, bombarded by boobs, touched by the gentle wonder of a beautiful lady, and now I was about to be coerced into cutting the heart out of the corpse of a dead dog.

"Say, Glory," I said. "This seems to be getting to be too much for me to grasp."

"I am sure it is. But do not worry, you'll be fine. Trust me."

"I do trust you. I just don't understand anything about what's going on."

"You will understand very soon."

"I hope so. It's not like the gas can, is it?"

"What do you mean?"

"Well, with rotting Jeremiah rolling around the back of this truck, don't try to tell me I've got to start deeply breathing in the Powers again."

"Fear not, Jackson. The lessons are not easy, but not that difficult."

"Tell me about Three Days, Glory. You said we're going there and it is the mountain of the Dark Spirits the hermit warned you about."

"You remember well."

"Then it's true, the Spirits of Three Days possess the power of the deadly storm?"

"Sometimes."

"God lives upon a mountain called Three Days?"

"By certain definitions, yes."

"Then why in the world would you want us to go to such a terrible place?"

"Do you fear this mountain?"

"I fear God, Glory."

"There are many Gods—some weak some powerful, some good and others evil."

"I fear them all. I fear Gods as I fear the vision of my burning wife."

"I have lived long. I have encountered the evil Powers many times and yet have survived. But, clearly, I understand what you say. Though I have discovered much of my own Power, I still fear the deadly bastards myself."

"So why do we seek them at Three Days?"

"When we first met and I called you by name you said you had many questions I might answer and I told you that answers would come. Well, now, my old friend, we approach the answers together. Surely you have not come so far only to flee at the first vision of truth looming before us."

"But Dark Spirits and a dog's heart?"

"It does seem bizarre. But how could a great search reveal discoveries that are less than bizarre? There is little within the realm of normal reason and experience to account for the forces that range and rage about us. What of a world of mortgage payments and new-and-improved laundry detergents approaches any notion of an explanation of the concept of death, the cruel truth of sorrow, the spinning wonder of seasons and sunsets? You said you seek answers and now that you approach them you expect them to be as comfortable as the childish myths of religion or the petty delvings of the sciences. So we are going to cut the heart out of a dead dog and take it to a sacred mountain. What difference does it make how sophisticated the supernatural systems are which control us? The end results are the same whether mandated from the Vatican or from some superstitious mountain: we are either alive or dead, happy or sad, enlightened or ignorant."

He pulled to the side of the street and stopped the truck. He looked deeply at me. "Are you with me, Jackson?" he asked.

Of course I was with him. "I suppose this means I have to help you with the heart, doesn't it?"

"What do you think?"

100

"Yuck. That's what I think."

He laughed and said, "Don't believe for a moment that I relish the idea of digging into old Rover back there, but there are certain rituals or procedures on the periphery of the supernatural which must be honored if entry is to be achieved."

"You know, my life would have been so much simpler if I had remained a Presbyterian."

"Much less gory, anyway."

"We didn't even have to kneel."

Glory grinned and said, "Do you know what they do when a Roman Catholic Pope dies?"

"Sure. They cut out his heart and take it to a sacred mountain in Arizona. Right?"

"You are close. They take a ceremonial silver hammer and tap him on the head three times, saying, 'Pope, are you dead? Pope are you dead? Pope, are you dead?'"

13 Day One

"I don't know," Carrie said. We were riding in the back of the pickup truck. Glory was driving.

"Good," I said. "It doesn't feel so bad knowing there are two of us who don't know what's going on."

"You know more than I do. He talks to you. He just smiles at me and I follow along like a loyal cocker spaniel."

"A cocker spaniel," I said. "When I was but a wee lad my father told me to be wary of things I was taught in school. 'Don't believe everything they tell you. Think it out yourself,' he said. And to illustrate his point he told me, 'Contrary to what is written in your first-grade reader, dogs do not say *Bow Wow*, they say *Ralph*.'"

"Ralph?"

"Yeah. As in, *Ralph!* I love cocker spaniels. Or, *Ralph!* I love to pet cocker spaniels. Or, *Ralph,* I'd sniff you in a second."

"You'd be a nasty dog."

"*Ralph!* You've got that right."

"So, what does this have to do with why we are bouncing along in the back of this truck heading for some strange place called Three Days?"

"I don't know. I guess I'm saying I'm just another cocker spaniel following along just like you. Wanna hump:"

"No thanks—not in heat."

"Rats!" I shouted to the road winds and the distant mountains," I thought you naked bar ladies were supposed to be easy,"

"Well, I guess your daddy was right, Jackson. Don't believe everything you heard at school." And then with sweet tease of a smile she made me shake by saying, "But I didn't say 'Never in heat.'"

I wanted her lips, I wanted her breasts, I wanted to embrace her with my fevered lust so I decided to talk about philosophy instead of going nuts. "Would you like to talk philosophy?" I asked. "I think Nietzsche was an asshole, don't you?"

She smiled at me. "You're funny, Jackson. I really like you."

"I'm glad."

"So, what do you know about Three Days?"

"Nothing, except that God lives there."

"That's all he told you, Jackson?"

"Oh, not all. But it's like math class back in high school. While you were sitting there watching the teacher and her lightning-fast chalk, working the problems was easy. But once you got home nothing came out right. I understand everything he tells me until I try to figure it out myself. I really don't know anything."

"Yes you do."

"I do?"

"Sure," she said as she huddled closer to me beneath our blanket and I knew that eventually there would be a perfect time and we would make love, and it made me warm and crazy.

"I know I'm going to make love to you," I said.

"That's not all you know."

"What else?"

"You know that Nietzsche was an asshole," she said and we laughed and I kissed her and there was such a wonderful wordless understanding between us.

****

Carrie and Kitty had called in sick, claiming that both had been stricken with food poisoning from eating bad tofu. In a matter of less than and hour we had packed food and pots and pans and socks, underwear, and toothbrushes for the road. We took the mattress off of the hide-a-bed and put it in the back of the pickup along with blankets and pillows. There was excitement to our frenzied activity. Without any trace of reason or common sense, we had blithely volunteered to follow Glory to the sunset and beyond.

It was fun. It gave me an opportunity to demonstrate my newly-acquired breathing Powers by carrying everything out to the car with the greatest of ease—even Carrie. We were all under the influence of a delightful trance and nobody cared if it all seemed insane. I was certain Glory Hallelujah was breathing through the three of us the same as I had breathed through the can of gasoline. We were so light.

Glory began our mystical trek by circling the city several times on the circumferential interstate highway. We were creeping along at a good forty-five miles per hour with red-faced commuters and Grand Prix semi drivers flashing lights and blowing horns and flipping birds at us from all lanes. Glory seemed oblivious to the madness and all Carrie and I could do was smile and occasionally shrug our shoulders.

"He might have the balls of a twenty year old, but, by damn, he sure drives like an old man," I shouted, hoping he would hear me and either speed up or get us the hell off the treacherous interstate.

"He can't hear you," Carrie said. By leaning close together and sheltering ourselves from the wind with a blanket, we found we could actually converse. "He's singing some kind of an Indian chant. Can't you hear it?"

"Oh, good. I thought we had a bad wheel bearing."

When in peril sometimes it is best to laugh and we did plenty of that. Finally, after at least three grueling loops around the metropolis, he took an exit from the dreaded interstate system and headed west on the old highway. Carrie and I stood up and banged on the roof, shouting our approval. From the cab, Glory and Kitty waved acknowledgment. She sat right next to him and they looked like a high school couple coming home from a date. As we cleared the last of the clutter of the city's outskirts I nodded at them and said, "It looks like true love to me."

"Why not?"

There was little traffic, and none of it was angry. About twenty miles out of town there was an old truckstop and we pulled in so Kitty could buy us some food and gas. She had generously volunteered to finance the trek. As we walked across the parking lot toward the restaurant I said, "For a while there it didn't seem like we were ever going to get out of town."

Glory smiled and said, "Sorry about the route. Some of these traditions can get tedious. But none of it will count if the rituals are not properly enacted."

"None of it will count if we all get run over by an eighteen-wheeler either."

It was twilight and the horizon was defined by a range of dusk-blue mountains. "Trust me, Jackson. We'll all survive the trip to Three Days."

"Do you really know how to get there?"

"Yes. We can see it from here. Our mountain is the one

farthest north—the tallest of the western range. I have known that mountain all of my life, though from my homeland it was to the southwest and cut a different silhouette. Taking a direct route, it's not that many miles to Three Days. But be patient. Some take as long as three years to get there."

"Then why don't they call it Three Years?"

"A Holy Man, traveling with spirits, could circle the villages for hours and still make it to the foot of the mountain in three days. It is part of our test to see how long it takes us to get there."

"Why would a holy one ever want to approach such a hellish place?"

"There are many realms of power upon the sacred mountain. Our journey to Darkness is but one."

We got a table and the ladies went to the restroom. "Glory, do you really believe all of this bullshit?"

There was rage but no anger in his answer. "If you mean have I actively practiced such superstitious rituals throughout my life, or do I actually embrace such beliefs and practices—hell no! I might be old and the color of the desert, born of fanaticism, educated in the ways of spirits, coyotes, and dry-land lizards, but I'm not stupid, Man. I know the difference between games and reason. Whether climbing some corporate ladder or joining a country club or approaching the dominion of a dangerous God, we must all make sacrifices of our own reason. Surely you know that."

"Kiss a little ass?"

"Exactly. We have to kiss a little ass if we are ever going to be in a position to kick a lot of ass."

And then his voice deepened. Once again his words took on a smooth and otherworldly tone. He speech became the poetry of a desert sage.

Breathe through your mind, Jackson, and listen to me. There is a reality cherished by the hearts and minds of all feeling and thinking human beings. A reality known only by the intuitive perception of the human spirit of the world of a greater self. There is a world beyond that which is condemned to suffer the plagues of disease and boredom that torment the laborious and lusterless path from screaming birth to whispering death. A world, no, worlds faintly expressed in the visions of man's greater eye—the music, the poetry, the painting and sculpture; the awareness of the artful blessings of nature in cloud-colored skies, mountain-rushing rivers, and the persistence of blood-red blossoms on the stark, sharp reaches of cacti. There are greater worlds as evinced by our driving need to travel the exhilarating impulses darting in shimmers of invisible energy through the velvet-black void of the heavens. There is a realm of higher essence than that which governs, with the fearful bark and howl of allegorical wolves upon the trail of our days, the mundane matter of finite existence. Coexisting with the world of life and death are the immortal worlds of spirit.

There are Gods who, with no qualms or logic and with no more than mechanical awareness, can pinch precious life from the warmest sources of human worth and cast it forever from the touch of the Earth. And, likewise, there are Gods manifest in the wings of birds and the petals of flowers, in the burst of geysers and the murmurs of brooks and poets. There are Gods of this Higher Order who stretch from infinite sources past the frail and petty curse of mortality and give us music, art, love—hints of the unquenchable light of the soul. And now, regardless of these foolish footprints we must make upon the blowing sands of this desert, you and I will confront the dark Gods of a holy mountain with the rage and illumination of our very souls.

"Jesus wants me for a sunbeam," I said.

"What?"

"I said, 'Jesus wants me for a sunbeam.' I never could understand how the God of sunbeams could also be the God of polio and spinal meningitis, war and famine. Hell, the God of indigestion and warts."

"Yeah, and premature ejaculation," said Kitty who with Carrie had joined us as Glory spoke. "The God of premature ejaculation sure couldn't be the guy who worked on sunbeams."

Glory laughed, "I think we're all getting it."

"And another thing," he added, "and then I will shut up about these celestial matters and let us feed our mortal flesh in peace.

These rituals associated with Three Days—they are unique to this corner of the planet. By no means is this the only region where ritual is required. There are many games implicit in the requisites of access, and in one form or another, we all must play them."

"And now we're just playing the wild-eyed-crusty-old-Indian version, right?"

"You could say so."

13 Love

Somewhere well into the darkness, Glory turned from the highway and onto a deserted road to the northwest. Desert nights are chilly and Carrie and I had bundled ourselves in a couple of layers of blankets. We were actually comfortable. Before leaving we had taken the truck to a carwash and flushed away decades of dust and debris. With the mattress beneath us and a couple of couch cushions at our backs it wasn't a bad ride. The moon had not risen and the sky was alive with stars. The road was smooth and straight.

"Sometimes I find myself in the strangest places," I said. "Places haunted by painful memories, or just haunted by anybody's fear and dread—generic horror and gloom. Sometimes I'm in places so normal I hardly know I exist. I'm seldom really lost but there are times when I have no idea where I am."

"And tonight?" she asked.

"Tonight I know exactly where I am. I'm not navigating by the stars or a *Rand McNally Road Atlas*. All they can tell is that you're a hell of a long way from any place safe. I'm navigating by my heart tonight and it's right next to your heart. That's where I am."

"Is it haunted here?"

"No. It is frightening."

"You're afraid of me?"

"No. Us."

"Why?"

"Glory was right when he said I'm afraid of love—afraid of more than just physical passion. I've been this way for a long time now, Carrie. Eleven years ago my wife was killed because I loved her and someone or some thing was angry at me. Since then, though I've known some fine women along the way—known the comfort and pleasure of a night's closeness against the scatter and chill of this journey—I have never risked the involvement of my heart or the commitment of my life since Lori died. I guess it seems like I'm one of these macho male pigs who hides from intimacy by dealing with women as objects instead of people. You know the type, seeing a body and not bothering with the heart and soul that dwell within it."

"You're no pig, Jackson. You might be a chicken, but you're not a pig. There's a big difference and, believe me, it's plenty obvious to a woman as soon as she meets a man. Pigs we detest; chickens we just pity."

"Now that's really comforting."

"I'm kidding. I don't pity you, Jackson. But I don't want you to be afraid to know me."

"Well, I am afraid. I loved with my whole heart only once and it proved to be deadly."

"Tell me about your wife."

"I don't know…"

"Please."

"Okay. I'll try, Carrie."

Then I just had to take a breath. Let the air and the nightscape roll by for second.

"Her name was Lori. I think about her most all the time and I know, even though she is dead and buried, in some invisible realm she's always with me. She whispers through me even now. I think about her all the time but I don't talk about her much."

"Why?"

"Too damn sad, Carrie."

We rode along with just the road sound and the rattle of the old truck for a while.

"So," she said, "you're afraid of 'us' because love made you sad eleven years ago. Love made you sad and it's kept you sad all this time."

"I guess so. That, and I know my love might still be dangerous so I tend to move on when I start feeling the kind of stirring I get when I'm next to you."

"Are you stirring right now as we speak?"

"Well, yeah. You see, I've been dealing with women as pleasing collections of exciting parts for so long I thought I might be safe from feeling this way."

"Parts. That's what we sell down at the Naked Rose."

"I know. Some really nice parts at that."

"And tell me, are you excited by my parts?"

"You bet."

"And..."

"And, Carrie, how long ago were we formally introduced in the front seat of this truck? It must have been about midnight last night. So, I've probably been in love with you for at least twenty-two and one-half hours now. And, damn it, it's not just your beautiful parts either. You made that joke about the topless sandbox and slipped right past a decade's defenses and it was just a matter of a few more laughs and the gentle way your eyes peered out from your soul and looked at me with such kind amusement and I was a goner. I haven't felt like this since Lori and it is truly frightening."

"Chicken."

"I'm serious."

"You're not only shy, you're also a chickenshit."

"Damn it, Carrie, I don't want to get you hurt."

"Jackson, you don't want to get yourself hurt."

That really hit hard. Truth can be like that. Especially when it's so obvious and has been denied for so long.

"You think?"

"Yes."

"Honest to God, I thought I was being noble."

"No way. You're just a shy chickenshit guy. But you're kind of cute—you've got some nice parts, too."

"And, even with demons all about me, you're not afraid?"

"Of course, I'm afraid," she said and I could see her lovely face smiling at me. "Okay, tell me, where are you right now."

"Next to your heart."

"And..."

"And next to your wonderful lips and your breasts and your panties and, by God, your socks and your pearly buttons. I'm next to your skin and where the hell are you?"

"I am here here and I'll bite the buttons off your shirt if you don't make love to me right now."

****

.... and lovers we were, Carrie and I in the bed of the pickup truck the night of the starry blackness on the road with no traffic. And in the ecstasy of our nakedness and our lust and our love we reveled timeless miles upon the dark road to Three Days.

14 Reflection

Glory said that without reflective enhancement love would be over when the energies were discharged.

Sometimes the zigs and zags of elbows and butts and knees are like pieces of a jigsaw puzzle. Our loving had been incredible. But the frightening part, the addictive part—the stuff of reflection—was how comfortably we zigged and zagged in naked warmth beneath the blankets after all the panting and growling and all the weaving of passionate intimacy was brought with artful crescendo to explosive exhaustion. It was so comfortable with her.

We were wrapped up together, but not constrained or bound—just wrapped up.

The world slowly returned and we were giddy. In the old movies great sex is followed by deeply inhaled cigarettes and meaningful silences. In truth, great sex is followed by intimate, sometimes nearly hysterical laughter. We were laughing because it all felt so good and because it was so comfortable there and the questions had been answered by our bodies. It was funny as the world returned.

And it was a different world. Sometime during our erotic absence from matters of the journey the world had changed. It had the same stars and the same sky, but in the smooth sweep and angling of the land, the eerie stillness, clearly we had left the real and reason-measured world behind.

It didn't matter. We were laughing and feeling so good. "I hope our clothes didn't blow away," she said.

We were laughing and the world was refocusing and I realized the truck had stopped.

"I've heard of passion's fireworks," I said, "but have you ever gotten it off with red lights and a siren?"

"You, too."

"Oh, my God. It's the Highway Patrol."

15 Them Bones

"I'll bet Glory doesn't have a driver's license," I whispered as, surrounded by a blinding aura of flashing lights, the silhouetted figure of a state highway patrolman slowly approached us. "I don't think it matters anyway," said Carrie. "There's nobody in the front of the truck."

She was right. The cab was empty—they must have slipped out and hidden in the deep shadows formed by spotlights cast out upon the irregular terrain of the desert.

"Get out of the truck, please," said the steel-cold voice of the policeman.

"Could you give us just a minute," I said. "We're kind of naked, Officer. We're getting dressed as quickly as we can." Carrie and I were digging through the blankets trying to retrieve our modesty but we both were laughing and it wasn't the most orderly and efficient search.

"To hell with the underwear, just give me my goddamned pants," I said under my breath.

"Find your own goddamn pants," she giggled. "He's looking at my ass."

"Hey, so much for blind justice."

With no words, the figure advanced slowly toward the truck and, ignoring our comedic struggling for clothes and irrepressible snickering, he began circling. As he passed directly by us, our mirth ceased. He was a huge form and beneath the polished leather brim of his cap were deep black recesses where eyes should have shown. A glimpse of his moving profile revealed the stark, horrid features of a fleshless skull.

Following the movements of the creature with the corner of my eye, I said, "Gasp."

Carrie had very sharp fingernails and they were steadily digging their way through the meat of my right arm.

Eyeing the creature as one watches the hypnotic motions of a snake, we, with the laborious ineptitude of flight from the antagonist of a nightmare, fought for freedom from the web of the blankets and pillows.

The figure stopped at the front of the truck, and, facing the direct illumination of the headlights, revealed the total horror of its visage. Before us stood the body of a large man—clothed in the brown uniform of a state patrolman with stripes running the length of his trouser legs, a large military-style belt upon which hung a dark pistol, a tailored shirt with indications of rank on the shoulders, a badge over the heart, and a gold name tag pinned neatly over the right pocket. And sitting atop this body, upon the blood-dried gore of torn sinews and vessels, where once sat the mind and face of a living human being was the desert-whitened skull of a demon. The hat fit loosely over the bone.

We were both still half naked. I had my pants on, Carrie had put on her blouse, and grabbing as much of the rest of our clothes as we could, we were stepping over the tailgate in need of solid ground and miles of running with the terror falling far behind us. But then, with shocking swiftness, the fiend spun about and in the crisp dry voice of a skull, demanded, "WHERE IS HALLEUJAH?"

We were frozen. "Just what we needed right now," I said. "Catatonia."

Frozen in the act of escaping, only our mouths were capable of movement and they were both frantically trying to form the words, "Hallelujah who?"

"WHERE'S HALLELUJAH?" the horror shouted again and started rounding the truck toward us. With great, slow, swaying steps the thing came nearer. We heard its boots crunching in the gravel of the roadside. We saw the black depth of the void within its eye sockets.

It stopped short of us.

"Carrie, do you realize that lurking just beneath the very surface of the delicate, God-sculptured beauty of the fairest of women, the most handsome of men, the cutest little Gerber-cooing babies—within all of us—just waiting for the curtain of death to rise, are the hideous features of a skull?"

"What?" she whispered.

"I mean there's nothing to be afraid of here. We're all the same under the skin, aren't we, Big Fellow? We've all got skulls. It's just that this fellow's is a bit more public than ours—at least at the moment. We'll all shed this mortal flesh eventually, won't we?"

"In the great by and by," she said with a nervous laugh.

"Yes, yes. You're beginning to understand. And when we meet on that beautiful shore we will take off our skin and really get naked."

"What a lovely thought."

"You can rattle my bones anytime, baby."

"WHERE IS HALLELUJAH?" it shouted again, this time with chilling rage.

"Carrie," I said and never for an instant had either of us taken our eyes off of the state highway patrol-thing, "I think I might be capable of running now. How about you?"

"I'm willing to give it a try."

And in a perfectly matched pair of streaks we leaped from the truck and plunged into the dark desert beyond the headlights.

We truly were in a different world.

We crouched in a shallow ravine and watched as the fiend moved restlessly about the pickup moaning and periodically raging, "HALLELUJAH!"

We were panting. It was difficult to stifle the rushing sounds of our breath.

Between gasps I whispered, "Where did Glory and Kitty go?"

"We are over here," Glory said in a disturbingly strong voice. He and Kitty were calmly sitting beside a large boulder holding hands.

"You don't have to shout," I said. "That gruesome son of a bitch will find us."

"Trust me, Jackson. We'll all be safe."

I was angry. We had been confronted by a devil in a highway cruiser and the two of them had sneaked off for a little nocturnal picnic.

"Well Carrie and I didn't feel very safe up there facing the rage of that cadaverous cop."

Glory laughed out loud at my indignation.

"Quiet!" I yelled, totally negating my purpose, "You'll let him know where we're hiding."

"You make more noise than I do." he said. "Believe me, we are in no danger from that unfortunate creature. He only has the power to terrorize the unknowing by being so ugly. Did you notice he stopped short of grabbing you?"

"Not by very damned much," said Carrie.

"You should have seen it from here," Kitty said, trying

unsuccessfully to control her laughter. "The two of you frantically burrowing through the blankets with your bare asses sticking up in the air glowing in the spotlights. It was hilarious."

"I'm glad we were able to be so entertaining," said Carrie in her cocktail voice. "If you liked it so much have a few more beers and catch the next show in an hour."

She and I were not at all convinced that the pacing creature posed no danger to mortal folk.

"HALLELUJUH!" it cried out—apparently ignoring the fact that, with all of our shouting and their laughing, our location had to have been obvious.

"I am right here, you bonehead!" yelled Glory.

"'Bonehead.' Now that's funny." I jabbed Carrie in the ribs with my elbow. "Isn't that funny?"

"We're going to die," she said.

"Right here!" Glory repeated. And nothing happened.

Glory said, "See, there's nothing to fear at all. Remember this. The dead are only the dead and have no real physical properties. As long as we don't allow them to frighten the energy of life out of us, they can't harm us."

"Tell that to the highway guy who had his head pulled off by that mere spirit up there calling your name."

"That's not what happened. That's the body of a highway patrol officer named Lankin. I recall the report. He was decapitated sometime back. He apparently fell asleep and drove his car beneath a large truck."

"Don't tell me," I interrupted. "It happened right after he gave God a speeding ticket. Right?"

"How did you guess?"

"Ahhhh!"

"Easy, my friend," said Glory, "I never said this was going to be reasonable."

The cop-thing was pacing, Carrie was putting on her pants, Kitty was looking good, and Glory was making fun of me.

"Let me get this straight. I think I've finally figured out what's going on. We're not going to Three Days; we're going to Oz, aren't we? If we all get into our magic truck and follow the Yellow Brick Road all of our wishes will be granted. You'll go the source of Music, Kitty will dance to that music, Carrie and I will find a soft place safe from highway patrol terror and continue our beautiful lovemaking, and then we'll fry up the heart of your dog and all have dinner."

"HALLELUJAH!" bellowed the beast.

"Oh, yes. Let's not forget Patrolman Lankin—if we all pitch in together perhaps we can lift his corpse into the back of the truck and maybe the Wizard will see fit to give him a brand new head."

"Jackson, you have uncanny powers of deduction."

"Sometimes I hate being right."

"HALLELUJAH!"

"Pardon me, friends. I'd better go up there and take care of the guard."

Glory walked up the sloping side of the ravine and onto the pavement.

"So there you are," said the demon. "I've been looking for you. You've been hiding. You must be afraid of me."

"Not really," said Glory as he stepped toward the huge form of the man. "I just decided to watch you for a while before I run you off."

"I don't dispel so easily as you think, Hallelujah. I am not only a guard upon the Road to Three Days, I have also been designated a messenger. An angel, so to speak, of the Gods."

"A messenger," said Glory, "I would have come sooner if I had known you had something to say."

From where the three of us sat in the darkness, the voices carried to us as clearly as if we had been standing on the side of the road. There was a strained quality to Glory's words I had not heard before.

"I thought that would get your attention. You're not so confident now are you?" crackled the fiend.

Glory responded with fierceness, "There is nothing of your grotesque form that frightens me in the least. Now get on with your mission before I scatter your spirit from the frozen Peaks of Doom to the fiery lakes of Hell!"

Glory took another step and the messenger stepped backward, keeping his distance.

"Speak!" commanded Glory.

"Indeed I will speak. My message is simple. Continue upon this road and you and your friends and all the living world you have known will be dead. You will be cast to the vast desert of soulless reach to eternally perish. My message is: Welcome to the hopeless Realm of Death, Hallelujah."

There was a pause. Silence. Deep, cold silence and then Glory said, "Is that all?"

"Continue and die."

"Then be gone, you pathetic shade. Tell the Gods of this land I thank them for the warning. However, give assurance, we'll see Them in two days."

The lights began to dim. The messenger was waning. "Look at me, Hallelujah. Look at the horror of what I am." Its voice was becoming the invisible wail of a dying wind. "Don't you fear this fate? Don't you fear my death?"

"No," asserted Glory. "I do not."

And the Ghost of Officer Lankin faded to transparency and then was gone. The lights darkened, and the four of us were alone on the desert with an old pickup truck and the heart of a dog.

16 Another Love Story

Carrie and Kitty were sleeping in the back of the truck. Glory and I sat on opposite sides of a small fire. We had made camp behind a cluster of large rocks some distance away from the road.

Much had happened yet I felt little weariness. We hadn't been talking, just sitting there breathing in the Powers for some time. Or, in my case, the Powers and an occasional drift of smoke.

I opened my eyes and realized Glory wasn't meditating anymore so I spoke. "I've been wondering. If you weren't afraid of that headless son of a bitch, then why did you hide in the shadows?"

"I don't have a driver's license."

"No kidding. Maybe you ought to take a look at the rule book. It says you can travel faster than forty-five miles per hour on an interstate highway."

"Sometimes we travel too fast to ever get where we are going."

"Too fast?"

"Yes. There is an African tale about porters who refused to move after several days of a forced march. Regardless of threats or bribes, they said they weren't going to budge until their souls caught up with them."

"I know what you mean. Sometimes I need to sit down and wait for my Spirit Guide to catch up to me. But that sure wasn't the problem back there on that superhighway."

"You seemed to have survived."

"It didn't seem likely a while ago when you and Kitty crept off into the wilds and left your companions to deal with Officer Death."

"I saw a police car coming up on us when he was still a mile or so behind. You and Carrie seemed preoccupied at the time so I didn't bother alerting you when Kitty and I ditched the truck. If it had been a real policeman our journey could have been delayed by legal technicalities. We couldn't risk that. I knew if you ever found your pants you would be able to show the law proper credentials and probably get off with a warning for indecent exposure."

"I thought our exposures were pretty decent."

"Not bad," he said. "Actually, it was quite a show."

I threw on a couple more pieces of dried pinyon wood and the fire rose and glowed warm against the rock. "Why aren't we tired?"

"Too much to do," he said. "We have left the world of our earthly wandering behind us. There is much to say yet, Jackson. Sleep will come in time."

"If Officer Lankin is any indication of this region, it might not be a bad idea to head back to the land of sitcoms and traffic jams."

"In all the worlds we travel, we must be wary. But I don't think we'll see any more Halloween characters for a while."

"So, what's next? What needs to be said?"

"Tell me more about your years. What have you done with your life in the time since your wife was killed? Surely you haven't spent the whole time being thrown out of cars and having starlight sex in the back of pickup trucks."

"Oh, yeah. This is typical."

"I find that hard to believe."

"In fact, Glory, the short time since I rolled into your life has been the best I've had in a long decade. Mainly, I've used up the years working empty jobs for meaningless wages. I've been an oil field hand, a truck driver. I taught English in a junior high school. I was even a banjo player with a traveling bluegrass band."

"Were you any good?"

"No, but they agreed to let me play if I promised not to sing."

"And you've not been in love since your wife died?"

I looked over at the truck and said, "It's tempting to seek love but I've generally avoided it. When anyone has gotten close I've gotten far away. You were right last night at the bar—I am afraid of love. I usually run at the first signs of a swooning heart—it's too dangerous for me to love someone."

"There has been no one?"

"Not really. At least, not until tonight. What am I going to do, Glory? I've gone and let myself fall in love with Carrie."

"I know."

"I've been so careful to avoid such feelings. But it's all been different here." I paused and thought for a split second and then realized what had happened. "It's you, isn't it? You breathed through me and I became as light as that 'damned gas can.'"

"She is a beautiful person, Jackson."

"Well, that's the truth, but is what I'm feeling real or is it just part of a spell you've cast?"

"Oh, yes, my friend. You are really in love with Carrie. I do not create this world, I just sometimes facilitate the inevitable with my humble powers."

"Okay, so I'm in love with her—what did you do to Carrie to make her fall for me?"

"Not a thing. All I did was meditate on your defenses and the rest just happened."

"You sure are an ugly old cupid."

"Yes, but believe me, penetrating the callouses of your road-hardened heart was no job for some bare-assed baby with a bow."

He was smiling, but with an honest chill of seriousness, I asked. "Isn't this this dangerous for her?"

"Perhaps. But does not love always entail a degree of risk?"

"Sure, but we're not talking a broken heart here. We're talking "lightning bolts and hideous death. There's more than a degree of risk for any heart involved with this curse of mine."

"Life is a risk we must take. Without the sweet ache of love alive within you, how could you be worthy of this quest? Jackson, if life were not so fragile, it would never be so rich."

"I don't want to get her hurt."

"Of course, neither do I. However, avoiding the truth is no solution to its challenge. Besides, it is only you that these fiendish Powers will wish to crush up on the mountain. They will be much too busy swirling away at our souls to bother with the ladies who accompany us. I know this to be true."

"Hell, Glory. I don't want to get myself hurt either.

He just laughed and then so did I. It was a fine mix of fear and excitement I sensed as the fire snapped and the night stayed at bay.

"And you, Glory. How about your heart?"

"Love?"

"Yeah."

"I love Kitty."

"And... "

"It was a long time ago, my friend, and she is dead."

I studied him in the flickering light of the campfire. I saw much pain.

It wasn't easy for me to ask. It wasn't easy for me to confront but I had to.

"Was she struck dead by lightning?"

And through the smoke I saw him nod his head. "Yes, lightning."

17 Resonance

Dawn had begun to define the rocks and crevices of the surrounding desert. Glory was resting in a deep trance. He might even have been sleeping. In any case, I was alone and there was no sleep in me. During the night he told me his tale and it had spoken decades of what I had known but briefly. His ancient words of love and death had resonated through the novice sorrow of my own heart.

Glory had been in love. He was young man and he had known the innocent, playful sensuality I had cherished with my Lori.

He told me his story of love and tragedy:

By the ambiguity of my parentage and driven by the bittersweet sacrilege of late youth and early manhood, I relished being an outcast from any of the several cultures of my homeland. I lived unbound and wild in the desert lands and, consequently, I both excited and disgusted the dwellers of custom and civilization. Some called me a devil who preyed upon the sacred tenets of order and control. I was the hated enemy of politicians and their priests, and priests and their politicians. I was the elusive inspiration of time-trapped poets and lovers. An outlaw who broke no laws, my only crime was living a life that shunned the oppressive restrictions of mainstream society—mocking, by my very existence, the façade of decency and order sustained by the forces of inhibition and fear. I was living a legend and having one hell of a good time of it.

Oh, what times I knew in those irrepressible days. Women would steal themselves from the cloak of their households and clasp to me with writhing abandon in the black nights then, with pouting masks, curse me in the daylight streets of their villages. Respected men would drink my whiskey and howl at my moon and then in public meetings call for my hanging just as an example for youth. Though I had never stolen as much as a crust of bread, I was the greatest thief of my time. I had broken into sacred coffers and had pilfered the most well-guarded secret of the controllers of society—the feeling, the style, the devastating and wonderful irresponsibility of freedom.

I knew no cloudy distraction between myself and the diamond stars under which I slept each night. I would have terrorized the petty fools until they either destroyed or worshiped me.

But then I met the dark-haired daughter of a desert priest.

I could tell you so much about her—of the beauty and poetry of my lady-child, of her delicate and raging sensuality. She had known no other man and, even with my worldly experience, when we first made love she gave me greater pleasure than I had ever known. And with each successive encounter we discovered deeper and wilder and more intimate levels of our passion—for we transcended the mere embrace of flesh. Truly we were in love.

It is a story too familiar to repeat in detail: the impossible love of Montague for Capulet, the love of a princess for a pauper, the love of one who rode the wind-swept distances of lands beyond the boundaries of society and government for one who was by birth and rearing inextricably woven into the fabric of that very society and government.

Her father was priest of a desert people. He had traveled to Three Days and been granted a limited mandate by the Force of Death. His people feared him. Within his venue, he was a very powerful man—accumulating great wealth and enjoying the extent to which the people of his land would humble themselves to gain his favor.

Though hated by most, few people voiced their loathing for fear of their lives. In the scheme of the mortal world he was nothing—a low-level bureaucrat in a vast system. But to those who were unfortunate enough to dwell within the reaches of his petty domain, he held absolute authority and, though lacking the massive Powers of the Mountain, would on regular occasions take pleasure in demonstrating his ability to direct the forces of nature against individuals who had threatened his realm.

The story is so often told it nearly becomes cliché. This despot had a beautiful daughter who had been insulated from the truth of his capricious and cruel control of innocent subjects. She was dearly loved by her father, and, in turn, she felt for him such affection as to blind herself to his evil.

It is exceedingly difficult for me to recount these events. Let it suffice that I tell you fate crossed our paths and a great love developed between us. A love that lives, yet to this very moment, in the pangs of teasing memory and waves of raging sorrow within me.

She would secret herself from her father's home and meet me to ride across the moonlit desert to my camp and there to love me until the morning light would steal her away.

Months passed before her father discovered our love. He summoned me and I came for I had no fear of him. The priest warned that he would use his powers to destroy me if I ever saw his daughter again. I was young and foolish and I laughed at his threat, knowing he was merely the potentate of a tiny cluster of frightened people and far too weak to harm a rider of the great desert. "It would take God Himself to keep me from my love," I told him and then stormed away.

"Jackson, even now, over sixty years later, when I recall this time it draws close about me and chokes the breath from my speaking."

But he went on:

It happened in the crisp cool of a cloudless autumn night. We had known our love's teasing lust, its explosive touch, and were embraced within warm

124

blankets knowing its soft ecstasy.

Then with sudden and startling fury, her father rode into my camp, raging upon thundering hooves and shouting that I had defiled his greatest treasure, his beloved daughter.

We rose, pulling a blanket about our naked bodies and I proclaimed my love for her and my desire that we marry. He replied that before he would allow me to marry his child he would first see me dead.

From the black night, with all the power of his hatred, he conjured a bolt of deadly lightning and cast it toward me. Its impact tossed me from the arms of my love and out upon the sand. But he had not the power to harm me.

So, failing in his attempt to destroy me, with a second bolt of lightning he struck his own daughter dead.

18   Day Two

It was a pensive day. Not a sad day, but rather a day of introspection and quiet.

We drove only a short distance into the land that was becoming increasingly surreal. Daylight had revealed subtle elements of color and shape that gave the desert an alien tone. Salvador Dali would have loved the Road to Three Days.

It gave me the creeps.

Even in daylight there were ghosts and terrors in the shadows of massive rocks and spiny, twisted desert plants.

We traveled together, the four of us, but also we each traveled alone. Glory gathered the quiet Powers as he moved about in a waking trance. We were approaching his Cosmic showdown with terrible forces and he was preparing himself for the battle.

Kitty sensed the gravity of the day and she too drifted into inner realms. While we were stopped along the side of the road for a meal of cheese sandwiches and potato chips, she stared out at the desert for several minutes and then said, "You know, if it wasn't for the blood I think I could have been one hellava great nurse."

As we made camp in early afternoon at the base of a huge phantom-shaped eruption of dark red rock, Carrie moved about gathering firewood, singing, in a soft and melodious voice, a chant-like wordless song just beneath the surface of her day.

And I spent the slowly moving miles and hours of that cloudless day seething with silent anger and anxiety in contemplation of whatever Power it is that creates death from the impersonal might of nature exploited upon the vulnerability of flesh. I had known for years that such dreadful weaponry as the power of natural phenomena could be possessed by evil men. The self-proclaimed holy vigilantes of the refrigerator factory were proof of the deadly implications of fanatic ignorance. All my years of searching, learning, groveling in frivolous waste—and all to find that Dr. Fintin and his cluster of pathetically impotent committeemen had been so close to the answers they could not bear to confront. And now I was square in the middle of the hateful territory of such a ruthless and terrible God as to be the source of the petty tyranny of the vile and self-righteous. I was ready for the fight. Glory was seeing to that. He was right, it was good the rage had not diminished with the years. I was ready, and, of course, I was dreadfully frightened.

So, when the day had finally spent its strange light and we were gathered around our campfire mumbling small talk and losing ourselves in the flame, I determined it was getting a bit heavy for my sanity to bear.

"I think it's time for a party game," I said in a sudden voice that effectively shattered the depth of everyone's thoughts. "Enough of this seriousness—this is the stuff of deep thought and meaningful conversations, both of which I avoid like poison ivy. I want to have some fun. How about a round of Pin the Tail on the Joshua Tree, or Spin the Rattler. How about A-Tisket A-Tasket, There's Sand in My Dirty Undershorts."

"You can forget that old favorite, Jackson," said Carrie. "You're undershorts blew out of the truck yesterday."

"Damn. And I did so much want to skip."

I wasn't the only one who was about to lose it. Kitty jumped in with enthusiasm and said, "I have an idea. We do this at the club every now and then. Why don't each of us tell the funniest dream we can think of. It gets pretty kinky, but what the hell, it can be fun."

"What the hell," I said.

"But everyone has to agree to tell a dream. Nobody gets to just listen to other people's crazy confessions."

"Fair enough. What about you, Glory?" I asked. "Are you up for a round of dream-and-tell?"

"Why not? I have had about enough of this seriousness myself. Count me in. It will be worth it just to hear Kitty's contribution—I know it will be nasty."

"Not necessarily," she said.

"Really?"

"Well... "

"I thought so."

"But I'm not telling unless Carrie agrees too. She's always so proper."

"'Proper' you say," Carrie said with amazement. "I work at the frigging Naked Rose peddling shots and beers to pocket-pool playing cow-creeps and you call me 'proper.' I mean instead of showing up for my interview with a resume I showed up with a tape measure. 'Proper'!"

"You've been to college. You're not as down to earth as some of the rest of us girls."

"Kitty, you don't know where some of those five dollar bills have been."

"I never," she said.

"Not to mention the long-neck Buds."

"Carrie, I have my standards and you know it."

"Well then, don't call me 'proper.'"

"Ladies," I interrupted, though I was thoroughly enjoying the conversation. "On with the game."

"I'll go first if Carrie promises."

"Don't worry, Kitty. You won't be the only one to tell a nasty."

"This does sound like fun," I said.

We put a few more dried branches on the fire and three of us listened as Kitty began our Freudian version of *The Canterbury Tales.*

"I have this dream all of the time and it's so funny. In the dream I'm a football team. I mean I'm the whole team, there's nobody else on my side of the field and I'm wearing a frilly dress that my mother would make me wear to Sunday School when I was about thirteen. The dress was all starch and ruffles and I always hated wearing it— it was so old-fashioned looking and uncomfortable. But my mother was a very strong woman and when she told me what to do or what to put on I wasn't going to argue with her. You all might not believe this, but I was actually a very good little girl.

"Well, anyway, in this dream I'm lined up on one of those chalk lines that go across a football field in my pastel-pink Sunday School dress which, of course, is too small for me because I'm full grown and it fit me when I was a girl. Facing me, on the other team, is one man. He's a big guy with great big muscles and he's all hairy and horny looking with a thick black mustache and a smile that really turns me on. I'm real excited and I want to play football with him. And another thing, he's completely naked and really excited too, if you know what I mean—really really excited.

"Then a voice, which I almost recognize but I'm never sure about, yells, 'Play ball!' and we both lean over like football players do and face each other. I can see his face right now, just like it's really happening.

"The next thing is I start saying, 'Hike, hike, hike,' over and over again and he comes for me and pushes me down on the grass and I know that I'm in trouble for getting a grass stain on my dress but I don't care. I keep saying, 'Hike, hike, hike.' When I fall down my dress comes up and I'm not wearing any panties and he forces himself on top of me and just as he is beginning to thrust himself into me and I'm really going crazy, a goddamned whistle blows.

"And this is the funny part. The man and I both stop playing and slowly look over at the official who had blown the whistle. I recognize the guy. He's a fat little man with a tiny little mouth and cheeks that are puffed up and red like they were going to explode. It's Pastor Wally. He was the assistant pastor at the church where my mother sent me in my fancy dress."

"My first reaction is to feel ashamed and that my mother will find out I've been playing football. But then I remember something and start to laugh out loud. Pastor Wally would never tell on me because he would be afraid I might tell people about the time he cornered me all alone in the Youth Fellowship Hall in the basement of the church and felt my breasts and told me they were mounds of the devil."

"So then the two of us are laying there on the field laughing at Pastor Wally while he furiously, then helplessly continues to blow on his whistle until it turns into a Snickers Bar and he just stands there sadly chewing on it while I start whispering to the guy, 'Hike, hike, hike.'"

"Isn't that a funny story?"

No one spoke for a moment. we just sat there catching our breaths and giving it a moment to settle.

"Really funny, Kitty," I finally said, wiping the sweat from my brow.

"You're a hard act to follow, Kitty," said Glory.

"I'd follow her anywhere," I said.

"Are you always this faithful in your relationships?" asked Carrie.

"Jeez-o-peezo, Woman. Can't a man have a stray thought?"

"Heavens no. The wedding's off, Jackson."

"What'll we tell the kids?"

"May I go on?" asked Glory. "It's a game of dreams and I have one to tell if you children will quit your bickering."

Carrie leaned against me, I put an arm around her, and we shut up.

"Some of my dreams are disturbingly prophetic. It is almost as if the future is impatient with the speed at which I approach it, and thus, in both symbol and likeness of reality, visions of my subconscious are often more than mere psychological musings. It can be so serious.

"But I recall one dream I had that made me laugh even if it did lead me to accurately predict the coming of a flash flood.

"Before I was deposited back at the trading post, you knew I was coming, didn't you? Was that from a dream?"

"No, that was more of a nightmare."

"Why does it seem like I've known you for years. There is something so familiar about your abuse."

"We live many lives, Jackson."

"Have I always borne the brunt of your humor?"

"Of course."

Kitty said, "Tell us about the funny flash flood. I don't like all this weird talk."

"All right. But first I'll tell you a dream I had about my nephew. There was little symbolism to it and it did foretell the future. One morning I awoke with a vision clearly in my mind and was able to tell my nephew he was finally going to marry the pretty young girl he had been courting for years. His perversely jealous mother had all but negated his natural energies in guilt and repression. In pleasing his doting mother he was endangering his masculinity and his future."

"What did you dream?"

"Sometimes dreams are clouded with complex symbolism and are difficult to understand. But then there are times when they come in on a very clear and direct frequency and require little in-depth analysis. In this case, I saw my nephew kicking his fat mother down a sandy arroyo and shouting after her pitiable fury, 'To hell with your chocolate chip cookies, I'm going to marry Sally Yellow-Feather!'"

"And did he?"

"Well, he didn't literally kick his mother down an arroyo, but he sure did marry Sally."

Night was deepening, but our spirits and the warmth of the fire stayed its dark messages.

"So, Glory," I asked, "how much of what is going on right now—this trip to Three Days and all of us—have you seen in your soothsayer dreams?"

He looked at me whimsically for a moment and then said, "Almost all of it. Right to the last and then it's more than I can see. But, damn it, Jackson, you're going to make us all serious again. Let me tell you about my hilarious dream."

"Is it a dirty dream?" asked Carrie.

"More sandy than dirty."

"Is it about sex?" asked Kitty.

"No, but it tickles."

"Would Freud have thought it was about sex?" I asked, accepting my cue that this was no time to pursue visions of the next day.

"That is a stupid question," said Glory. "Now, does anyone care to hear a man's dream?"

"Tell it."

"In the beginning I was high up in the branches of a great tree, crouched in its wind-rustling leaves. The tree stood on a rocky cliff overhanging a mighty mountain stream at the head of a steep-walled canyon.

"Suddenly, in a raging voice of thunder and wind the azure sky boiled to gray and black and the gentle limbs of the tree were tossed wildly about like whips. My grip was no match for the force of the storm and in a long slow fall I was pitched into the blackening waters.

"The dams of the heavens burst and, riding high upon the face of a massive swell of water, I rode the crest of the wave into the deep canyon as it dropped violently from the verdant mountain land toward the arid desert miles below. Though the unleashed furor of the water dashed viciously against the rocks and trees in its path, and the terrible waters were about me, I felt only the exhilaration of the ride and none of the torment.

"Upon the violent waters I descended the falling canyon until, with a rushing sigh of winds and waters the river spilled widely out upon the thirsting desert floor. The stream divided into numerous rivulets. I rode the most momentous of them out from the mountain land and upon the meandering channel of a large smooth-floored wash.

"As the water grew thin about me I gently settled down upon the land until beaching in the warm dry sands of a mere waterless wrinkle upon the surface of the white-tan desert.

"I recall waking from the dream laughing at the sensation of the tickling sand."

It was quiet but for the crackling of the campfire.

"You people are so symbolic in your dreaming," said Carrie. "Your dreams are all about repressed sex, the powers and sensations of nature—you could probably sit down and figure out all kinds of hidden meanings in football games and in the twists and turns of a dark canyon. Most of the memorable dreams I have had can be traced directly to late-night pepperoni pizza or a lump in the mattress."

"What would Freud have to say about lumps in the mattress and pepperoni pizza?" I asked.

"Or Timothy Leary," said Glory thoughtfully. "Could it not be true that the voluntary ingestion of pepperoni pizza late at night is similar to taking LSD in hopes of producing hallucinogenic dreams?"

"Not only that," said Kitty, "but I think she is pulling a

lousy, damned cop-out. I never said my horny dreams were caused by gas."

"Okay, okay, I take it back. In truth, my dreams are technicolor productions of a sick mind. They are filled with fiendish lusts and twisted motives. Dreams of porcupine lovers and dancing with serpents. Is that better?"

"You are definitely getting closer," I said.

"Carrie," said Glory rather soberly, "What is wrong with your dreams?"

"My dreams aren't funny. They don't tantalize and they don't tickle. They are acted out by a cast of thousands: ugly things in familiar faces. I don't like to think about it. Most are gone by morning anyway."

"It could be that you have too many dimensions trying to exist on one level. Thus, the convolution of reality in your dreams. Your mind is like an overcrowded tenement. Your thoughts, like rats and slum dwellers of the inner city, begin preying upon one another in the madness of their density. Perhaps you need some kind of a creative outlet, Carrie. Some activity or purpose in your life which will allow those thoughts to expand in a less restrictive environment than your current life allows. Perhaps you are not haunted by demons so much as by the clutter of suppressed potential."

"Rats in a tenement," she said.

"No—talents, hopes, aspirations trapped in topless bar."

"What's wrong with a topless bar?" asked Kitty.

"Nothing at all when it provides a place for you to express a talent. You are a magnificent performer upon a rowdy stage, my love. Carrie is naked bartender there."

"Very naked," Carrie said. "But that reminds me of a funny dream I had last night while Kitty and I were sleeping in the back of the truck. Kitty rolled over on me and I dreamed I was hang gliding and had crash landed in a field of cantaloupes."

"For God's sake," said Kitty.

"Well, I tried, didn't I?"

Glory turned his attention to me. "Tell us your dream, Jackson. We've got to get on with this. Kitty and I need to walk out into the desert and perform some purification rites tonight before I greet the Irate Gods of Three Days tomorrow."

"I don't know what the hell he's talking about," said Kitty. "But I'll bet I enjoy it."

Glory just smiled and I began my tale:

"This dream is only funny because it was so unusual. How many people can say that they've had a dream with absolutely no motion to it? I mean it was just exactly like looking at a painting or a photograph. The people didn't even blink an eye, the curtains in front of the open window didn't stir. There was no sound at all. In the dream picture my Aunt Wilma and Uncle Louis were sitting at their kitchen table. The only element of the dream which had motion was my consciousness as it surveyed various portions of the picture. I first noticed the partially eaten chocolate cake which was on the table. My Aunt Wilma made the best chocolate cakes of my childhood. Then my attention moved to my uncle's face. It was kind and open. He was wearing a characteristic pair of bib overalls with the top of his pouch of chewing tobacco sticking out of the center pocket. I noticed his strong, rough hands and thought about how he had tossed me about with them and delightfully tortured me to say 'uncle' with such painful devices as Dutch rubs to my head and Indian burns to my wrists. There was a clock on the wall which was frozen at twenty minutes past twelve. There was a bowl of apples and oranges on the buffet which sat against the wall beside the table. My Aunt Wilma looked exceedingly young though she was well into middle age. She was smiling and her eyes glowed with a moist luminescence which traveled through my consciousness in a wave of warm sentimentality. Behind my aunt and uncle and the table was an open window edged by airy white curtains. There was nothing visible outside the window except a gray sky and, to the amazement of my awareness, immovable like my aunt's eyes and my uncle's hands, and preserved like the moist crumbs of the chocolate cake—I saw my eight-year-old face peering innocently into the kitchen."

And then we sat for quiet moments by the fire realizing

how much better we knew one another from the telling or not telling of our funny dreams.

19   Holy Business

"Good morning!"

And it had already been a good morning. Carrie had awakened me in early light with a glass of cool water and a warm kiss. It had been a wonderful morning by the time Glory and Kitty started banging on the fenders of our bedroom truck and shouting "Good morning!"

I figured it could be the last day my life. I laughed with the joy of Carrie's pleasures and the abandon of a warm morning's love. "Good morning!" I shouted as we joined them by the campfire.

"How much farther to Three Days?" I asked. "Are we going to make it in time?"

"But for a few more turns in the road, we are there now. We camped within the very shadow of the Great Mountain. So, let's have breakfast and then you can perform the marriage ceremony for Kitty and me."

"Me?"

"Yes. We have a license and I will grant you the religious authority. You see, Jackson, I shall appoint you the High Priest of my Spirit Nation of Hallelujah. You shall be the High Priest of Hallelujah."

"Me?"

"Yes, Jackson."

"This is just some more of the dance and gibberish to get us on the mountain, isn't it?"

"Yes and no. Yes, it is crucial that you marry us. No, the Priesthood of my country is not a matter of gibberish. I have been the ruler of my own nation for many years. My realm begins with the grains of sand upon which I tread as I walk this planet and reaches far beyond the dimensions of the mind.

"Even during the past few years while cloistered by the obligatory good will of my relatives, there was never a time when anyone doubted I was an autonomous state—coexisting with local worlds but always as an alien.

"And now," he said with a sweeping gesture to the three of us, "I wish to invite my friends to become citizens of the desert and Cosmic country of Hallelujah. With such a dedicated population as yourselves, the Gatekeepers of this wicked mountain will most certainly be impressed."

"Does this mean I'll have to give up my right as a natural born American to abstain from voting for lying politicians every couple of years?"

"Dual citizenship is quite acceptable."

"Am I likely to get drafted into your army?"

"Too late, you've already enlisted."

"Where do I sign?"

"Step right up, friends. There is little obligation—no examination or required oaths of loyalty, no taxes to pay—for the most part you already speak the language. It is all so very simple. Just give your favorite old monarch a hug—a handshake will do for you, Jackson—and congratulations, you are citizens of Hallelujah."

"And all for the price of... " I questioned.

"...your honest friendship and belief."

Carrie and Kitty descended on the old bastard and so did I. What the heck. "How's it feel to have subjects," I asked as we huddled together affectionately at the foot of the Great Mountain of Three Days.

With a great smile he answered, "Wonderful."

* * * *

One of the reasons I had chosen to wander the paths of my life alone was that I was never a leader and, hence, when a leader was around, I became a natural follower. Alone I had climbed high mountain peaks, choosing each step I took, creating, in the steep ascent, my own patterns of success or failure. Whenever climbing in a group, like a pack horse, I would fall into place, nose to the tail of whomever happened to be there to take the initiative. I don't know whether to chalk it up to a weakness of character or just to a lack of competitiveness. One who wanders alone is never a follower.

I had pledged with a hug and an honest smile, my allegiance to a leader for the first time since Boy Scouts, but, for reasons as strange as the land through which we traveled and as powerful as the positive energies of Hallelujah and the dreadful energies of Three Days, it seemed right to me.

We ate and then packed the truck and pulled it into the shade of the large red rock. "It's a short walk to the trail from here," said Glory.

"How do you know? You've never been here before."

"When we first met I knew your name to be Jackson and I know the trail to be just up the road a few turns and over a rise."

"What else do you know?"

"I'll tell you. I know that Katherine and Carrie will accompany us past the stone gate and from there you and I will go farther up to a region of jutting rocks and deep chasms. I know when the Forces of this mountain confront us, Jackson, it will take all the might of our combined hearts and souls to survive. I know it is your mission to join me as it is Katherine's mission to marry me and Carrie's mission to travel with us on this journey. There is to be terrible fear and pain in the hours ahead, but, also, there can be the some resolution of life-deep injury. There can be the promise of eternity in the jeopardy of these fragile hours.

"Jackson, I appoint you The High Priest of Hallelujah and in doing so make you as vulnerable to the rage of this mountain as I, but, likewise, potentially as blessed by the enlightenment we seek. Do you accept?"

Life can be so comfortable—so safe, peaceful and calm if it's played out carefully. So damned dull and meaningless and comfortable and safe. Life can be a dozen variations upon the all-summer monotony of an ice cream truck's jingle. It can be elevator concert halls with violins humming "Let It Be, Let It Be," and great sensory feasts serving heaping plates of canned laughter, and life can be such a grave-certain glide from the erotic splashing of ovum by the mad hunger of sperm to the arrhythmic spilling of dirt upon a coffin's lid.

"Yes, my friend, my king, I accept. In these short days since I began this trek with you I have learned the absolute truths of Cosmic wit—everybody do-dos; I have drunk the sweet and dizzying wine of Carrie's loving passion, and I have sensed the raucous and holy depths of my being—hell yes, I'll be your High Priest—bring on the bloody bastards. I love life—let them just try to wrench it from my fierce soul."

"Katherine," said Glory and she moved to his side and they stood hand in hand before the great red rock glowing in the desert-morning sun.

"Help me, Carrie," I said and the four of us joined hands. "By the sacred and beautiful Powers that breathe through the vast Universe, the Music and the Light of the Immortal Spirit, and by the Power vested in me as High Priest of Hallelujah, I pronounce you, Glory Hallelujah, and you, Katherine... what's your last name, Kitty?"

"Morgan. I'm Katherine Morgan."

"... Glory Hallelujah and Katherine Morgan husband and wife."

20 The Metaphor

"And regardless of what changes you witness, what sounds and sights and distortions of form, you must not desert me. Your loyalty must never weaken even in the face of the most bizarre developments. I need you."

We were sitting in the shade of a large rock near the gate and Glory talked to us with hypnotic strength and we listened as he spoke and as he breathed the Powers through us.

I have been a man of flesh in your fine company for these marvelous days—a being as rooted to the earth by mortality as the most fragile life form, a man whose breath and flowing blood of life were as open to the fatal wounds of brutal time and happenstance as any creature of this measured world. I have laughed and pleasured and loved in the good closeness of our short times. In the warmth of Katherine's loving bed, in the joy of Carrie's subtle goodness, and in the humor and terror of Jackson's strange world I have known more of the human touch than decades have afforded my searching.

But now, before we enter this land of enchanted evil, I must reveal to you that I know of worlds that are invisible to this dimension and beyond our mortal struggle for breath against the suffocating reality of fatal destiny. These old eyes have seen more than the shifting of sands and seasons, more than the damp and grasping wonder of birth and the dry and gasping horror of death. I have seen Light and, Jackson, before this night has passed you shall see that Light emanating from within me. I have heard more than the tones of sadness, pain, and pleasure, or the howling of the wind. I have heard Music, and you will hear that Music in your own soul as I sing it to the darkness and the silence.

With the Light and the Music within me I am eighty years old and yet as strong as a youth—as sharp of wit, as virile of loin. But all the vision, the vibration, the strength I have gathered from the Immortal Powers is harbored in the frail and death-weak port of this eighty-year old flesh.

I am Humanity, my friends, and as I have basked in the wonder of Eternal Light and have wept in the joy of Celestial Music, all who will know the heart of the Human Spirit may also know such marvels. So, I enter this deviled land of death's pungent rot as a man who seeks to defy the imminent destruction of his vision. I intend to defy the curse of death. I am Humanity and I shall either evolve beyond this mechanical trap of mortality or all that I have known will perish. I am Brahman, I am shaman, I am Kachina Spirit Dancer, I am a thousand-year-old holy man, I am man and woman, laborer, philosopher, and, bless you Kitty, barroom ballerina. I am the vessel of all the sacred fluid and blood-red life of a species and I shall fight the obliteration of all that has gathered about my eighty years and about the millennia of humankind.

Have you heard the melodious torture of Beethoven exploding with the petty wrath of a hundred raging instruments against the deaf and apathetic certainty of maggots? Or Bach's frenetic fugues, pacing with interwoven intricacies of brilliance the claustrophobic cage of unrelenting years? Have you heard the screaming, self-destructive electric hysteria of heavy metal rock-and-roll? Have you read the poets? Have you read Dylan Thomas as he raged, raged "against the dying of the light" and then died of too damned much whiskey? I have heard only short measures of the Great Songs, brief verses of the Great Poems. I have seen but glimpses of the Great Light and, I'll tell you, what we have known from Shakespeare, from Mozart, from Michelangelo is only a crude teasing touch of what is out there—like the games of children who imitate the grown-up behavior of their parents. The works of the

141

most inspired of our human artists are only the groping caresses of a little boy who, having secretly watched his parents making love, fondles the nonexistent breasts of a little girl who only giggles and thinks him pleasantly mad.

And I have sensed these immortal wonders with both mortal feet standing firmly upon the dirt, the "dust to dust" to which I am doomed to return.

Our friend, our leader, Glory Hallelujah, was not just a man. He was truly a man who had been touched by Powers beyond normal perception—blessed by Their beauty, perhaps cursed by Their distance.

"What can you do upon this mountain? How can you stand upon this earth and not die upon this earth?"

"I have prepared myself. As I told you, I have studied well the works of man. The sounds, the images, the creations of humankind in imitation of the Gods. I have read books, I have listened to music, I have studied paintings and sculpture, I have even watched television. I have sampled the best and the worst of our groveling efforts at saying what is integrally a part of us and infinitely denied us. And I have spent countless nights in the most intimate company of million-starred galaxies.

"And, amazingly, Jackson, the secret I discovered began with my book of Cosmic connections. It started with 'Beers rhymes with tears.' Few expressions in the annals of mankind have been so flatly banal. There is a chapter I didn't recite for you, Jackson— one of the more lengthy truisms in the book. It was Shakespearean:

Like Hamlet, Macbeth, King Lear, and Ophelia;
Death is the last card the Fates ever deal-ya.

"Somewhere between the word-wild spirit of poets and the earthly truth of beers, do-do, and death, I knew I had to discover a link, a connection more powerful than either the obvious or the futile. And I think I did in the most unexpected circumstance. It was from the libraries, the concert halls, the star-swirled nights that I found my source, but it was from a garage that I discovered my technique.

"It occurred to me one afternoon as I watched a nephew of mine as he arc welded two pieces of metal together. Wearing a protective helmet I was able to watch the blinding arc of electricity as it melted the hard metal. The heat generated by this energy was great enough to form a molten pool of steel out of the edges of the separate pieces that, when cooled, united them into one. My nephew explained to me that the skill involved in welding is to position the welding rod at a distance which is far enough from the surfaces being fused to avoid direct contact with the metal— because the rod sticks if you get it too close—and, yet not so far away from the surfaces as to be at a greater distance than the electricity is capable of gapping. And, also, interestingly enough, the intensity of the arc increases as does the distance between the rod and the metal. In other words, the greatest heat is generated at that point where the rod is farthest from the surfaces without disengaging the flow of electricity across the gap. Sometimes, he told me, just in the act of pulling the rod away from the metal, that point of maximum heat is reached and a hole is burnt through the material being welded.

"I stood there in his shed watching the process and then it suddenly came to me. Just like the electricity flying across the gap from the rod to the metal, the most powerful poetic and musical and visual imagery is produced by the same flow of energy across a gap. You see, the reason the electricity jumps toward the metal is because a ground clamp is attached to it. Do you understand? It's an energy source attempting to neutralize itself by leaping to a ground or a place of resolution—much like a controlled arc of lightning.

"When electric power is harnessed it flows smoothly through our air conditioners and televisions and peacefully returns to a ground. It is only when a gap occurs that super intensity is produced. A wire breaks, a charge leaps to ground itself, and the radio goes up in smoke. The creative use of such a gap is what gives the finest works of art their greatest power—the power to express that for which no word or image or sound exists: the power of the metaphor. No offense to Charlie Brown and Company, but happiness is not a 'warm puppy.' Happiness is the metaphor struck between the concept of a feeling and the reality of a cuddling dog. Happiness is the inexpressible essence experienced in the gap between the word and the known image of the puppy. The metaphor.

"Now stretch that metaphor and the power increases and we may speak of love. Love is sweet-smelling sweat and a single dream. Love is a mother's closed coffin and a son's gentle children. Stretch it more. Love is Cupid's searing, breast-splitting scalpel. Love is a winter-cold mmoon."

And then he looked at me with eyes of glaring and dangerous intensity and shouted, "More! Love is an Indian Princess destroyed by the sky, and, Jackson, love is a lady-child called Lori. Love is death's cruel gift."

"Lori!" I gasped.

"Yes, Jackson. Lori. The deepest love is by death's eye known."

"Goddamn you, Hallelujah." I spat.

"Yes, Jackson. Yes. Goddamn me. Goddamn the metaphor which reached too far for the energy to gap. Too far. The heat won't reach."

He put a hand on my shoulder. "I'm sorry, my friend. But do you understand? You must understand. Life is the energy, death is the ground. With no gaps, the motors run evenly, the process is smooth, the birth becomes the death. But it is the arc, the gap, the resistance to the fatal flow that creates the heat of joy, of pleasure, of enlightenment. It is only when we become the metaphor between spiritual life and its inevitable grounding in biological death that we are most human.

"My method is simple. I believe, by concentrating all of the essences of my being into a single force—all of the knowledge, feeling, Light and Music I have accumulated from this earth-bound, eighty-year journey—in a confrontation with the most vile of deadly grounding Powers I know, I will become the metaphor that is the heat of the Infinite. When I become the absolute metaphor between my living will and the enveloping, grounding vacuum of death, then, in that raging glow of balanced opposition I might create an optimal gap and burn away the very ground that draws me to expiration.

"I know it sounds crazy. It all seems so superficially symbolic. But I believe it will work—if you haven't surmised it already, I will tell you. It is an allegorical land through which we travel."

21 The Gate

"Are you scared?" Carrie asked me. We were holding hands.
"Yes."
"So am I."
The Gate was a huge stone arch. Beyond it the trail climbed steeply to the base of the mountain and there became a narrow ledge ascending the sheer rock face in switchbacks.
Glory and Kitty entered first. It was late afternoon and the shadows were long. There was a chill to the place that had little to do with the weather.
About the arch were monolithic spires of wind-etched rock rising hundreds of feet above us. Dropping away from the path were deep dry canyons twisting and turning like mazes.
There was an audible hum, partially an effect of the constant wind, but there was more to it than that. You could feel it on your skin and in your hair like static electricity. There was a perceptible energy and it seemed to be searching us, our bodies and our minds.
Carrie and I hesitated before the arch,
"You don't have to do this, you know."
"Yeah I do." she said.
"I was afraid you'd say that."
"We're all part of this strangeness. He said he'll need all of us, and that includes me, Jackson."
"And me too."
"The jerks back at the bar need another beer, Kitty needs a roommate, you need a hug—but Glory needs me and I'm going in."
"You sure you wouldn't rather go to a movie or something?"
"I don't think so, Jackson."

The electrical intensity increased as we walked beneath the arch and, like fierce watchdogs, the winds rushed upon us. The Gatekeeper, though having no visible form, had accosted us with an undeniable presence. The humming energies were clearly driven by a dark and awesome rage.

22 The Altar

If it were not sitting dead center upon the path to Hell it could have passed for just another big ugly rock belched from the bowels of the earth in a volcanic fury. But this was the Land of Three Days and this massive stone was the Altar of a merciless God.

"Jackson," said Glory, "with priest-like pomp, place Jeremiah's heart upon the flat lap of the stone."

With as much dignity as I could muster, I stepped up to the face of the Altar and dumped the dog's heart from the plastic vegetable bag and onto the eroded bowl of stone. The rock was blackened by ancient and not so ancient stains and crusts of blood. I stood solemnly before the awful rock and felt a deep and terrible trembling. Perhaps it was the shudder of my frightened bones. Perhaps it was the tremble of the entire planet.

I turned and rejoined Carrie.

Glory and Kitty stepped before the crude Altar. He spoke and I understood why it was necessary that he and Kitty be married.

"My friends," he said to us. "Citizens of Hallelujah, sixty years ago a petty priest of an Order of this Mountain, in a vile act of rage and hatred directed at me, struck dead his only daughter with a bolt of lightning. Later, in the madness of his guilt and pain, by proclamation of his Powers, he forbade me to ever in my life know the blessings of marriage. Upon this day," Glory said as he turned to the stone, "I defy those Powers and stand before this blood-filthy shrine of death as a man married by both legal and holy rite by Jackson Blake, High Priest of Hallelujah, to Katherine Morgan, wife by love and beauty, and witnessed by Carrie Nelson, friend and patriot."

I don't know where the clouds came from. It was an autumn afternoon in the arid clarity of a blue-skied desert, but from somewhere the soot-black bastards swirled across the sun and filled the moment with ominous shadow. The raging energies danced upon our flesh and the winds did howl. Glory spat upon the Altar and turned away. "Jackson, I believe we can go on now, there is no Power here to stop us."

He faced Kitty and holding her hands he said, "We must not give way to sentiment here, though my heart is filled with its sweetness. It is time to depart and we must say little. Katherine, my lovely, my only wife, love endures the flesh. I shall be with you. I need you and Carrie to go back to the truck and wait there for Jackson's return.

"Are you sure? I'll stay if I can help," said Carrie as she fought tears.

"No, Carrie. The rest of this journey requires the special and terrible knowledge that Jackson and I share of the wrath of such Powers. You have helped make my entry possible. Without you we would have failed. Now you must go. And, believe me, friendship, too, endures the flesh. I shall be with you."

Carrie nodded.

"I love you, old man," said Kitty and tears streamed down her pretty face.

"Old man, hell," Glory said as he patted her gently and directed her toward the arch and the road back home

"I love you," she said again as she and Carrie walked away from us and down the path. Carrie glanced back at me for an instant. I smiled and she left.

Without speaking, Glory and I walked past the Altar and headed up the side of the rock mountain.

23   The Coming of Death

"How long do you think we'll have to wait?"

"Not very long, I suspect."

"It sure is dark." I was shivering. "Do you think they fell for the dog's heart?"

"Oh, yes. I told you Death was powerful and hateful—I never said it was smart."

The climb had been strenuous but neither of us was fatigued by the effort. Glory had instructed me in a breathing/walking meditation that had considerably lessened the rigors of the trail. If we were to survive the encounter it was critical we be as strong as possible and the gathering of Powers was imperative.

Throughout my life I had consciously avoided taking myself very seriously. Life had proven to be many things: joyous, tragic, painful, beautiful, and cruel. But never serious. And, as a player in this drama, I had never felt compelled to strut too profoundly upon the stage. For me, sarcasm had not been a weapon. It had been a carefully refined attitude intended to both entertain a potentially hostile world and to protect me from ever believing the myth of such a world's significance. But some of Hallelujah's meditative magic had begun working on me and vision that I normally would have dismissed as delusion was becoming believable. Life upon the very threshold of death had, at last, become real. "We're here," I announced as we entered the high mountain valley of jagged peaks. Glory had briefly described the terrain that morning but my recognition of the shape of the rocks and the distant vista of the great flat and the sound of our steps upon the stone and the feel of the darkening airs about us had the clarity of personal awareness. The rock-strewn landscape, a huge, natural amphitheater, was as twistedly familiar as a childhood backyard. "This is where we fight Death."

Again the mixture of anger and fear that had recurrently stalemated my life stirred within me. The clouds at the gate had dispersed as quickly as they had appeared—apparently props for a supernatural bluff. The evening sky was a clear twilight blue and the jutting rocks formed a broken wall of grotesque silhouettes about us.

"Are these sons of bitches ever going to become visible or are we to combat whirlwinds and force fields?"

"Soon they will become quite visible. Visible, audible, tactile— we will even know their stench. They will swarm from the crevices of this evil mountain and we will know them as manifestly real as the heat of the desert sun or the bite of a serpent."

"I might not be ready for this. I could just as easily run as fight. It's like the thunder. I hear it and I never know for sure if I'm going to rage against the storm or cower beneath the nearest rock or barroom table."

"I believe in you, Jackson. You are much stronger than the circumstances of your life have revealed."

"I wish I were as confident as you."

"You are my sole support in this confrontation. If I am willing to entrust my destiny to you, you should at least share in some of that belief."

"I'll try. It's just that I can feel the chill of death all around us here. This is no place for weakness."

"You shall never be weak again, my friend."

We waited as night settled about us. Light breezes became vicious gusts and the sky became a harsh and heartless realm of cold sparkling eyes.

"As you know," he spoke above the wind sounds, "I shall not survive this evening in human form. There are three possibilities. It could be I will become the ashen remnant of Their victory— scattered by the fury of the winds. If not, if my being is not disintegrated we shall either have won and I will have embarked upon a journey of infinite exploration of the ecstasy of the Higher Realms, or, in loss, I shall return to the desert as a soulless form whose body remains but whose mind was extinguished in the conflict. In any case, I want you to know this is the moment for which my life was lived and, regardless of the outcome, there shall be no regrets. It is a glorious conflict—the best of our lives."

And in that moment the Legion of Death's hideous kingdom arrived. With growl and crackle, and the shrieks and calls of a thousand agonized souls; the brutal gasping sounds of untold masses of death-grasped lives; the lonely sobs of a million heart-dead nights of nightmare-lucid visions that gave nearness to the memory of the living glow of beloved flesh only to have it torn away by the rake-like fingers of metal death. And the distance drew away the precious beings—their bodies dragged down long black vacuums forever. Then with sudden and choking sensation, silence sucked it all away—the utter irredeemably absolute absence of the sounds of life, the sounds of life's heart and swirling blood and the perception of the moving earth. It was the non-sound of the stark, cold stillness of my own death. Then silence was banished by terror. In panicked resurgence, came the sound of my own horror-driven heart drumming, madly striving to escape the frail confines of my body through my ears. I heard them coming. Coming for Glory Hallelujah.

24   The Battle

It is difficult to describe. Most experiences are centered upon one or two of our senses. The meal looks good and smells good; the lake looks beautiful and its waters are cool; the wind sounds like wolves; the woman has a fine visual form, a soft voice, and she smells like a sweet flower. With further awareness it is possible to express the presence of other senses—the taste of her lips, the feel of her smooth flesh. The senses can be examined singly or in harmony with one or two other senses in a coordinated effect.

When the Legion of Death appeared upon the battlefield, arriving with a swirl of cold wind tearing violently across the plain and scattering the rock-dust of eons of eroded rubble, all of my senses were simultaneously bombarded. The sounds I had heard as they approached intensified and out of the mass symphony of suffering I began hearing individual voices crying out the names of the loved ones from whom they were torn by the wrath of Death. And as the Legion swept close I could see them clearly— the dozens of devilish figures attacking us. They wore black hooded capes which waved in trains behind, connecting them with the night through which they flew. They were faceless, having only glowing embers for eyes. And as they rushed past I could feel a dark pulling force like the undertow of a black-night sea drawing me toward the depths. The emptiness of their visage tore at me with terrible powers—like black holes, drawing with almost irresistible force the very light of my soul. And with a putrid taste in my mouth and a piercing, gut-wrenching odor in my nostrils, I instantly and intimately knew of the patently physical nature of death. I felt the damp cold chill of their enwrapping will as it hungrily lapped about my flesh. The mental anguish, though, was far worse than the physical assault. As if to smother even that ambiguous area of a sixth sense—the presence of the Legion forced **upon** me a myriad of mental manifestations in full dimension and vivid detail. A holographic magic **lantern** show of a thousand macabre variations upon the theme of the destruction of life flashed indelibly upon the screen of my mind. And somehow, as if guided by the reaction of my own thoughts, the progression of corpses convoluted with fatal agonies came closer and closer to exploiting the inner horrors of my own life. There was a subtle shift from the impersonal shock of viewing the generalized horror of twisted automobile accidents with limp arms draped from jagged windows, to levels of vision more and more fine-tuned to my personal vulnerability and experience. In rapid succession I suffered the deaths of a dozen children—with silent mouths agape in disbelief and fear at eternal separation from the promise of life. Next came the burning of the children, and I could hear their screams and smell the flame-raged consumption of their flesh. And then there was the burning death of a single child—a death I had witnessed when I was a boy. It was Scout Camp, a burning tent. A friend trapped and me just standing there helpless. And upon that wretched mountain I again knew the flames and the choking smells. And I heard so plainly the pain-tortured agony of a child trapped in a burning tent. And it was real and it was vivid. In a hollow, echoing voice from the heart-vacant realm of loss, my own subconscious reservoir of latent horror was clearly the source of my own torture. How I despised and feared the presence of Death upon that mountain as I knew what was coming. The Fiends had invaded my mind and stolen instants of my life long repressed for the sake of my sanity. I knew the next vignette of death could easily be more than I could bear to reenact within my mind. I tried to cry out but the Force had already absorbed my voice. I would have run, but likewise, there was no movement left to me. The ruthless projection went on. With crazed and brilliantly lucid awareness I watched as roiling sensations turned in timeless detail before me. From an ominous, green-gray sky there appeared a bolt of lightning. And with stopped images catching it a dozen times as it descended, I felt Death stop the breathing in my throat. And with a face more lovely than even the most generous glimpses left to my memory I saw her laughing, rain-splashed face smiling love toward me as she glanced back from the grassy knoll upon which she ran. And then I watched as it hit. The blessings of suppressed recollections stolen from me, I helplessly watched as her eyes boiled and her arms flung wildly, and her heart exploded. And then I heard the moan within my throat as sound returned and I struggled to run but Glory, who was at that exact moment recoiling from the horror of his own forced visions, placed a firm hand upon my shoulder and I stood my ground. There was, in the strength of his years and knowledge and internal powers, a resistance to the terrible Force and I felt it rising in the blood of my own being.

A sound, not really a voice but a sound, came from the surrounding cluster of the forms of Death. It said, "Glory Hallelujah, Jackson Blake you are dead."

And after a pause during which he must have gathered all the energy of his eight-decade quest for life, Glory replied, "No! By the songs of the Gods who dwell beyond this petty realm, we are alive. We shall live!"

The battle was but an instant. I felt the vibrations of Death—the throbbing cessation of life's functions, and then I felt the thrust of living force coming from Glory, who, still grasping my shoulder, cast off the fear that had been foremost within me and unleashed the truth it had suppressed. And I felt my Powers joining Glory's Powers as together we stood in opposition to the Fatal Legion. With the wild-rushing passion of our collective rage we defied the Forces that had ravaged our lives and our minds.

"No!" spoke the single voice of our resolve.

The metaphor, the arc, the balance of countervailing forces had been created. The Light, neither glaring nor bright yet so intense as to dispel the darkness that had engulfed us, glowed from all directions and within that Light there were sounds of richness and joy beyond any that had graced the finest of mankind's music. It glowed and sang with such beauty that I could barely stand to know its existence within me. I laughed and wept and staggered at the force of it all.

And Death was burned away by the Light.

* * * *

"I'm going up and take a look. I'll come back and bid you farewell before I leave."

He walked up a path into the heart of the Light and peered into its living clouds. After a moment, he turned back to me. He had changed. He had no age, the edges of time had vanished from his face. He had become a source of the Light.

He came back down and placed his hands upon my shoulders. In his eyes were sunsets and rainbows and spectra of color beyond imagination. When he spoke his voice was the rhythmic sounds of ocean waves and the crescendo of symphonies and delicate harmonies of the spirit. "You are the High Priest of Hallelujah, Jackson. Life is your mandate." And then he **laughed** a laugh of windchimes and burning stars and wonder-spinning rushes and said, "It's just so beautiful, so rich, so complete."

And he turned and walked back up the Celestial Path—taking the Light with him, yet leaving some of the Light with me— and then with more **laughter** and song than mortal man had ever **laughed** or sung, he stepped slowly into the realm of Immortal Art, and Beauty, and Love.

PART THREE

Surreal. You bet it was surreal.
And then the best part—more real than ever.
The beauty, the vibrant essence of just regular old everyday sunshine and local flesh and the taste of a glazed doughnut— wow.
You'll see.

1   From the Mountain Toward the Forest

I wasn't really stunned. It was the weight of what happened that held me motionless for untold moments—not the shock of it. Witnessing Glory's transmigration into a mortally unfathomable dimension had seemed as natural as sensing the fascination of sunsets and ocean tides or feeling the touch of wind upon my face. I had no fear of the Death forces which surely were lurking in the shadows of that wondrous Light. And, when the Light had departed and the incredible depth of the lightless night returned, I had the quiet confidence of one who has been freed from the quavering self-doubt and fear of frail humanity to one blessed by the soaring potential of mighty humanity. I felt no loss at the departure of my good friend. Instead, I knew the companionship of his Truth and his Powers within me.

I wondered if anyone would notice I had become a Holyman without my donning robes or spinning prayer wheels.

Though previous to my amazing encounter with Glory I had no notion of any clearly defined purpose in doing so, like Glory, I too had been making preparations for that grand night. The walking meditation Glory had taught me was not totally unfamiliar. Years earlier I had spent a whole evening wandering the streets of a small town in a similar state of transfixed awareness. Walking itself can be a form of meditation, and I soon drifted into a trance as the night-closed rows of houses passed and the blocks and hours fell behind me. I spoke with my mind and called all of the various selves which dwelled within my aura together into a single being and together I viewed the world. With steady-cadenced concentration I felt the presence of my total being pressing the confines of my body. Then, directing all of my vision on the sidewalk upon which I walked, the Earth became as loosely-strewn straw and I saw through its insubstantial mass to the universe beyond it. The night became a full sphere of stars and blackness with no real barriers to the full view of the orb of reality.

But no one noticed. The next day when I went back to work at my job, I was surprised my coworkers were so dense as to be unaware I was a larger being than I had been the day before. I had seen the blazing sun as a peer to its heaven-vast brethren. They couldn't see it in my eyes, though from within my mind I saw them from an entirely different perspective than I had ever known before. And, even after I had foolishly bared my soul and described my experience, the only reaction I got was, "That fool Blake has taken a couple of high voltage hits too many. I know he has."

I knew it then, and I knew more so than ever up on that cold magic mountain: It is the nature of enlightenment that such experience be internal and invisible to all who do not share it. Paradoxically, the more lucid that the Great Truths become, the less we are capable of telling them. Back then I was a wanderer who had stumbled upon a universe. That night upon Three Days I had become The High Priest of Hallelujah who had been guided to a vista of the Infinite. And I had learned, regardless of the depth of my experience, the world to which I was to return was unlikely to know the difference—just like the boozers back at Sassy Sally's tavern, there would always be the ninety percent fools and ten percent philosophers so self-blinded as to miss the glory of the days through which they passed. It didn't matter anyway. My mandate was of life, not evangelism. I'd leave the missionary work to assholes like Brother Earl and his ilk. In the exuberance of that fantastic night, I felt as if I could kick Earl's butt anyway.

I walked back down the mountain without the slightest trepidation at the unseen things rustling about in the darkness along the path. I didn't even fall off the narrow trail and break my neck. I didn't trip over any rocks or even my own big feet. But I did breathe the Powers through the symbol of the air. And I realized just as these magical energies were perceptible in the invigoration of that clear, cool air—the body into which I breathed Their symbol was, likewise, but a symbol of an equally and vast and invisible Force: the Human Spirit.

"Wow!" I shouted to the rocks and the canyons, to the world beyond the crude beasts of death. And I heard the echo of my shout for, at least in the moments of that night of a single victory, the howling winds were stilled. So I started singing. Why not. And what better song—with mumbled recollection accentuated by a precise refrain—what other than *The Hallelujah Chorus*.

"Dum... dum... dum, dum, dum-dum: Hallelujah! Hallelujah!"

Downward I marched in solitary celebration of triumph. "Hallelujah! Hallelujah!"

I was not deluding myself. I knew well that, once the circuitous trail reached the archway and I passed from the realm of the singular authority of this mountain, there were a hundred other kingdoms of death, some good, some evil, to which I had no such immunity. But, what the heck. An hour's immortality I would flaunt and relish, and let the fall of days to follow wend their way as they must.

"To hell with the wimpy Death of Three Days!" I bellowed and the humbled fiends whispered and the ancient mountain faintly trembled beneath my feet.

Beneath me, in the now full light of the risen moon I could see the Altar and the Arch beyond it. And, laughing and shouting and nearly dancing I descended the final turns of the trail.

"Not by the hair of your chinny, chin, chin," I taunted as I rounded the Altar and then, with startled gasp of terrified breath, I stopped rigidly still before the awful rock—as silent and as chilled as death itself.

Upon the lap of the Altar, as if discarded like the skin of a snake, and ripped and torn to horrendous distortion by the hideous claws of a beast, lay the lifeless flesh of Glory Hallelujah.

2 Whew

"Glory," I said in a subdued, almost trembling voice. "Are you there?"

And from somewhere within my soul, some place in the mystery of my newly-discovered being, from wherever it was within the entity that yet bore my name where the Light persisted beyond Glory's exit, came the voice of distant Music and it said, "Of course, Jackson."

"Whew, I said. I looked at the carnage that had just hours earlier been the living, breathing form of a briefly known but deeply beloved friend and said, "I just thought I'd tell you these guys are really pissed off."

And with more of the deep, wild, and melodious laughter that had been the voice of his departure, he said, "No kidding. They really scattered my old bones, didn't they?"

And, again relieved of fear, catching the infectious mirth of his spirit I said, "So, do you want me to slap these chumps around a little more, Boss?"

With more of the Musical energies he spoke again within me saying, "That won't be necessary, my friend. Now will you leave me alone, I've got so much to experience."

"Sure," I said. "Live it up. So long, Glory."

"Farewell," he said. I left the Altar to the next desperate pilgrims from the Road to Three Days, walked through the Arch back toward the pickup truck and a world forever changed.

3   Meanwhile Back at the Rock

The truck was gone there was no sign of Carrie or Kitty. I thought of the mutilated remains of Glory and a shiver of dread coursed my soul.

I sat down in the dirt before the great red rock and awaited the dawn. My life was yet immune to the mountain, but what good to survive only to know again the death of love? It didn't make sense, though.   We won the battle, the loss of a corpse withstanding, and no harm could have befallen the ladies of our entourage. It wouldn't be right.

"Damn it all. It wouldn't be right, Glory!" I shouted.

No answer.

"Glory! You can't leave me now. Where are they?" No words were spoken but I knew by the faint sensation of Music within me that all was well. "Okay," I said out loud to the vacant desert. "A nice long walk will probably do me some good. What's another hundred or so miles to the spirit-lightened feet of a Priest? Hey, maybe Officer Lankin will give me a ride."

Jesus Christ wandered the desert. Mohammed wandered the desert.   Howard Hughes bought the desert. Why not Jackson Blake, nomadic Holyman, wanderer of the sand and rock?

I lay flat upon the ground and tried to not think about how thirsty I would be by noon.

With a long and smooth exhalation of breath, I scattered perplexing matters to the distant corners of the night, closed my eyes and, seeing nothing, fell to deep and dreamless sleep.

"Wake up, Jackson," she said. She was kneeling beside me gently touching my face. It was bright, well into the morning. She glowed above me like an angel and I loved her.

Awareness joined the day and I drew her to me and kissed her. "Where were you?" I asked. "At first I thought the beasts had gotten you and then somehow I knew you were all right. I was so relieved when I thought the only thing that happened was you had abandoned me out here to die."

"We've been best friends for so long—what is it, four days—do you honestly believe I'd abandon you in such a time of need?"

"I guess not."

"That's better. Now let's go home."

"Home. Our friend Glory went home, the rest of us will have to stay out and play for a while longer."

"At least we're all still playing."

"Where did you go last night? Our leader said you were supposed to wait for me. Where's Kitty—I need to tell you both about Glory."

"It's strange. We already know what happened up there. We heard the terrible sounds and we felt the awful sensations from down here. It was almost as if we had gone up the mountain with you. It must have been horrible up there."

"It wasn't easy."

"And then we knew you had won. It suddenly felt so good and we knew that Glory had found his other world. Then Kitty started crying, I guess I did too, but she couldn't stop even though she wasn't really sad. Glory had told her what was going on and she explained that the whole thing—meeting Glory and you, giving her heart to Glory, coming here, getting married, and then living through last night like an incredible dream that seemed so real. And she said when it was over up there on the mountain it was like waking up. When the dream is over you feel an emptiness but you're not really hurt by the loss. But she had to go home. She said she hoped you would understand, but she had to go home. So I drove her back—it's only an hour and a half to the city from here if you take real highways and drive over fifty miles per hour. I let her off, then came back out here to find you."

"I'm sure glad you're not dead and that I'm not going to die of thirst or starvation." I was sitting there. The sun was aglow upon her. I looked at her clearly for the first time that morning and it was amazing how lovely she was and I knew the Light and the Music were as close as her embrace.

"Jackson, you look different. Your eyes are different, they're deeper, warmer."

"The better to see you with, My Dear."

"Well, you might have walked with God, but you're still a smartass."

"Do I really look different?"

"Listen to me. I mean it. You're the same old almost handsome guy you were yesterday. But, yes, there is something definitely different about your eyes when you look at me like that."

"I'll try to uncross them. I mean you are really looking good."

"This is serious."

"Impossible. Remember to whom you are speaking, child."

"Jackson," she said with an unguarded smile that was almost apologetic. "When you look at me I feel beautiful."

"I stood up, and grabbing her hands and pulling her close to me, I said, "Well, you ought to see what you look like from this side of these wild eyes of mine. You are beautiful, Carrie. Before, you were pretty and sexy. It fascinated me just to look at you and excited me when you looked back. It must be part of the miracle of last night. I've been to the very source of Beauty and I can recognize its presence in you. Not only can I see you more clearly, but I can see the Light within you. I'm not just looking at what you are, Carrie. I'm looking at who you are."

"It feels strange. I've never felt like I was beautiful before,"

"Well, don't be so damned modest about it. Let's take a look at the rest of your recently beautified body."

"In time, Love, I think I'll just walk around and feel beautiful by myself for a while."

I took her in my arms and knew, just as the horrors of the mountain had been multi-sensory nightmares, the joys of Enlightenment also scanned the full spectrum of perception and communication. She pulled away from me giggling like a young girl, but then her mood changed suddenly. She glared at me as if she had been betrayed, "You're going to leave, aren't you."

"Yes," I said and only knew it then myself. "I must."

She smiled at me sadly. "I understand."

"Carrie, I have no choice."

"Send me a postcard from time to time, will you?"

"Wait a minute, Love. You've got to really look into these eyes of mine."

She looked away and then she looked back, "Yeah, I see. But will I feel this beautiful when you aren't here looking at me?"

"Carrie, you are this beautiful. I didn't make you so. I simply see you so."

She blushed a pretty glow and then said, "Sure." She took a few steps away from me and let it go. "I saw a tavern about thirty miles down the road from here. You want to go get a beer? I'm buying."

I walked to her and held her hand and we walked toward the truck. "Are you sure us Holy-guys are allowed to drink?"

"Unless you happen to be a Baptist or a Mormon High Priest of Hallelujah, I think it will be okay."

"That's a relief."

She looked at me and said, "Jackson, you're all dusty again— just like you were the night I first met you."

"You cheated, didn't you?"

"Well... "

"You sneaked a shower at the apartment. For all you knew I could have been out here choking my final breaths and you wasted precious minutes on personal hygiene."

"The better to smell to you, My Dear."

"And you washed you hair, too. I can tell."

"What of it? My big fluffy bed looked pretty good to me, too. I could still be there getting my beauty sleep."

"Oh, no," I said, and for a moment the good feelings were all around us. "I don't think I could stand you to be any more beautiful. It could burn my brand-new eyeballs right out."

"I'll try to be careful," she said.

As we approached the pickup she said, "You drive. I'd better get some rest. If I'm fortunate enough not to be fired, I have to get to work by six this evening. It's time to get on with my career. I'm just dying to get back there with the guys and splash beer all over my boobs."

"Listen to me. You don't ever have to go back to work at The Naked Rose. I realize now that Glory's mandate to me was not only concerned with the preservation of life but also with its quality." I didn't know the extent of my own powers but it was with genuine authority that I said, "Carrie, you'll never have to work as a naked lady again."

Suddenly she was angry. "What are you going to do about it? Will you take me away from all the sin and sadness of my seedy life and make a lady out of me? Are you going to marry me, Jackson? Are we going to run away to some place so distant that every cowboy in the county can't describe the dimples in my ass? Are we going to raise a little family together, you and I? You've already said you have to leave. I can understand that. Everyone has to leave.

164

But don't tell me lies. That's cruel."

"I'm not lying and I would never intentionally be cruel to you. Hell yes, I'll marry you and then the ghastly Devils can kill you just like they did my first wife. They can drown you in a flood. They can burn you in a fire. They can smother you in snow or crush you with rock. There are a thousand varieties of death, Carrie, and I have only conquered one of them."

"Then you'll spend the rest of your life hiding from death?"

"No, I won't be running anymore. But, until I understand just who Jackson Blake is after this wild night, I won't jeopardize the safety of love. Never again. And, by the way, I wasn't lying. The last thing Glory Hallelujah told me before he left was that Life was my mandate and, by damn, I'm starting to believe I have some Power to back that up."

"The whole thing has gone to your head. How can you help me?"

"I've got the magic, Baby. I can feel it. Shazam! You're a certified public accountant. Shazam! You're a nuclear physicist. You call it, Carrie, and I'll grant the wish."

"You're crazy."

"You call it."

"I want to be a naked bartender."

"This is going to be entirely too easy."

"Let's go get that beer," she said.

She walked on ahead of me and I watched her. "My God," I said to Glory Hallelujah whose body was a ripped up mass of gray-dead flesh and whose spirit was at that moment doubtlessly ballroom dancing with goddesses and drinking Budweiser with the Bards of the Universe. "Isn't she lovely this morning?"

4 The Poet Priest and the Bad Bikers

It was midday by the time we came to the biker bar that was one of three businesses still open in a crossroad cluster of sand-blown wooden buildings called Dibble, Arizona. The other two enterprises were a gas station and, strangely enough, a hobby shop specializing in rare coins. No matter how long I live or how much I glean from the wisdom of the ages and the Powers of the invisible, I'll never begin to figure out everything.

"If I had any money, I'd buy you a rare coin."

"It's a nice thought," she said, "but I think I would settle for a cold beer."

Well, as long as you're buying—why not."

I knew it was a biker bar by the assemblage of Harleys parked outside. But, just as with bankers and teachers and plumbers and preachers, there are good bikers and bad bikers and, generally, if you don't mess them, most will leave you alone. So, we headed on in.

When you walk from the blazing brilliance of high noon upon the desert into the dim confines of a bar, it takes a minute for your eyes to adjust. We stood just inside the doorway and waited for the interior to become more visible. As details emerged I could see there were about a half a dozen men standing at the bar and several more seated in the corner of the room sitting at a table. The bartender was a skinny old man wearing a dingy tee shirt. I could tell it was not a good place for us to drink but it was certainly the only bar in miles and, what the heck, Carrie was buying.

She sat down at a table and I went to the bar to order. I stood there for a minute or so before the ornery old bastard finally acknowledged my presence and glanced at me. "Two Buds, please," I said.

With a lack of enthusiasm that could easily be interpreted as disdain, he pulled the beers out of the cooler and sat them on the bar. His only words were, "That's ten bucks."

"Ten bucks!" I said in amazement. "It must be a long way to the next bar."

He just stared me and I counted out Carrie's dollars. It sure wasn't a very friendly place.

"I hope you brought a bunch of money, Carrie, beers cost a fortune here," I said as I sat down at the table with her. "I didn't get you a glass either. I was afraid to ask, he might have shot me."

"That's okay. I don't mind drinking out of a bottle. At least it has a chance of being clean. And don't worry about the cost—you're worth it."

"I'll drink to that," I said and with a clink bottles we took a drink.

"Say, Jackson," she said as we sat our bottles down on the table. "If I'm so beautiful and pure, then why are all of those guys at the bar looking at me like I'm some kind of five-dollar trash?"

I took another long, cold swallow and casually glanced at the gentlemen at the bar and, sure enough, they were a lusty looking bunch to say the least. They were mumbling amongst themselves. "Carrie, my darling, as much as I would thoroughly enjoy spending the remainder of this devilishly hot day sipping refreshment with you in some cool and shaded tavern, I don't believe this is the place to do so."

"I think you might have a point there, Love. Why don't we get the hell out of here?"

"Indeed."

We calmly set our partially emptied beers on the table and stepped as inconspicuously as possible toward the exit. However, before we could slip past the vigilant lechery of the crowd, three of them moved to the door and blocked our way—a fleshy barricade of leather, big guts, and ham-sized arms covered with tattoos.

"Ain't you all leavin' kinda soon? You ain't even finished your beers yet," said one of the self-appointed doormen.

"We hate to drive on more than a half a beer," I said. "Safety first, you know."

"Well, we don't want you to be takin' any chances out there on the highway, but, all in all, it might be safer for you if you didn't leave right away," said another of the fellows and there was an eddy of guttural laughter at the bar and from the table in the corner of the room.

"Thanks for the advice but I think we'll just be pushing on, we've got a long way to go today."

The apparent leader of the pack stood up from the table and spoke. Where the other two had been taunting and sarcastic in their remarks, he was blatantly threatening.

"You ain't goin' nowhere. Sit down and drink your beer, Mister. I'm gonna put some money in the jukebox and this here lady is gonna dance the same way they do down at the Naked Rose. I seen her down there tending bar and I'll just bet she's got the moves just like the rest of them naked bitches do. Ain't that right, Boys?"

And, of course, the boys all agreed.

"I've seen all over her body down there and now we're gonna have a little hometown show. What do you say, boys? Are we gonna have a show here this afternoon?"

"Yeah," said the boys, the bastards, and in seconds a space was cleared and the jukebox was banging.

Carrie was frightened. So was I. "Jackson, you promised. You said I wouldn't have to do this again."

"Oh, what's one more dance?" I said and I'm not sure that I was joking.

We stepped back toward our table. "You'd think a Holyman would have a backbone," she said to me.

"I do have a backbone. It's just that it's engineered more like a palm tree than a mighty oak."

"Why don't you just shut up and sit down so the pretty lady can go to work," said the terrible leader of this desert outpost— no doubt the mayor of Dibble. With his words the huge man gave me a shove. There was a flash in Carrie's eyes as he pushed me. What an endearing glimpse it was into the sheltered interior of her heart. Danger and love were the modes of that moment.

"Leave him alone," she said. "I'll give you creeps a fucking show."

Whatever element of a sex drive that causes men to seek voyeuristic pleasures in topless bars or burlesque shows must be much more akin to the excitement of violence than the intimacy of lovemaking. In that instant, there came the scent of blood to the barroom. As soon as my lovely lady had demonstrated a protective interest in me stronger than her obvious distaste for performing for the bastards at the bar, I became the center of their attention and Carrie was relegated to some secondary level of the aggressor's awareness.

It was almost as if the pack, with salivation and glowing red eyes, had discovered a lame brother ripe for slaughter.

"What do you do when you don't have your mama along to take care of you?" said the would-be rapist.

Forces were assembling within me. Escape was impossible without confrontation and, damn them, they were messing with a Holyman's lady.

"I get by somehow," I said.

"Jackson," said Carrie, "It's okay. I'll dance for the sons of bitches and then we'll leave."

"No," I said. "I wasn't lying to you. You're not going to dance here, and you're not going to dance in the city."

"I'd rather dance than see you hurt."

"Well," said the big fellow, looking about the bar with a twisted grin, "it looks to me like you ain't much of a man without this here lady takin' care of you."

A couple more of the boys stepped over from the bar and joined in.

"I'm not sure that he ain't one of those converted ladies hisself. He's ugly and ain't got no tits, but he sure don't got no balls either."

"Is that right?" said my central adversary with darkness of eyes and a voice rumbling with overtures of violence. And then with a sway to his body which I recognized as a John Wayne windup for a punch, he said, looking back at the coterie of bar-chums gathered about him, "Well, I ain't never been one to hit no lady before, but I guess there can always be a first time."

I watched with a curious objectivity as his large fist uncoiled toward me and connected with my face, sending me crashing across the room.

From the rubble of chairs and tables I looked up as the man swaggered toward me. Beyond him I saw the expression of pain upon Carrie's face. All about me I felt the ugly presence of the wolf-vicious dark side of humanity.

I wasn't seriously hurt, but noses tend to bleed impressively when struck by giant fists.

"Get up, you son of a bitch, get up and fight!" shouted my attacker. I stood up and, wiping the blood on my shirt sleeve, in total defiance of his violence, I refused to raise my arms in defense.

He struck me again. This time I bounced against a wall and didn't go down. "Fight me, you chickenshit bastard," he raged.

He was fooling with a Holyman. He shouldn't have been fooling with a Holyman. Forces were chiming within me like the deep, throbbing vibrations of huge church bells. Not the kind of forces that answer violence with violence, but rather, forces counter to the ever-lurking potential in my fellow human beings for fomenting such acts of cruelty and viciousness. Though I was neither frightened nor angry, I was definitely being pushed to a point of taking action.

"That's enough," I said in a flat and dangerous voice.

There was a nervous pause in the reaction of the boys, then with a high-pitched, hooting voice a man in the shadows shouted, "Watch it, Ed. I think he's gonna be a fighter after all."

I took a step toward the man and said, "Get out of my way. We'll be going now."

"Like hell you will," he said, but I perceived a crack in his resolve. I knew with certainty that nobody in that snake pit of a tavern could stop us from departing. I was the High Priest of Hallelujah and Carrie was with me.

"Step aside, sir, the lady and I will be leaving and you would be ill-advised to further delay our parting."

The man was perplexed by the disquieting tone of my voice, and, having doubtlessly lived with the pitiable limitations of rage and fear all of his life, was ill-equipped to handle my calm and passive aura of confidence.

I was invincible and he was beginning to realize it.

He glanced about nervously. "What's the matter, Ed," said another of the voices from the pack. "You scared of this sum bitch?"

"I ain't afraid of nobody," he said as he raised his fist to strike me again. "Goddamn you, fight me! You hear?"

"Get out of the way. We're leaving."

I took another step—my arms hanging loosely at my sides. Another step and he would either have to give ground or punch me again. I watched as his eyes lost their confused aspect and became the crazed glare of one pressed to the brink. "I'll give you something to fight about," he said. He grabbed Carrie's arm with one hand and with the other he ripped open her blouse and there, in the dead, dark air of the dimly lit barroom, with the leering eyes of the crowd upon them, were her lovely, intimate breasts.

And the words of Glory Hallelujah filled my mind. "When the man becomes the metaphor."

I would destroy these fiends.

In voice, strong and steady, I said, "Beauty is the breeze-chilled quiver of a tiny forest flower."

"What'd you say?" said the man who intended on tearing my head from my shoulders.

"Beauty is a tear, a child-song memory, birdcall truths singing through the meadowland."

"What the hell are you talkin' about. You crazy?"

"Beauty is peace in the twisted rubble of deadly war, the taste of salt upon the flesh of a summer lover."

"Shit man! I just got your girlfriend's tits out for everyone to look at. Now, you gonna fight or are you gonna just stand there babblin' like an idiot?"

"Beauty is lust extinguished and slumbering forms with hands in a delicate embrace."

"Ain't I gonna break your face?"

He was teetering, about to fall. I knew that with one more bloody arc from my visions of the Upper Gods deep into the vulnerable ignorance of his incorrigible mortality, he would certainly be felled.

"Have you had enough?" I demanded. "Do you give up?"

"What?"

"I said, 'Have you had enough?'"

"Enough what?" he said. And then I grinned a powerful grin at him and he started laughing nervously. "Goddamn," he laughed. "What's so damned funny about this anyway?" And he and the other terrible people laughed with more air than mirth. The brute sputtered, "I'm gonna hit you so hard," but the hilarity of his total defeat was more than he could overcome with further violence.

And turning slowly like a gunfighter covering all the corners of the barroom, ready to strike forth with another blast of ruthless beauty if any in the place were still game to challenge me, I said, "Carrie, shall we go?"

5   Resolve

Kitty was working. It was late into the evening and Carrie and I were sitting at her kitchen table drinking her decaffeinated coffee.

"Don't you have any real coffee?"

"If you are dissatisfied with either the service or the products served, you certainly may take your business elsewhere, sir."

"I didn't think there would be any harm asking—but apparently there is. I've made the waitress snippy."

"Snippy, Sir, is but an irk away from full-out bitchy, sir. Would you care to comment further on the variety of coffee being served?"

Something was ajar. Crooked. We had sped away from Dibble and its dangerous dudes laughing and exuberant at our victory over the forces of filth and ignorance. Amidst sputtering laughter she had asked, "Jackson, is your nose all right? Did he break your nose?"

"No real harm done," I assured her. "Well, I'll probably be able to sniff around corners better than I used to, but no real harm was done."

And then she jabbed me in the ribs with her elbow and said, "'What's one more dance?' Is that what you said?"

"All a matter of strategy, My Dear, strategy."

"How clever of you."

It was Arizona hot and the long desert road was slow in the old truck but we were happy.

"In your own, strange way, you really fought for me today, didn't you?"

"Am I your hero? I've always wanted to be somebody's hero."

"Yes, you are my hero, Jackson. You saved me from the gang of bad guys." She leaned close to me and kissed me on the cheek. "Thank you, Hero."

"Aw, it weren't nothing, Ma'am."

"Yes it was. Why did you risk your nose, anyway. I've stripped for mangy bastards like them six days a week for most of the last year. It would have just been "one more dance."

"I promised, Carrie. Whatever you do, it'll be your choice."

"But your nose. He hit you so hard and you bled all over your shirt for me. You could have been killed."

"No problem, Miss. I have another."

"Nose?"

"No. Shirt."

"Really. Why did you fight for me?"

"Because, Sweet Lady, beauty is always worth fighting for."

When we got back to the apartment it was about seven and Kitty was already gone. We showered and shampooed and shined until the hot water was gone and then we went to bed. She had made no further mention of returning to work that night. It was so comfortable with her. We slept for hours.

But, upon awaking, harmony had slipped to discord and playful banter had taken on an aggravated edge.

"Hell, yes, I have more to say about this castrated coffee you brew. I'll risk escalation to all-out bitchiness. Let me have it full bore, Miss. Your coffee sucks."

It didn't work. Instead of becoming more feisty and belligerent, she just became sad. I was prepared to do battle, not to confront truth.

"I know two things right now and they both hurt."

"Don't you want to fight about coffee?"

"You're right. The coffee has no character. It's nice warm, safe, dull coffee with no risk to it at all. It won't make us hyperactive and keep us up all night, it won't turn us into caffeine addicts—it's so safe. I hate decaffeinated coffee, but I think I'll have another cup. It can't hurt me like the real stuff can."

"Are we talking about coffee?"

"What else?"

"You know, I've lived this long by being an avid coward. I have been known to run for years in avoidance of a single, meaningful conversation."

"Need a refill. It's very mild."

"All right, Carrie. Spit it out. What is it you know that hurts so badly as to defy escape?"

"I thought you'd never ask."

"You're nearly right."

"I know two things. I know that right now I ought to be down at the Naked Rose making money. That's one thing that I know."

"And what else do you know?"

"I know you're going to leave me tomorrow morning."

"Is that right?"

"Yes."

"And you're sad, aren't you?"

"Yes, I am sad," she said with quaver in her voice. "I'm trapped and I'm going to be lonely again, and damn you, Jackson, I'm in love with a worthless bastard who's going to leave me sitting here being beautiful all by myself."

"I'm leaving tomorrow morning?" I asked because I didn't know it for sure.

"Yes, or the next day or tonight. It doesn't matter, you said you can't stay with me. You said you have to go. I know that. And, besides, maybe I don't want you anyway. You're no damned good— we both agree with that. You don't have any money, you drive an old truck that's always going to be out of gas, you hang around with old men who fight with gods, you beat up bikers with poems, you're not even all that good looking when I really think about it— you're so dusty most of the time." Then she took a breath and said, "And, Jackson, you lied to me, even if you didn't mean to, because we both know I'm going to go back to the bar and be naked again just as soon as you leave. Isn't that true?"

"Wow! Let's make sure you've got it all. Let's see... I'm poor. I have no material class. I fight like a sissy. My friends are weird. I'm homely and, God forbid, I'm dusty. And, oh, yeah, I'm a liar to boot. Did I get it all?"

"And sarcastic, too."

"... and sarcastic."

"Yes."

"This woman is not the least bit decaffeinated this evening. I think she's said it all."

"No I haven't."

'Egads There's more?"

"Yes. You make me laugh, you excite the hell out of me and then you touch me and make me feel wonderful, you even make me feel beautiful."

"And..."

"And, damn it all. I don't want to love you. A year ago I quit a good job and left my hometown to get away from a lover-turned-

174

jerk. My old high school girlfriend Kitty said for me to come to the city—we'd have a great time, we could get an apartment together, she could get me a new job—you know, at the club where she worked. So, I came to the city. I'm not having a great time. I hate my job. Then you show up with your babble and your wild blue eyes and make love to me and tell me I'm beautiful and then tell me goodbye."

"I never said 'goodbye.' I just said I would have to go... and I didn't say I was leaving you. I just have to be gone from you."

"Whatever... "

"There is a difference. I could choke on it right now. I could weep for the difference between saying goodbye and saying I have to go." I turned away. I hadn't cried since Lori's death and God knows if I started, there might have been no stopping me. I stared out the window. The booming bass beats of the Naked Rose thumped the wicked night, the neon signs were flashing a gaudy glare into the sky, a couple of cowboys were angrily strutting violence in the blue-cast shadows of the parking lot. "I warned you I was dangerous. I said I never wanted to hurt you and now I have."

She sniffed a few times, searched her purse for a Kleenex, and blew her nose.

She came up behind me. Wrapping her arms around me and putting an end to the gloom. She said, "Bullshit. You haven't hurt anything that wasnt already injured. You just ripped back the bandages on some of my old wounds for a while and then dumped a little salt on them. That's all."

"Salt. My love is salt on an opened wound?"

"You could say that."

"I didn't say it. You did. I was thinking I might be more of a soothing salve, a balm for the traumas of your troubled times."

"More like a bomb, Jackson."

"I haven't been all that bad, have I?"

"Okay. I'll give you this much. Maybe you've been an aspirin, but my life's been a migraine."

"Come on. Quit being so dramatic—maybe your life's been a mild sinus condition—but a migraine... I don't think so."

"Well, it's true. I have known some poet-nasal drips in my time."

"That's better. I'll accept your metaphor. And, the fact is, I wouldn't mind being your aspirin if I were taken along with a little bed rest."

"Of course. What good is an aspirin without going to bed?"

"No good at all."

"It's probably about time for another dose now, don't you think?"

"Maybe."

Touching her cheek and stopping the moment I said, "Carrie, regardless of my questionable medicinal value—you are right about me being no good—but you're wrong about me lying to you."

I turned to her as her priest and her lover and said, "You are beautiful."

And with the Holy Mandate of Life, I gazed upon her upturned face. And with the Holy Mandate of Love I breathed the Powers through her body. And with the entirety of my heart, my mind, and my spirit soaring madly in loving lust I said, "You've never made love with a Holyman, have you?"

"Hell, Jackson. I've never even made love with a cowboy."

6 Consummation and Departure

Upon the warmth and purity of clean sheets and blessed by the honesty of our affection, we made love.

Carrie and I made love that night while Kitty worked at the Naked Rose and the deep evening air brought sounds of distant-muted music and howling crowds through the open bedroom window. And then we lay in each other's arms and marveled in near disbelief at the wonder of the mutual gifts we had shared.

While wrapped in the wild and delicate love of Carrie, and while moving in the physical and psychological matrix of her passion and my own, elements of Light and Music had vibrated within me and resonated throughout our beings. I sensed clearly that, dwelling within the seeming insignificance of our death-vulnerable selves there was a source of that very Core I had only glimpsed and into which Glory had committed himself. The entire symphony of our embrace—the physical and spiritual and sensual communication culminating in orgasmic bliss—was a direct link to the primal Power that drives all matters galactic and microscopic.

She spoke first, in a whisper, "Wow Jackson," she said.

"Hey, no kidding. Did you feel it, Carrie? Did you?"

"Oh, yes, I felt it, Holyman. I've never felt so special in my life."

"Well, bless you, my child. It's a Holyman's pleasure to touch you so."

"Thank you, Father Blake."

"We weren't just loving, were we, Carrie? We were singing with the Gods. And the strangest, the most wonderful part of this erotic and heavenly harmony is that I don't ever recall feeling so thoroughly human."

"You mean I'm not your angel?"

"No. Much better than an angel. You are my living, breathing, incredible, *Homo sapiens* woman. We didn't just make love for ourselves, or for the Gods, or for each other. Don't you feel it? We just did it for all humanity and, man, did it feel good!"

"Glory Hallelujah!" she shouted.

"No!" I countered. "Carrie Nelson! Jackson Blake!" We laughed and, so close to us as to ring within our souls, the limitless Heavens resounded with our laughter.

And for the rest of that incredible night our pleasures and our slumber were softly adrift in cloudlike abandon.

"I'm sure glad you're not a celibate Holyman," Carrie said to me.

"I'd be a lousy monk. There's too much to celebrate out here in the world of the living. But I can speak in tongues. Want to hear something in Monk?"

"How I dread what's coming. Yeah, sure. Say something in Monk."

"Abba-dabba-dabba-dabba."

In the morning, refreshed by a shower and clean clothes, fed by a quiet and loving breakfast, and with a pocketful of borrowed gas money, it was time for me to leave.

We stood beside the old truck holding hands and Carrie said, "This is going to be easier than I thought."

"Oh, yeah?"

"I might not even cry."

"Not a single tear?"

"Don't push it. I said 'might.'"

"Well, I might not cry either," I said and I wasn't being the least bit flippant.

"You'd better get out of here or 'might' is not going to mean a damned thing."

I looked at her with all the depth and the warmth of my loving eyes and said, "Do you realize we have consecrated your lovely flesh? That we have made sacred your spirit and your beauty?"

"So that's what we were doing all night."

"Well, that and some mighty fine screwing. But I want you to know The High Priest of Hallelujah has declared you to be a Holy Wonder. Now, how can you take the flesh and soul we have deemed to be sacred down to the Rose where they shout, 'Yahoo, jus' lookit the headlights on that bitch'? Kitty is a queen in that realm and, bless her, let her dance. But you go there again and you will defile what you know to be true: your beauty is a matter of love, not exhibition."

Her face was so soft and yet so serious, "It's all easy to believe with you standing here telling me."

"I made you a sacred promise. Now make an honest man out of me."

"Drive on away from here, Love. Then we'll see just how honest you are," A moment's embrace, a gentle kiss, and we let go and I climbed into the truck.

I started the engine. There was shouting from the apartment window above me. Kitty was trying to tell me something. I turned off the rattling old motor and heard her say there was an envelope in the glove compartment I was to open it once I got out of town.

"What's it about, Kitty?" I shouted back.

"I don't know what it is, Glory left it for you.

I said goodbye to Kitty and reminded her that decent women didn't hang out of their apartment windows in broad daylight unless they were wearing clothes. She giggled and, with a memorable shimmy, disappeared into the bedroom.

I restarted the engine.

"Be careful," Carrie said with averted eyes.

"You're so pretty," I said. And with the same resilient spirit that surely would break her free of the Naked Rose, she looked me squarely in the eyes and with tears spilling down her reddened cheeks and a ferocious smile she said, "And don't forget I lent you a hundred bucks."

"Hey. I'm an honest man. I promise I'll pay you back."

"You damned well better, Jackson Blake!"

"I promise," I said.

7   West

When I don't know which way to go, when travel and distance are my primary objectives rather than a specific destination, I usually travel west. This tendency stems from an old tradition originating in the belief of those of us who grew up anywhere east of the Rocky Mountains that all the neat stuff, i.e., mountains, canyons, raging seas, cowboy country, and California women, was to be found by following the afternoon sun.

It hadn't really been as easy as Carrie had tried to bluff. As I slowly made my way through the clutter of mid-morning traffic in the city, I was not only encumbered by a rattletrap of an old vehicle, a cracked windshield, and a lack of familiarity with the streets—I wasn't just fighting traffic; I was fighting tears.

I was miles, hours, and over a half a tank of gas west of the city and Carrie before I stopped to open the envelope that Glory had planted for me. It wasn't that I had forgotten about it being there. I had intentionally ignored the thing.

In the years I had survived since Lori had been killed I had consistently avoided major commitments and their accompanying serious issues. I was certain whatever message Glory had left for me would involve some kind of obligation or awareness of a greater scope than my personal traditions would normally tolerate. Embracing the higher Humanity revealed to me had felt great in bed and in love. And it wasn't just sex. Everything I had experienced since the Mountain—sunlight and the dazzling clarity of the sky, desert vistas, Carrie's bottom, the taste of orange juice—the whole wondrous bombardment of sensual stimuli through which I journeyed had taken on an incredible richness, an intensity I had never before perceived.

It was marvelous. But also, undeniably, it was scary. I was beginning to know elements of the common world that openly, blatantly challenged the ugly, grounding, life-cursing, and powerfully deadly Forces that ruled the mortal plane. And, not only could I sense the presence of vast and beautiful energies, apparently, judging from Carrie, I was also capable of revealing them to others. I was not only touched by the Power, I could also touch with the Power.

To the Darkness, I was a dangerous man. I thought again of the mutilated corpse of Glory.

I put off opening the envelope.

I was thinking about hiding out. Maybe I could turn the truck around and head back for some flatland suburb far away from the desert, from Carrie, from any portion of the enchanted existence I had discovered. Maybe I could lie low for twenty or fifty years or so—there are plenty of life-consuming options that are so innocuous as to make existence nearly invisible. What about all those murdering Nazis who disappeared after World War II?

Or maybe, to save time and boredom, I would just run the old truck dry of gas and then walk until my shoes were gone and then crawl until my skin was gone and then blow away like the rest of the dust and the sand.

I was deeply frightened. I didn't fear death so much—death alone is no tragedy. But I had known the fiends as they sorted through my mind in the creation of my own personal Hell. I didn't fear death. I feared knowledge.

But I did pull the truck over to the side of the road. I had to—the engine had blown up.

I had no choice.

8   The Letter

I thought of the rainforest of the Hoh River Valley up on the Olympic Peninsula of Washington. It is a gray-green, ancient place of ferns and two-hundred-foot fir trees. A place of mist and cushioned paths and the soft and haunting company of memory's laughter.

I was probably as far from the Hoh Valley as was geographically and spiritually possible.

The midday sun was bleaching the textured desert terrain into faceless monotony. The smell of oil and the simmering wisps of black smoke coming from beneath the hood of the truck foretold a return to the unprotected realm of the roadside.

It was hot, but I could stand the heat. I wasn't particularly hungry or thirsty.

The Hoh River Valley—I'd have to go back there some day.

I opened the large, manila envelope and examined its contents. There was a note from Glory written in a firm and artful hand. There was a stack of time-worn hundred-dollar bills—twenty of them. And, hanging upon a silver chain, there was the silver ankh with a large piece of rough turquoise set into its center that Glory had worn about his neck.

It was very quiet. The only sound was a slight hiss coming from the expired engine. An apathetic wind occasionally rocked the creaking truck.

Dear Jackson,

I'm writing this note while you and the ladies are sleeping. Tomorrow we will arrive at Three Days. I have much I could tell you but I will make this brief.

First, I am enclosing a portion of my life savings for you to spend and, thus, enable you to travel freely, for a short time anyway. I believe this will be a necessary mode of existence for you, at least until greater matters are resolved. You are not unaccustomed to such a life.

Second, I am giving you my ankh. It has no special powers or properties other than those given it by the priests and artisans who created the symbol back in ancient Egypt. Supposedly it represents the continuation of life and a reverence for it. I pass it on to you simply because I wore it through a good bit of my own life and would be pleased if you would keep it. Perhaps this trinket has protected me on occasions—I'm not certain.

That takes care of business. Now for the advice. No matter what the result of my impending conflict with the Death Creatures upon the Mountain of Three Days, by the fact that you shall accompany me, you will be identified as an enemy of Darkness throughout the world. Admittedly, my friend, I am knowingly placing you in grave danger. I have no regrets. The only course of action they can take against you is to attempt to destroy your present manifestation. It will be regrettable if they succeed prematurely—you are a most likable life form. However, the experience you shall gain by joining me in this encounter, regardless of how difficult or painful, will more than justify dropping back one rung on this great ladder toward Truth that you and I and, hopefully, many others have been climbing throughout the epoch of our species. Humanity was born of The Light and The Light resides deep within us. It is our quest, through lifetimes of search and growth, to return to the Source from which come the Immortal Powers.

Be careful. If I succeed in this venture, and I believe I shall—particularly with the infusion of your heart-deep rage as an additional resource—then you will become a most despised conspicuous enemy of the Darkness. If we win, you will accrue a greater power than the authority of this province. However, once you leave this area, as you certainly must—as you will feel compelled to do—I cannot guarantee you any immunity, though, it might exist, to the forces of other regions.

And I can tell you now, no matter how mediocre you may appear to casual observers, I recognize you as being my dear and trusted companion throughout eons of search.

You, Jackson, are truly a High Priest of Humanity.
Try not to screw it up.
I"ll be seeing you sooner than you think.

Glory

And there was just the hiss of the engine, the occasional shudder of the wind.

9   Flight

I heard myself whisper, "They're after me now."

Trapped in a dead truck. A gust of wind-scattered sand in a rush across the hood. A giant diesel truck roared by, shaking me with a blast of air.

"Thanks a whole hell of a lot, Glory!" I shouted. "You've been a real pal. I could have wandered around this life forever. I could have recycled simple times over and over until the empty journey was finished and I was just dead. But you couldn't let a man just fumble on in mediocrity, could you? We had to piss off the Gods, didn't we? I saw what They did to your body, old friend. And I know what they did to my mind up there on that damned mountain."

"Is anyone listening? Glory, are you there? I never asked to be a crusader. I am every bit the meek and clumsy fellow I seem to be on the surface. I'll forget the visions, the horrors, the vengeance, the Holy calling—just get these Bastards off my back, Glory! Do you hear me? Off of my back!"

Of course he didn't answer. Either he was too busy playing the back nine at the Celestial Hills Country Club, or hang-gliding along the coast of the Golden Seas using his own wings, but in any case he was obviously too busy to help a friend in need.

"Thanks a lot, Glory," I said again. I was condemned to be the sole Priest of a defiant order. It wasn't going to be easy. I was sure of that.

I got out of the truck and began circling about and finally sat upon a large rock to decide what to do. Afternoon was moving right along and the thought of the inevitable darkness of evening was frightening. I had to figure some course of action that would give me anonymity and distance. He had said I was safe from the demons of the mountain, but also, as I had guessed, there was no telling how far their powers reached and where I would cross over into the jurisdiction of some other realm of Evil. Glory, in his zeal for encountering and knowing the Powers of Light, had exposed me to the Powers of such Darkness that I feared, more than ever, for the vulnerability of those precious to me. I had seen these sons of bitches in action before and wasn't about to lead them back to pretty Carrie and have her wiped out as another example to me.

But I was committed. By the very experience that, even in the anxiety of the moment, was singing through me with a purity of sound and sensation and perception making the afternoon of the arid and thorny desert a world of glowing wonder, I was cursed by the Bullies of Hell.

Bullies. I don't like bullies, I didn't like bullies in grade school where they made me spend my precious few pennies buying them sticks of red licorice at Carbismeyer's Candy Store. I hated the pushy big kids who reveled in my terror.

"Get your own fucking candy," I said to the wind.

And the wind said, "Say, what?"

"Get your own fucking candy," I repeated.

Something was happening to me again. Just as it had up on the mountain, I was getting mad. Anger, no—rage was beginning to overshadow the reasonable course of my fear and I could feel the swell of courage rising up within me. I felt the change and tried to resist it. I recalled a poem I had written on a bathroom wall.

I fear no fool
but the fool be I,
and I'm half the size
of the other guy.

It was one hell of a time to be picking a fight with the Gods.

I walked back to the truck and got in. I was going to sit there and ponder the situation for a while longer when I noticed a Highway Patrol car swish by going the opposite direction and then slow down intending to turn around to check my nonexistent registration or title. I was in no frame of mind to discuss with the law the legal technicalities of the bill of sale Glory's nephew had written on the inside of the cardboard wrapper from a six pack of Nehi Root Beer: I Sell this truck to J. Blake for...

"All right, Blake," I said to myself. "If you're so damned powerful, then make this miserable truck run." I turned the key and the engine that was never to run again started right up. I quickly ground the old beast into gear and pulled back onto the highway. Looking into the rearview mirror to make sure the police were leaving me alone, I said, "I don't want this kind of power. Do you hear me? I don't want it."

At a later, more rational time, I thought about what had happened and realized whatever condition had caused the motor to die had been temporarily remedied by cooling off. But, at the moment it happened my mental state was not so analytical. To me the amazing resurrection had been a result of nothing less than the application of my own magic.

For a while there, I must admit I was somewhat impressed by my prowess as a Priest. For a short time illusions of grandeur stayed the fear that had been plaguing me and a sense of giddy power asserted itself. As I steadily rolled westward, thoughts of the possibilities of using the amazing talent dashed madly about my mind. My final thought brought me to near hysteria. Speaking aloud I said, "Wouldn't Glory be proud of me if I utilized his enlightenment by opening my own garage."

I laughed and laughed and then, just as I approached the first sign of human life in fifty miles, the damned thing died again. At first it didn't concern me. I allowed the truck to coast right up to the front of the only building in the town of No Hope, Arizona. Then, exhaling a casual breath, I calmly said, "Start."

I turned the key and nothing happened.

"Start!" I repeated, this time in a louder, more desperate voice.

Of course, nothing happened.

In power only an hour and already usurped. "Damn you, truck. I'm Jackson Blake, the High Priest of Hallelujah, now start!" I yelled at the thoroughly inanimate vehicle.

The most I could raise from the engine compartment was a reluctant moan.

"I don't know a whole lot, mister," said a voice from the shade of the front porch of the combination grocery store, post office, and gas station, "but I don't think that wreck you're drivin' really cares who you are. It ain't never gonna run again."

Startled by the realization that someone had witnessed the madness of my attempt to resurrect my Lazarus of an engine, I sheepishly climbed out of the truck and walked toward the porch, squinting to see the face of the man who was seated there. "It does seem to have some kind of a problem," I said.

"I reckon so," he said.

"You want to buy it?"

"What?"

"My truck. You want to buy it?"

"It don't work. What would I want with an ugly old truck that don't even run?"

"It's got a good front seat," I said. "Really comfortable—it would make you a fine couch for your porch here."

"I got me a good seat."

"The bed's in good shape."

"What good's a bed if the damn thing don't move?"

"Plenty good. You take the thing off the chassis and turn it upside down—then your dogs will have a nice place to crawl under and stay out of the sun. Flip it back over, weld the tailgate shut, fill it up with well water and you've got yourself the only spa in town. You paint your name on it and set it up out beside the highway for a billboard. I can see it now—big letters saying 'No Hope Gas Station Just Ahead.' Hell, you can put a lid on the damn thing and use it for a snake-proof coffin."

"Ain't no snakes in the graveyard."

"Why not?"

"Ain't no graveyard."

"Why not?"

"I'm the only one here and I ain't dead yet," he said, exploding into a storm of wheezing laughter.

"I wouldn't press my luck if were you."

He sputtered back into control of himself and said, "Hell, Mister, I ain't got any luck to worry about. If a man had any luck at all he sure wouldn't be livin' out here, would he?"

"I guess not."

"How much you want for it?"

"Does a bus stop here?"

"Sometimes. If I put out the flag and the driver feels like stoppin', he'll pull in here. But only sometimes. Not all the time— it just depends."

"Well, saying we can get him to stop, you get me enough money to pay my way to the next real place west of here and I'll give you my truck."

"Whew," he said. "It'll cost me twenty dollars to get you clean out to a real place."

"The radio works."

"Sold."

"Thank you, sir."

"Sure. But I told you, didn't I?"

"What did you tell me?"

"Anyone damned fool enough to buy that truck of yours deserves to live out here, don't he?"

"I wouldn't know," I said.

"Ain't got no luck at all," he said laughing and coughing to himself.

10 Greyhounded

The man of No Hope bought me twenty-dollars' worth of distance and to that I added most of what I had left of the money Carrie lent me and paid my way to the coast. With local turns and stops and the discovery of a dozen towns every bit as well developed as No Hope. the ticket was good for over twelve hours of relative security. As little kid, in the early light of day when the house was deathly quiet with sleep and scary dreams were still fresh within my mind, behind the scrunched up barrier of my small legs I would hide so the "big bad wolf" could not see me through the window. Tinted windows, the anonymity of the night, and the high-backed seats gave me a similar illusion of safety.

I loved it, and the longer the hours dragged on, the happier I was. There is nothing like being physically and psychologically exhausted and having listless hours to lull away in sleep and semi-sleep while cruising the smooth roads of the continent within a great big bus. Yes, sir, I'll gladly "leave the driving to them" if they'll leave the drifting and dreaming to me. I was freed of all worldly possessions except for a change of clothes and a toothbrush in my small canvas suitcase, and the ankh I wore on a chain of silver links about my neck. Glory's stack of hundred-dollar bills didn't count in the summation of my worth. I had no idea what the purpose would be for the money but I didn't count it as part of my operational budget.

Broke and alone, I was experiencing a suspension of human obligation. At that moment, there was nobody on the face of the Earth who was expecting me to show up or expecting me to be anything. No touches; no one to touch—I was in that euphorically blissful state that precedes devastating loneliness once an awareness of the extent of one's isolation settles upon the situation.

I knew it was a fragile feeling of well-being I was experiencing but I didn't care. It felt good. I indulged myself in guarded moments of dream and memory. I bought the ticket and, by damn, nothing was going to spoil the ride. As the gentle weariness of escape carried me across the evening and deep into the night, parading visions of the best times of my real and fantasized past and future filled my mind.

And, of course, I thought of Carrie. I daydreamed the wild beauty of her touch and the distant call of her love. I thought of Carrie and a beautiful, sweet sadness pulsed my heart. Swirling times, thoughts, the turning of highway wheels toward the west, the gradual filling of the seats and the mumble of conversations, the turning of dry black hills and service station lights into the deepening darkness in our wake, the mesmerizing hum of physical movement through the timeless immobility of memory. And Lori was there, too. Dwelling as she always did as a whisper of timeless song within me. It was tireless travel upon a good and gentle road.

And then, in harsh violation of the sanctity of my painless revelry the voice of doom spoke out into my special night, shattering the pleasant delusion of safety. With the utterance of a simple question, streams of reality with their vast portent for terror, cruelty, neglect, and hatred flooded over me.

"Does y'all like country music?"

"What?" I said, obviously startled by the piercing effect of the question. The young man who was sitting next to me was likewise startled by my emotional reaction to his inquiry.

With a halting voice he said, "All I said was, 'Does y'all like country music?'"

I pondered my reply to the question. The seemingly harmless young man who had taken the seat next to me somewhere back in the lost hours of the night had vibrated the taut fibers of my past. Surely it was the madness of the previous days driving me to overreact to an innocent attempt at making conversation. To cover my inappropriate reaction to the question I smiled with false warmth and lied as I had to Brother Earl, the factory fanatic, so many years previous. "Sure. I love country music. I listen to it all the time."

The young man stared at me for a moment and an expression flashed across his bony face with haunting familiarity. It was the cold and arrogant gaze of the piously ignorant.

With quiet and practiced fervor and a voice quavering with conviction he said, "I know the Way of the Serpent and the words of the sinner. I know the path of the irreverent. You're lying to me,

Mister. Y'all don't like country music."

"Who taught you to say that?" I snapped bitterly.

"I know the way of the Lord, and the Lord he carries a mighty sharp sword."

"Where did you learn that bullshit about 'the irreverent' and 'country music?'" I said with anger burning in my words.

Looking about quickly as if seeking a place to run, with fear he said, "You-all devils can't frighten me. The Lord's gonna protect the faithful."

I grabbed his necktie and pulled his chalk-white face right up to mine and in a harsh whisper said, "You miserable fucker, who taught you about irreverent behavior. Tell me or I'll choke the life out of you right here. I swear I will."

The terrified young man gasped, "It's everywhere, Mister. Honest it's everywhere—on the radio, in the churches, on the TV. I don't know which one give it to me. Honest, it's everywhere."

I let go. He closed his eyes and while panting and praying he pressed the button on his player and through the hiss of his earphones I could hear the song and the song said:

> *The Devil's a drinker's companion,*
> *he'll set up your soul every night.*
> *You'll lie and you'll cheat on your family,*
> *'til your life is the Devil's delight.*
>
> *But I gave up the barroom for Jesus,*
> *and that was a beautiful day.*
> *He gives us his love and it frees us,*
> *so the bottle can just stay away.*
>
> *To the beat of sin songs on the jukebox*
> *and the clink of ice cubes in a cup,*
> *the sinners all booze down their evenings*
> *and the Devil just swallows them up.*
>
> *But I gave up the barroom for Jesus…*

He was right. The sons of bitches were everywhere.

11 Sojourn in the Familial Web

Daybreak in the plush Los Angeles suburb of Huevo del Oeste.

The sun was large and orange—magnified by the haze of human fumes. The street of prosperous- looking California homes was just beginning to stir. People appeared momentarily, stepping from doorways to scoop up morning papers and briefly survey the close warmth of the morning's weather. As I slowly progressed up the long street, the near silence was occasionally broken by the sound of a car door shutting and an engine starting in the ritual of the daily commute. A police cruiser crept by and carefully scrutinized me. I smiled and waved. I was relieved when it continued on without any more than visual harassment.

I was looking for my sister's house. Janice and her urbane California family had always been so distantly removed from my life as to seem inhabitants of a different world altogether. What better refuge from the demons of Three Days and the venom of Brother Earl than the "like burbs" of Orange County?

I knew I was on the right street, but there was a great deal of similarity in the outward appearance of the houses. Most of them had few windows opening to the front, had backyards surrounded by six-foot cedar fences, and front yards landscaped with palm trees. The first time I had visited the place, years earlier, it puzzled me that an architect of my brother-in-law's renown would live in a home with such a bland exterior. When I asked him about it he replied that to be distinct was to invite invasion by motorcycle gangs and murderous cultists.

As I approached a house that seemed familiar to me, I noticed a beautiful young lady standing on the sidewalk. She appeared to be in her early twenties, had long red hair falling in waves across her darkly tanned shoulders, had a full and vibrant figure, and was staring at me intensely. She suddenly burst into a great warm smile and rushed me. With a storm of hugs and kisses to my unshaven cheeks, she cried, "Uncle Jackson, Uncle Jackson."

She was my thirteen-year-old niece, Ashley.

Later, as I ate breakfast with my sister who just sat there gazing at me and uttering such phrases as, "Praise the Lord, Jackson, for all I knew you might have been dead." I said, "They sure do grow up fast out here. I didn't even recognize her."

"You must be referring to Ashley's bosom."

"Well, not only her bosom—but I'd have to say, she's got quite a chest for a thirteen-year-old."

"Jackson, Jackson, you haven't changed at all. You still view the world with lustful eyes. It would seem that time would have eliminated some of your adolescent attitudes towards life by now. But no, not my little brother Jackson, it's still a world full of boobies and bottoms."

"That's my big sister—always finding something to preach about. Come on, Sis, admit it. You're just jealous because Ashley's got a better bod than her mama."

She glared at me for a moment and then remembered I was her long-lost brother, that a Christian is rarely discouraged, and that I was never to be taken seriously.

"Jackson, Jackson, for all I knew you could have been dead for all of this time."

"Nonsense. I sent you a letter not more than a year ago and in it I believe I made specific reference to the fact that I was yet among the living."

"A year is a long time to go without hearing from your only brother."

"Don't you still stay in contact with Mom and Dad?"

"I call them once a month."

"Didn't they tell you I was still alive? I send them a note or call them collect at least every three or four months or so. Well, at least twice a year."

"Of course. I talk with our parents regularly, but somehow you seem to have been totally removed from our conversations. We talk about the weather, the cost of groceries, and how my kids are doing in school. And then they say good-bye. They seldom mention you, and I rarely ask—it seems to upset them so."

"That's real sad. I mean Mom went through a bunch of pain and inconvenience to have me. You'd think I would occur to her every now and then."

"I'm certain she thinks of you, Jackson. It's just that she and Dad are not good at handling disappointment," she said with a missionary smile.

"Ouch, Janice. So un-Christian to smite your brother's little pink cheek."

Once again she hovered on the brink of scorning me and then again considered the source and dismissed my comments with a polite, if somewhat caustic laugh.

"Jackson, Jackson, praise the Lord, you might have been dead."

"Remember the time I caught you and Hank Smith down in the basement? Oh, boy, did you do some fast snapping and zipping that afternoon."

"Remember the time I caught you in the upstairs bathroom handling yourself?" she retorted.

"Hell yeah, I remember. It was likely the thrill of your young life, wasn't it?"

"Do you remember the time you borrowed two dollars from Mom to buy school supplies and instead you bought all of those used dirty magazines from a kid you met at school?"

"Yeah, I remember. You got mad at me for not showing them to you and ratted on me."

"And you got into such big trouble with Mother. I loved it. And then she burned the filthy books."

"Not all of them."

"What do you mean?"

"She didn't burn all the magazines. She and Dad kept a couple of them. I know because I found them when I was going through their dresser drawers looking for rubbers."

"Jackson, you didn't."

"Sure I did. I couldn't find where they hid the condoms but I found the magazines underneath a stack of underwear in Dad's drawer."

"You're kidding."

"I swear."

"What on earth would they have wanted with such smut as that?"

"It might surprise a pure and upward lady like yourself, but there's a touch of good old-fashioned perversion in all of us. It's what makes an otherwise listless life worth living."

"Look, Jackson," she said with her eyes blazing. I was finally getting to her. "Just because I happen to be a Christian and believe in leading a life the way Jesus wants me to, doesn't mean I don't like to fuck, I mean...make love with my husband."

"Praise the Lord," I cried. "At last, a crack in the exterior. We are truly brother and sister. You fuck, don't you? I mean you don't just 'have sex' with old Wilber—you really screw him, don't you?"

"That's enough, Jackson."

"Admit it."

"Admit what?"

"Tell me the truth, Janice. You really like to do the deed, don't you?"

"You make it sound so filthy."

"Admit it."

"Well... "

"Well, what?"

"'I am a healthy woman, you know. Of course I take pleasure in having sex with my husband."

"You'll never know how glad it makes me to hear you say so. There might be hope for you yet, big sister."

"Thank you, Brother. I wish I could say the same thing about you."

"Oh, you can, Janice. You can."

"Hope for the heathens?" she asked.

"Sex for the Christians," I said.

She quickly changed the subject. "Wilber Junior won a medal at his high school for the one-hundred-meter dash."

"He always was a speedy little devil. What was it—six months after you got married?"

"You bastard," she said, almost smiling; her defenses diminishing. I loved my sister Janice. Sometimes I even halfway recognized her through the cloak she wore. Sometimes while we talked I could see her little-girl eyes flashing out at me from within the dense layers of her propriety. Seeking her within such a proper exterior was like going back to an old neighborhood and trying to find a familiar sight. We talked about our childhood together and forgot, for a few moments, how we had grown apart.

"You pulled the head off of my favorite doll. I never did forgive you for that, you barbarian."

"I swear it was an accident, Janice. I just turned it upside down to see if it had any interesting parts and the damned head just fell right off. I didn't do it on purpose. I swear."

196

"An accident, you say."

"I swear on my baseball mitt."

"It was terrible. You laid her out on the couch and I picked her up and her head rolled off on the floor."

"Boy, I can still hear your screaming. I'm really sorry and, honest, it was an accident. Even I wasn't mean enough to set you up like that. I wouldn't have intentionally decapitated old... what was her name... Penny, was it?"

"*Yes*. Penny was her name and she was my favorite."

"Well, anyway it's been almost thirty years now—do you think you might find it in your extremely Christian and charitable heart to forgive an old doll molester?"

"No way, Creep-o."

You know, we had some pretty good times back then, didn't we?"

"Sometimes."

"It's been a while."

"Yes, it has."

"I kind of miss my little sister. Here I am talking to a grownup version of my sister trying to find the little girl who snarled at me and ratted on me and loved and protected me for all of those years. I know she's still in you somewhere—I can see her in your eyes."

"I guess we are always everything that we ever were, aren't we, Jackson?"

"At least."

"But time can make us so much more than we were, too."

"Or less, Big Sister?"

""Yes, or less."

"Have you got any beer, Sis?"

"Praise the Lord, Jackson, for all I knew you might have been dead."

12 Disquiet

I was sleepy. The house was empty. The children were at school, brother-in-law Wilber yet to make his appearance that afternoon upon returning from a business trip to Texas, and my sister on some mission of charity and goodness involving pornography and children of the ghetto.

It was warm in the sunshine out by the pool. I put on a pair of Wilber's trunks Janice had left out for me and stretched out in a great soft lounge chair.

"At least I'm safe," I had said to myself just before going to sleep.

I woke up hours later, hot and groggy in the mid-afternoon sun. With great effort I forced myself to rise from the plastic cushion of the chair and make my way to the edge of the pool. For several moments I stared at the hypnotic rhythm of light shimmering on the surface of the water in the slight breeze. Just as I was about to dive into the pool I sensed the presence of a disquieting force somewhere about me, and then noticed an object lying upon the bottom at the deep end of the pool beneath the diving board. I walked to the edge nearest the object and was able to clearly see what it was. There in the tranquil depths of a family swimming pool which seemed so deeply recessed into the fabric and security of suburban existence lay, with a tarnished link of its silver chain severed, my ankh.

"Gee, I wonder how that fell off," I said out loud.

"Were you talking to me, Uncle Jackson?" came Ashley's sweet, soft voice from inside the house.

"Why, no, Ashley. I didn't even know you were home. What time is it anyway?"

"It's almost four-thirty. Wilber, Jr. and some of his chums were here but I sent them away so they wouldn't disturb you while you were sleeping."

"You're so kind, Ashley," I said, eyeing the ankh lying like a dead snake at the bottom of the pool. "I think I'll take a dip and try to wake up."

"Good. Daddy and Mama will be home in an hour or so and I'm sure they'll want you to be awake for the little party they've planned for you this evening."

"Party?"

"Yes, Uncle Jackson. Mama is so happy that you're not dead."

"So she says."

I dived into the water and it was surprisingly cool. It could have felt good and refreshing to me but instead it felt dangerous. I resurfaced, took a deep breath, swam to the bottom of the pool, and retrieved my ankh.

12 The Party

"I'm like really into sex," she said. She was **probably** twenty-five years old, a little too blonde, a little **too tan**, and a lot too skinny.

"So's your mother," I said.

"Then you've been to the kitchen."

"Yes, several times, in fact. She's a very warm person. Does she always station herself next to the refrigerator at parties?"

"No, she didn't used to be so proactive in **her** sexuality. Actually, until a year ago when she became like a convert **to** the Church of the Liberated Libido she was pretty much of a prude."

"Praise the Lord."

"**Do you** think she's **like** cheap **for** grabbing guys in dark kitchens?"

"No. Not at all—just very warm."

"What's your name again?" she asked.

"Jackson Blake, I'm Janice's long-lost brother."

"I like you, Jackson. I think we might be sexually compatible."

"Thank you, Erika. But, how can you tell so quickly? I mean you don't even know my sign."

"Don't be like trite, **Jackson**. I can feel your power."

"How?"

"Between my legs," she said with a seductive gesture.

"I didn't ask where; I asked how?"

"Vibes."

"I thought 'vibes' went out with **the** sixties."

"Like no way, Man," she said sarcastically.

"Glad to hear it—I always kind of liked good old vibes."

"So, once I made love with a Jesuit priest for a week. He was just **like** you."

"Really?"

"I met him in a bar. He was in disguise at **the** time. When priests go on vacation some of them like wear regular clothes and pretend **that** they're normal guys. He was like ridiculous **looking**. He wore a gaudy **Hawaiian** shirt and plaid pants. He **looked** like an Iowa corn farmer on his second mai tai—a real joke."

"And I remind you of this guy? Well, that's great."

"Have you taken a good look at yourself in like your brother-in-law's retro leisure suit?"

"So the pants are a little short?"

"Yeah."

"And the sleeves?"

"Yeah."

"And a bit out of style."

"Ages beyond 'retro,' just creepy old."

"Go on with your story about the yokel priest who was so much like me."

"So, when this funny-looking little man sat down next to me I tried to like ignore him completely, you know. I was like really into surfers then and this dude was hardly the bronze god I was looking for. But, he wouldn't leave me alone. First he like asked if he could buy me a drink, then if he could sleep with me, and, as a last resort if he could hear my confession. I finally turned to him to tell him to take a flying leap and saw his face and his soul which were like vibrating from behind the orchid-covered shirt and the clumsy line he was coming on with. When he saw that he had my attention, he said he hadn't had oral sex with a woman in like six years. I asked him if he was always so subtle and he laughed and I laughed and we made love for a week. He's the best that I've ever had and you're just like him."

"Wonderful. So, do you intend on making love with me for a week now?"

"I can't."

"Why not?" I asked more out of curiosity than disappointment. "We're compatible and I'm holy and surely your mother wouldn't disapprove."

"I can't. I'm like joining a convent next Tuesday."

"Oh, bad luck."

"God bless you," she said in the nastiest way as she drifted away.

There must have been seventy-five men, women, and California questionables at the party—not a bad showing on a couple hours' notice. It surprised me that my pious sister would have such a diverse group of friends. It pleased me too—there was a comfortable element of artificiality to this gathering of liberal

American society. In the varied and sophisticated conversations I heard as I wandered through the clusters of wine-sipping, successful, artistic, and eccentric people—I sensed none of the fanatical ignorance life had taught me to fear so much. Of course, I was miserable in the mass of upper-middle-class, pseudo-humanoids, but, at least I didn't feel threatened.

"Jackson!" came Wilber's voice from across the room.

"Wilber!" I replied.

"Jackson!" he countered as he made his way through the tangle of boisterous conversations to my side. He took my arm and led me to an unoccupied corner of the atrium that was the entry chamber of the house. "Sorry I've been so involved with the other guests, Jackson, I'm not trying to ignore you."

"Oh, that's all right, Wilber. I understand. Who are all of these people? I had no idea you and Janice had so many friends."

"These aren't real friends—just party people. Through my business and the contacts Janice makes doing her volunteer work, we've managed to accumulate a decent sampling of humanity."

"I'd say."

"Are you having a good time?"

"Oh, yes. I really appreciate you having this get-together for me," I lied.

"Wonderful. I'm glad you're having a good time. You know you've worried your sister half to death over the last few years. Why, for all she knew, you could have been dead."

"So I've been told. I'm sorry I've worried her so much. It's good to know there is someone who cares if I'm alive or not.

"We all do, Jackson. We all do."

"I'll try to stay in closer contact in the future."

And then, trying to change the subject, I asked, "How's your golf game, Wilber? We haven't played in years."

"About the same, I'm afraid to say. About the same." And eluding my strategy, he went on. "She's never totally given up on you, but there were times when she really despaired. Let's get you another drink, Jackson. Shall we?"

"Good idea," I said as we headed for the bar that had been set up on the deck next to the pool. I knew Wilber was dwelling on my lack of substantiality in the shifting world for some reason. I knew Janice was concerned for my well-being but couldn't believe my parents had completely failed to mention my continued existence to her at least occasionally over the previous two years.

"Could I get you a glass for that can of beer?" Wilber asked.

"No thanks, Wilber," I said. "I prefer to drink it right out of the can."

"Always the nonconformist, ay, Jackson?"

"Just saving glasses for the unfortunates of the world who require them for the ingestion of vital fluids."

"I see," he said as he directed me to a seat on a couch and sat down next to me. And, knee to knee, leaning into my face he began, "Now, let's get down to business. I want to ask you a few questions about your life. Will you answer honestly?"

"I'll try."

"Where are you going?"

"With my life?"

"Yes, Jackson. Where are you going with your life?"

"You didn't say this was going to be hard."

"Answer the question."

"I have no definite idea. But I'll assure you I have come a long way toward getting there."

"You're well past thirty."

"That's the truth, Brother-in-law."

"Aren't you worried about not having anything to show for all of these years?"

"If you mean, am I concerned about not owning a swimming pool or a leisure suit I can call my own—no, I'm not. I don't regret the course I've taken—or rather, the course I've followed. It hasn't been the easiest life I could have ended up with, but I accept it."

"It's time, Jackson."

"Time?"

"Yes, time. Time for you to grab hold of the real world before it spins away without you."

"And if it spins off without me I'll end up down at the bus station bumming dimes and telling people I'm God."

"That's somewhat extreme, but you get my gist."

"I think so."

"Think about it. It's time."

"You're not going to tell me about a future in 'Plastics,' are you?"

Daunted, but not dissuaded, Wilber just grinned at me

and shrugged his shoulders.

Janice appeared from out of the crowd. She was wearing an elegant casual outfit.

"Janice," I called, hoping to change the serious tone of the conversation, "you look wonderful tonight."

"Thank you, Jackson. Now, what are you gentlemen discussing with such gravity?"

"I'm not certain," I said. "I think Wilber is trying to tell me he's jealous of my lifestyle."

"Don't think you can discourage me so easily," he said. "I'm not through with you yet."

"Well, as they used to say in Caesar's time, 'You buy the beer, and I'll lend you my ear.'"

"Mother always did say you were a poet," said Janice.

"That's right—she did call me a poet on a number of occasions. That was usually right before she would ask the rhetorical question, 'So, who needs poets?'"

"So bitter."

"Not really. Mom did her best—I was a good-natured little fart but hardly a cherub."

"Honor thy father and mother... "

"Wilber, quick, get this lady another Perrier. I'm afraid she's about to recite the Bible. You know how that goes—by the time she gets halfway through Deuteronomy this party will be dead."

"All right, Jackson," he said rising, "I'll get Janice a mineral water, but don't wander off—I want to talk with you some more."

Janice sat down and stared at me for some time before speaking. "You never got over Lori's accident, did you?"

"No, Sister, I haven't. But, as far as that goes, she hasn't gotten over being dead yet either."

"Jackson, I worry about you so much."

"Don't. I'll be fine just as long as I stay out of the rain."

"Be serious for a moment, please. I know what Wilber is going to ask you and I think it deserves more than your joking consideration."

"You should know by now that I am always serious and I never am really joking about anything unless it's about being serious. Life is a serious matter that must be continually given our most fervent laughter. I'd like to know who the fool was who decreed that seriousness was necessarily a somber matter. I'll bet he was surprised when he died and found out that worms and maggots tickle, and, once deeply secured in the very serious confines of a coffin, one giggles oneself to dust."

"Jackson!"

"Yes, Mother," I said laughing.

"You'll joke about anything, won't you? Nothing is sacred to you. You must be very much afraid of death to make light of it like you do."

"The old whistle in the dark?"

"Yes."

"Horseradish, my dear, horseradish. I've recently been on an expedition that took me right to the brink of death and I saw it faint at the sight of a crusty old desert rat. I saw it cower in the presence of unfettered life. I have no fear of death, believe me. But, I must admit I'm damned scared of dying—I'm certain it can be very painful."

"Will you please listen to Wilber?"

"I know what he's getting at, Janice. He's going to offer to find me a job—get me established with one of his corporate buddies as a high-class money-maker and potential purchaser of one of his square little houses with the customized floor plan. I know that crafty old devil; he knows as long as I'm worthless I'll never need the services of an architect."

"You're wrong about his motive; but, you're right about what he wants to discuss with you. I talked to him on the way back from picking him up at the airport. He has a friend who's looking for someone to train. I don't know much about the job except that it will pay a great deal of money and Wilber thinks with your education and his recommendation you might be able to get it."

"No thanks, Janice. Jobs are for real people with measurable needs. I've had a few professions and all they ever gave me was respectability and a place to spend my days."

"Mother was so proud of you when you were a school teacher."

"I was respectable, wasn't I?"

"What's wrong with being respectable?"

"Nothing at all. It's just too expensive. The purchase price for respectability is exorbitant—you pay with your whole life. I have nothing against those of you who are hard workers and steady debtors—I just can't afford your lifestyle."

"Exactly what can you afford, Jackson?"

"Nothing."

"And what do you want?"

"Just what I can afford."

"You can be so exasperating."

"We go back a long way, Sister. I've been driving you nuts since I was born. But, getting back to your compulsion about money, in fact I'm quite wealthy."

"What do you mean?'

"'I've come into some money of late. A sizable sum. You might have thought me worthless all of these years, but you were mistaken, Dear Sister, your little brother has considerable fiscal depth."

"How much?"

"So crass."

"How much?"

"A bunch."

"Show me."

"Remember when we were kids and we spent an entire summer collecting scrap metal—cleaning garages, scouring dumps, picking up hubcaps along the streets? And then, just a week before school started up again we loaded it all into Uncle Fred's pickup truck and he hauled it to a junkyard and they gave us twenty-six dollars. Do you remember?"

"Certainly, I remember. It was the most money either of us had ever had in our lives."

"Well, I'm not nearly so rich as we were that day, but I do have more money now than I have had in years and years."

"How much, Jackson?"

"Can these people be trusted?"

"I think you're bluffing. You don't have any money—you've never had any."

"Okay, Janice. You force me to show my hand," I said as I produced my wallet and then proudly spilled forth Glory's cache of hundred dollar bills."

Janice eyed the dingy stack of cash and then said with disdain, "What the hell is this?"

"My fortune."

"This money is filthy. How much is there?"

"Two thousand dollars," I said proudly.

"This is your life's savings, Jackson? A little stack of dirty old hundred- dollar bills."

"Yeah, Janice. Ain't that something?"

"Jackson, what is two thousand dollars?"

"Hell, Sister, it's nine hundred ninty-nine dollars more than my life saving before I got it."

"It's pathetic. Our house payment is nearly twice that every month."

"You mean I'm not rich. I can't afford to golf with the country-clubbers?

"You're so glib. You make me feel foolish for even trying to reason with you."

"I'm sorry. I don't want to alienate my only sister, but honestly, this is the only way I know how to deal with the kind of crap you and Wilber are dishing out here. I am not middle class material, Janice. Whatever shot I had at joining your notion of normalcy was blown away years ago in a lightning storm. Or, to be truthful, it was a long time before that. While you were gathering doll families about you for crumpets and tea, I was dreaming the dreams of a gypsy and sensing the crazed wonder of a baby poet. I never did fit, and it would be a fatal assault to my identity to attempt to wedge me into an approximation of proper dimension."

"I see," she said with a sigh.

"Really?"

"Yes, I'm afraid that I do see. I don't believe you are ever going to grow up."

"Are you just now realizing that your nuts-o brother is a hopeless case?"

"Maybe," she said in a weary tone.

"That's kind of sad, Sister," I said. "I'll never get big, right?"

"I doubt it. Damn it, Jackson, quit making fun of me. I really had hopes for you."

"Well, praise the Lord, Janice, I could have been dead."

Janice just stared at me with a sad contempt and said nothing.

"Excuse me," said a voice from earlier in the evening. "I hate to interrupt this like heavy conversation, Janice, but I wonder if I could get this holy man brother of yours to like give me a ride home?"

"Did you say 'holy man'?"

"Yes, don't you know that your brother is a priest?"

"Now I've heard everything," she said rising and moving away. "I'll get you the keys to one of the cars and also a house key—I'm sure you'll be late."

Janice left and the girl said, "She's really like upset with you. I can tell,"

"You're right. Are you heading for the convent next Tuesday?"

"Yes. Hey, like even nuns need a ride home sometimes."

"Just asking."

"I don't mind. I'm really like aroused by you, too. It's too bad we didn't like meet last week before I like committed myself."

"Just bad timing, I guess."

"True. And speaking of timing," she said glancing in the direction of Janice's hasty exit. "You really don't have to take me home."

"Yeah, I do. It'll drive my sister nuts."

13 Betrayal

Erika and I drove out to an all-night cafe in Newport Beach and did some "like eggs and hash browns" and then I took her home.

It was late when I returned my sister's house. The guests had apparently dispersed as rapidly as they had been assembled and there was no sign of the party left. I unlocked the front door and walked through the entry forest and into the living room. There was a light left on for me. It seemed the whole family had gone to bed. I was glad. I was in no mood to continue any discussions with either Wilber or Janice.

Something was wrong. The place seemed strange and hostile to me. My mind flashed back to the ankh and the swimming pool and Ashley. I tried to dismiss my misgivings as being the result of party fatigue and "like" hours of "like" listening to "like" Erika, the airhead nun. It was enough to stir anyone's paranoia.

I went into the guest bedroom where I had left my suitcase and changed out of Wilber's ridiculous leisure suit. Rather than getting into bed, for some reason I decided to put on my own clothes and stretch out on top of the bedspread. Someone had left me a copy of a book entitled *Lyrics for the Lord* lying on the pillow. It was a songbook and there was one song noted with a bookmark from a Christian bookstore. The song had many verses extolling the virtues of Heaven and the pitfalls of this earthly curse we must endure.

The chorus read:

> *I'm a sinner and I'm wretched*
> *from my feet clear to my head,*
> *and with the Heaven God has told.*
> *I can't wait until I'm old—*
> *and get my soul out of here when I'm dead.*
> *Get my soul out of here when I'm dead.*

"This all seems rather counterproductive to the joys of living," I said to myself as I put the book aside. Just as I was reaching for the light on the bedside table, I heard a murmur coming from down the hall.

I thought someone must be awake but I didn't recognize the voice as being that of any member of the family, though there was something chillingly familiar about the fast-moving, high-pitched, frantic tones I was hearing. I quietly stepped down the hall toward the source of the sound. It was coming from the master bedroom. The door was slightly ajar and I was able to see the image of my sister and brother-in-law reflected in their dresser mirror.

They were sitting cross-legged, side by side on the bed. On the bedspread before them was a small CD player. They were listening studiously to the affected rural whine of Brother Earl as he said, "I know the Ways of the Serpent... "

I stepped back from the door and stood tensely in the hallway listening to the stream of cliché revelations flowing from the savior of the lost flock of Sassy Sally's Blue Bird Cafe and Lounge on Skintz Bottom Road, the self-appointed moral and spiritual leader of the Getzman Refrigerator Factory, the cold-blooded murderer of my wife. I wanted to burst into their room and cram the disk right down Wilber's throat. Doubtlessly, my sister and her husband had seemed a bit more religious than the average middle class couple, but it was appalling to think that such shallow, hate-driven rubbish could have infiltrated this comfortable and sophisticated strata of educated and successful human beings. Wilber and Janice were not of the desperate, the ignorant, the superstitious, the fear-ridden. They drank imported bubbly water. They played Saturday morning tennis at The Club. They had kids with straight teeth. They had tax-sheltered annuities. What on earth could be the appeal of the obvious stupidity of Brother Earl?

I listened to what apparently was the exciting conclusion of a spiritual lesson.

So, here we are again, brothers and sisters, back to the word "responsibility." Yes, dear ones, responsibility is the key to cleanin' up this mess of a world. With the Lord tellin' us what's right and the masses of us worshippers just doin' the right works, just bein' responsible to ourselves and our families and our friends, and, most of all, to God and His Ways; we can put down the magnates of irreverent behavior; we can strike the foundations of wrong; we can run the devil of free livin' right off the face of this world; we can turn the tide, brothers and sisters, turn the tide of wrong thinkin', wrong doin', wrong feelin' and run it back out to the Sea of Oblivion. Are you listening? Are you hearing what I'm a-tellin' you? Are you taking in the Word? Is it in your hearts right now? Can you feel it now? Can you see the world more dearly now, beloved? Praise the Lord.

And Wilber and Janice, in their matching robes and sitting on their king-sized thermal massage bed said, in perfect unison, "Amen."

All right now. What does it mean? What is this matter of responsibility? Think about what I've been preaching ta you for the past half hour on this *Brother Earl Home Salvation CD #67*?
What does it mean?
I'll tell you what it means. It means that not only are you and I and all the believers and Righteous worshipers across this land held accountable for our own behavior. I say, not just our own behavior, but, now hear me, also we of the Legions of the Lord are responsible for every irreverent act committed in this world. Every single one. We're all in this together, brothers and sisters, all of us in the *Right* are responsible, I say, responsible for the acts of our lost brethren and sisters living in the *Wrong*.
And, you who play this *Brother Earl Home Salvation CD #67*, you heed Old Brother Earl—this means you. Even right now as you listen to the sacred lessons that this humble servant of the Lord is teachin' you, even as you lead a forward and up-righteous life of fear as a miserable sinner and in glory as one of His beloved; even though you may love the Lord and tell His Truth wherever you go, even if you never vary from the Golden Path of Goodness—you'll go straight to the sulphur-burnin' pits of Hell if you tolerate irreverent behavior in

anyone. Anyone! I say. Hallelujah! Beloved, we're all in this together. Blessed be the ways of Righteousness, we are not only the good, the right people, the sole possessors of the only genuine Truth ever revealed to man—we are all more than that, hear me, more than just right. We, you and I and your spouses and your children and your neighbors, are all in this together—and as bearers of the real Truth, we are, now here it is again: Responsible.

You know the number to call, the address to write. You know the only way to salvation is through the absolute purification of all of mankind. We need money to keep this great prayer a-rollin', we need money to fight the Holy War, we need money to cripple the unholy that they may be converted to the Truth or destroyed. And, brothers and sisters, we also need those names. Know thy enemy. Send me those names, and no matter how painful, don't spare a soul—if you do you're bound to lose your own. Look about you, Beloved, look at your neighbors, your co-workers, your friends, and, yes, even your loved ones—save them, give them the message, give them my address, tell them of the radio and the television broadcasts, tell them the Way—you know the evil Way of the Serpent and, praise Glory, you know the blessed Way of the Lord. Now, save those who contaminate the race of man and make it unfit for Heaven.

And, once you've given your best to the struggle, you've prayed your hardest, traveled all the routes to righteous thinking I've been teachin' with these *Brother Earl Home Salvation* CDs, then, if it all fails to move the heathens, send me their names and addresses and let Brother Earl's mighty army deal with 'em. We're combat ready and armed to save.

Call me on the telephone and tell me, day or night— Brother Earl never sleeps when there are sinners about. Get on that phone and call our Headquarters at the Brother Earl University and say to me directly with all of your heart, "Brother Earl, I've tried with these sinners. I've used all of the procedures and nothing has worked. I need your help with those who are truly lost to the Lord."

You keep those prayer requests and contributions coming, dear hearts. And give me those names, brothers and sisters, give me those names and then, Glory be, we'll all get there together. Do you hear? We'll all get to Heaven. Amen. We'll all get to Heaven!

"Amen," said Wilber and Janice.

After a moment's quiet reflection, Janice spoke. "It's getting very late, Dear, do you think we ought to put off listening to our second lesson until morning?"

"Janice," he chastened. "We pledged two lessons a night and we're going to make it. Besides, the next one is about the Devil and music—I'm really eager to hear it."

"You never tire of 'His Word' do you, Wilber?"

"No, I never do," he said as I heard him sorting through what must have been dozens of CDs. "Here it is, *#68*. By the way, Janice, what happened to Jackson? I missed him during the latter part of the evening."

"I hate to say, Wilber. I really hate to say. He left with that terrible girl, Erika. You know, the one with the mother who ravishes men at the refrigerator. They left some time ago and I just know they are behaving irreverently. It saddens me so to think about it."

"Well," said Wilber, "praise the Lord, at least we know he's not dead."

"It anguishes me to say this, Dear, but, praise the Lord, as far as I'm concerned he is dead."

"No more hope for him, huh?"

"We've done all we can. He simply refuses to change."

"I had hoped to get him interested in a job out here. Once we got him settled down maybe we could have worked on his soul."

"He's lost to us, Wilber. There's no hope for my brother's soul. I even think he's involved in some kind of religious cult. That wicked girl called him a priest and I don't think she was joking. I think she meant it."

"Responsibility," pronounced Wilber.

"Yes, I know," said Janice and her voice was shaking with emotion.

"Well, you can't say that we didn't give it our best effort," said Wilber as he reached for the phone. "What's the number, Janice?"

And how clearly I can yet recall the sound of my own sister's

213

voice as she said, "1-800-BRO-EARL."

14 Parting Is Such Sweet Sorrow—Not

I mailed Janice and Wilber a letter before I escaped the mire of Southern California.

My Dearest Sister and Brother-in-law,

Not only have you devoutly aligned your souls with the most ignorant tool of the Forces of Death; you have, in your awful piety, ratted me, your own brother, out to the very same people who cold-bloodedly murdered my wife so many years ago. I doubt if you are capable of believing this, but I can assure you Lori—remember Lori, remember the wedding, remember the funeral—was murdered by your spiritual mentor, Brother Earl. I find your stupidity abhorrent, but your betrayal is unforgivable. By the time you read this note, thanks to your unknowing generosity, one of your many family cars and I will be far away from you and, hopefully, the hateful grasp of your cult.

I can't fathom how people as intelligent and informed as yourselves could fall prey to such a petty excuse for Truth. You seek the simplistic temptation of some holy notion of death while a world, vital and brilliant in energy, sings about you in crystalline tones. Freed from the hatred and resentment of self-righteousness, I know the Song could be heard by us all.

You have given yourselves to such local powers.

I trust you will willingly lend me your car. If you turn me over to the police I'll just go to jail and be forced to be irreverent with men.

I love you, my sister. If I weren't so overjoyed at this moment thinking about how cleanly I have escaped the trap you two were setting for me, I would probably be very sad.

As ever,
Your no-good brother, Jackson

I lied.

It hadn't been a clean getaway.

I stood in the hallway while Wilber reported my name and description to the *Brother Earl Twenty-Four Hour Sinner Alert Line.* I heard him assure one of the operators "on call" that he and Janice would detain "the sinner" at their house long enough for someone to come for me. I heard Janice sob once and then the sound of Brother Earl beginning his CD #68: *The Devil and Country Music.*

"Does y'all like country music?" he asked.

Deftly I had returned to the guest room, retrieved my bag, and taken the keys from the pants of Wilber's leisure suit. Then, with stealthy step, I had made my way toward the kitchen door and freedom.

Just as I reached the doorknob and began carefully turning it, the quiet was shattered by a voice saying, "Leaving so soon, Uncle Jackson?"

I was noticeably startled when I spun about and said, "Why, uh… yes, Ashley. I thought I might just be moving along. It's time to be going."

"Without even saying good-by, Uncle Jackson? You disappoint me."

"Sorry, Ashley. But a sudden change in events has occurred and I feel I must be leaving."

"Leaving your family like this, it's terrible." She spoke in a soft and excessively sweet voice and moved slowly and smoothly about me with her eyes fiercely aglow and intense. "All those years without us seeing you and now you're leaving so soon. Do you really have to go, Uncle Jackson? Really?" She paused directly in front of me—her pretty lips almost in a pout, her eyes opened wide like in one of those maudlin paintings of children and poodles crowding the art galleries at discount stores.

"Why do you want me to stay, Ashley?" I asked with tension

tightly and warily suppressed from my voice.

"Because I love you, Uncle Jackson."

"You love me. How sweet."

"I've always loved my Uncle Jackson. Please don't go away so soon."

I pulled the ankh from beneath my shirt and watched her eyes. They darkened.

"You're one of them," I said.

"What are you talking about, Uncle Jackson?" she said as she began circling again—moving like a cat, eyes never leaving me.

"You're one of them," I repeated.

"You sound funny, Uncle Jackson. Why don't you lie down for a while and rest. Maybe by morning you'll feel like staying with us a little longer."

"Ashley."

"What?"

"Why did you cut the chain on my necklace and throw my ankh into the deep end of the swimming pool?"

She stopped moving. "I don't know what you're talking about."

"Sure you do, Ashley. You're one of them and you're lying to me."

"You're talking mean. Don't talk mean, Uncle Jackson." She had glided herself to a position between myself and the door.

"You're one of them. You're lying. You cut my ankh. Now admit it."

"You sound crazy, Uncle Jackson. You'd better get some rest."

"Does y'all like country music?" I asked.

And with eyes turning to black rage and a spring-like voice recoiling with involuntary speed she snapped, "I know the Ways of the Serpent!"

I don't know where she had been keeping the butcher knife, when she had picked it up or how she had hidden it beneath her robe while we talked. But there it was, sharp and menacing in her upraised hand as she spoke in a harsh whisper, "You cannot leave. You are irreverent and you cannot leave."

And, as I left, I knew the Powers of Death were yet weak upon the High Priest of Hallelujah for the vicious thrusts of her butcher knife only pricked my skin like the bites of mosquitoes.

15 Wind-sound and Country Music

Driving through the night with the shapes and shadows of the California high desert a dull backdrop to the momentum of my flight, holding a direction in the grip of a steering wheel and, with a rate of change controlled by the touch of a pedal, rushing toward the anonymity of distance: I fled.

The purpose for Glory's hundreds was beginning to focus.

And the rushing wind-sounds of air against the moving car caressed my thinning consciousness so, in defiance against sleep, I played the radio.

Where is National Public Radio when you need it?

Through the rock-rimmed night of vacant land only the 50,000 watt voice of Trucker Radio could reach me.

And the radio said:

> *When I seen you cookin' breakfast this morning,*
> *that you hadn't been to bed was plain to see.*
> *Well, you busted my heart*
> *then you busted my eggs—*
> *it seems ever-thing is runnin' out on me.*

16 Hoh Bound

Two or three hours northeast of the mega-sprawl of Los Angeles, I decided to take the highway north and west over Tehachapi Pass. As I drove, the moon broke through clouds over the stark hills and cast the subtle marvel of its cool white light across the desert. Along the high rock ridges were hundreds of windmills, sentinel silhouettes stilled by the un-stirring night.

Man, was I tired. Before morning light I pulled over and parked in a secluded spot. I sighed, locked the doors, reclined the seat, and slept for most of a day.

I awoke late afternoon with a plan.

I would drive up to Washington State and head out to the Olympic Peninsula where, in the rainforest up the Hoh River Valley, giant trees and whispering ferns would surely bode silent repose from my plight. Lori would go there with me—Lori and her soul's sweet laughter within me. Then perhaps we would drive over to Idaho and stop by Craters of the Moon National Monument. Glory would buy the gas and Janice and Wilber had provided the car.

Sister Janice, the thought of her shuddered through me with a fatal sadness. I drove on through the void of empty miles toward dusk and then on into the night.

Having abandoned the main highways, I was winding through the deep-forest roads over the coastal range when the terrible thought enveloped me: Janice knew about Carrie.

It had happened during a momentary lapse in the sarcastic chatter between us. Janice had asked me about my love life and I had told her about Arizona and Carrie. It seemed safe then. I wasn't spilling my heart to some beady-eyed zealot encountered along the road. This was my educated, affluent, Southern California sister to whom I divulged the doings of my lonely being.

"Her name is Carrie?" Janice had asked.

"Yes, Carrie."

I was trying to be open, honest, and intentionally vulnerable. What a fool I had been. She immediately went on the attack.

"So, what does this Carrie person do when she's not

cavorting with vagabonds such as yourself?"

"Well," I snapped, with defenses and sarcasm fully restored, "actually, she's a topless bartender at an eastside dive called the Naked Rose." Oh, how Janice had recoiled from that volley. And, driving along the night-empty highway, how deeply I felt the pangs of regret gnawing at me for giving up my beautiful Carrie. I could hear Janice telling it all to the "Brother Earl Twenty-Four-Hour Rat Line." "Yes, he sneaked out of the house before we could stop him but I'd bet he's living in sin with some slut named Carrie who works at a den of iniquity called the Naked Rose."

What nerve! Janice, the sanctimonious bitch, calling my beloved friend Carrie a slut.

It was late evening. I pulled into the lot of a darkened service station. If Carrie had returned to her job at the Rose she could already have been murdered. If, and believe me I was praying that I had succeeded in making a believer of her, she had determined never to be a naked barkeep again and had stayed away from the miserable night club, she would probably be safe for a while. Brother Earl's guys would likely take some time to summon the courage to barge on in for a direct encounter with the devilish allure of full-out, flesh-toned, naked ladies.

I knew I had to take action quickly if I was to save her from the wrath that destroyed Lori. There was a phone booth. I made two calls.

It was late and if Carrie didn't answer it would mean she had given up on herself and was working across the street. I nervously crammed coins into the slots. The phone rang and rang. My heart was choking the air out of my throat—and then she answered.

"Hello," came the sweet and sleepy voice.

"Carrie?"

"Yes, who is this?"

"Are you okay?"

"Is that you, Jackson?"

"Yes, Carrie. It's me and you're home, thank God, you're home. You answered the phone."

"What'd you expect? Where else would I be at 11:00 p.m., working at a topless bar?"

"Well, of course not. Perish the thought." I could have cried. I almost did.

We talked until I ran out of quarters and then she called me back. We had become such good friends in such a short span of time.

"So, have you made and decisions about your life?" I asked.

I talked to people at the university here the day you left. I'm getting my transcripts together—Jackson, I'm going to use my college degree... "

"... 'college degree?'"

"Well yeah.   You didn't know it was a prerequisite to employment at the Naked Rose?"

"Who would have thought?"

"Well anyway, Smartass, I'm going to take my college degree and the money Glory left me and apply to law school."

"Egad, Carrie. I saved you from the Naked Rose so you can become a lawyer?"

"Disgusting, isn't it?" she laughed

"Couldn't you   have   decided on a   more respectable profession, like streetwalking?"

"No. I'm sorry. I suppose I was just born to be bad."

"Carrie the Lawyer. That doesn't sound too bad."

"I like the idea. I'm going to give a try."

"Did you say Glory left you some money, too?"

"Yes. Kitty and I found envelopes in our apartment after you left. It turns out your old desert buddy was far from broke. He left a bundle for his family back in Indian country and gave each of us... well, some tens of thousands."

"Tens?"

"A few."

"He only left me a lousy two grand, and I'm a priest!"

She was laughing. "I know. In his note he said to be sure to rub it in."

"Well, rub away, my friend—what am I here for if not to be abused?"

"He wrote that a hungry priest is much holier than a fat one and that what you seek in this world is free anyway."

"Truth and Beauty may be free, but a tank of gas and a burger with fries still cost plenty."

I was beginning to believe she was in the clear and then she lowered the boom.

"Say, Jackson," she said. "The strangest men were here asking about you this morning."

221

They had found her. I had underestimated their resolve.

"These guys were so clean-cut looking it was creepy. I thought they might be urban missionaries or soap salesmen but they claimed to be private investigators."

"What did they do, Carrie?"

"They didn't do anything. They just said they were looking for Jackson Blake and I told them I had no idea where you might be. Then they asked me some stupid question about country music."

"Well, does *y'all*?" I asked.

"No, 'I-all' doesn't. I told them to mind their own damned business and they took off."

"Is that all that happened? There wasn't a big storm or anything, was there"

"No. The weather's been clear... why do you ask?"

"Just wondering."

"I did tell them one other thing, though."

"What was that?"

"I told them if they found the bum to remind him he owes me a hundred bucks."

"Yeah, that Blake character is a real deadbeat."

"We'll see. He'd better come back here and pay his debts."

"He'll try, Carrie. I'll tell you he really wants to come and pay what he owes."

Then she reached right through our light talk and said, "What's going on, Jackson?"

How close they had come. Right to her door. She probably had enough power from our victory at Three Days to stave off these petty messengers. It had been too close a call. Next time they would bring bigger guns to her front door.

"I'm on the road again," I answered.

"Where are you heading?"

"I'm not sure. I've got to do whatever it takes to make sure those jerks never bother you again."

"I can take care of myself. Don't get yourself hurt."

"Don't worry, Love. Remember how I took care of that gang of ruffians out at the Dibble Inn?"

"That is exactly what worries me, Jackson."

"Look, you stay strong, Carrie, and you can take on anything this world throws at you. I know you can. I've just got to make sure you don't have to field any shots from 'other worlds.'"

"Those guys were dangerous, weren't they?"

"They could have been if you weren't so powerful."

"You've got to be careful out there, Jackson. I really need that money you're going to bring back to me."

"I'll do all I can, Love. Believe me."

We talked for another hour saying words touched by love and then we said goodbye.

The second call I made that night didn't require any change. It was toll free.

I dialed 1-800-BRO-EARL.

17 Solitude

Maybe grief averted is grief prolonged. I don't know. I do know, in a decade of milling about most of the corners of this country, I had avoided the Hoh River Valley. And I know there was no doubt that in silent chambers of my soul there unrelentingly simmered the sorrow of Lori's death.

The place was special. Lori and I discovered the Hoh Rainforest while on the only trip we were ever to take together. For all the wandering of my years, I had not returned.

It was the summer after our December wedding. I was happily between factory jobs and college semesters and she was an elementary school teacher and had the whole summer off. We even had some money saved—enough to seize a couple of weeks and call them our own. We didn't designate the journey as a postponed honeymoon. Neither of us liked the idea of a sweet little trip for novice lovers. Sleeping on a mattress in the back of my old Dodge station wagon, cooking our meals on a Coleman stove at waysides along the road; we weren't cutesy little newlyweds, we were road poets. We were seekers of sunsets far beyond the edge of each successive day's grasp. And with our love and our laughter we were creating a bond of heart and flesh and soul as precious and fragile as life itself.

And just as soon as we cleared the limits of familiarity and knew the open road, we decided to travel on forever—love-gypsies, traveling troubadours harmonizing with the cacophony of little radio stations stretching like signal buoys across vast reaches with country hits and rock-and-roll oldies marking the channels of an infinite sea. I think it was probably Lori who reminded us of the finite reach of our finances, but that couldn't deter us from knowing the infinite distance of a good two weeks on the highway.

How flat the wheat fields of North Dakota, how wide the plains of Montana, how lush the mountains of Idaho... "Craters of the Moon National Monument," she read from the road sign.

And in unison we had said, "I don't think so."

From the top of the Space Needle in Seattle, on a rare and

radiant Northwestern day of clear sky and warm sun, we looked to the west and saw the splendor of the Olympic Mountains.

And then, the next day, up the eighteen–mile twisting road from the Peninsula Highway, we parked in the lot adjacent to the trail leading into the rainforest. Huge trees soared skyward, disappearing into the ever-mist and drizzle of low clouds. In the leaf-muted hush of soft rains we stood, holding hands, awed by the silence of the gray-green forest giants.

"It's like being in a magnificent cathedral," she whispered.

"Yeah," I agreed. "But, I think God might actually live in this church."

There was a National Park Visitor Center. Outside, a park ranger was gathering a group for a guided hike. We joined them.

In rote pattern with megaphone voice, the ranger began his forty-minute spiel, naming the vegetation, quantifying the height of trees and the depth of rainfall, and telling the genus and species of each fern remnant of the Age of Dinosaurs. Briskly we were herded from station to station as this "priest" spoke the measured chants of human ritual before the immeasurable essence of God.

And, of course, we got the giggles.

One of the immense trees lay fallen across the trail. A cross-section had been cut out so we could walk through. Its diameter was taller than a person and its hundreds of rings told the drought and plenty of centuries. The tree was so large it had been given a name, General Something-or-Other.

"And I had the good fortune of standing right here the day that the General came crashing down," Ranger Stumpy was reciting.

In a whisper to my love, I did us in. "Too bad the Old General didn't land on Ranger Blather-Ass," I said.

She gasped. He gave her a quick and disapproving glance and then moved on the next numbered stop on the tour.

Lori and I ducked into a damp thicket behind the corpse of the great tree and tried vainly to muffle our laughter.

It was like ditching class. It was wonderful.

The guide and his little group trailed on without us. Gradually the sound of his sealion voice grew farther and farther away, fainter and fainter.

We quit giggling and then in the silence realized we were absolutely alone. Abandoned in the heart of the forest.

The very scale of the place was at first frightening. The mass of the trees, the magnitude of their silence filled us both with a chilled reverence. I gripped her hand more tightly. She gripped mine and then, in a sweeping realization, we knew our love could dispel any of the fearful might of the forest. There was Lori, there was Jackson, and there was God. And there was in that moment an exquisite balance of flesh and love and all matters Holy and Infinite.

And that is why, in all the years of my rambling, I had not dared to return to the Hoh Valley and the cathedral of its rainforest.

More so than death itself, the forest represented what had been stolen from me by the petty wrath of local evil.

18 Solitude Confronted

So it was there, in the Rainforest of the Hoh Valley—the place where, years earlier, silence had melded Holy union of love and nature and God—that I stood alone in the damp chill and knew I would have to destroy Brother Earl.

PART FOUR

Once while traveling an obscure corner of a forgotten state, I encountered a disheveled man with a strange story that eventually helped tie up the bundle of this empty world.

This is what he told me:

Man, I used to be a real doper. Not just the small time stuff like pot—I did the big ones. My mind was a boiling kettle of soup and the steam coming from it was a lot of different colors and the smell was like flowers—you know what I mean. So, I would just hang out and score dope and make soup and I would have been dead a long time ago but then I got a job doing dope. Man, I know it sounds strange, but it's true. I actually got a job doing dope. The pay was great—heavy duty dollars, free food, a place to crash, and all the dope I could eat or sniff or smoke or shoot-up into the old temple of the body— and enough for all my friends to score, too. It was head heaven, man, I mean I had pills and blow and smoke and stuff I'd never even heard of so I just ate it—I was the proverbial kid in the candy shop and making a damn good living at the same time.

All I had to do was lie around this big estate and fly with my friends. It was crazy. I had been busted for a little marijuana possession and was coolin' it for a while in the slammer when these weird dudes busted me out on some kind of job- release program. They said if I would agree to do some work for them they'd take care of all my needs, if you know what I mean. They said all I'd have to do was create a dope scene out at their research institute so people would think it was just another commune or something. I was to be their decoy—so they could do their secret stuff without anybody taking it too seriously. I told them I didn't give a damn about what they were doing on the inside of the place—I'd be glad to do a dope gig on the outside.

You say you used to live back in the Midwest. Maybe you've heard of the place. It was called the Willow City Truth Center. Oh, you have **heard** of it, right. Just a hangout for hippies and dopers, right? Yeah, man, you got the scam. Everybody thought that. The local rednecks hated it and wanted to burn the place down. There were some high-powered preachers who used to come out and do their number in front of the place every week. One of them even did some live broadcasts for his radio show from **the** sidewalk. He'd stick his ugly head through the metal rungs of the gate and say terrible things about my eternal soul but I didn't care much because I was just a big bowl of soup and was going to stay that way forever—best job in the world.

What happened, you say? I really don't know. I mean it's been years now and I still haven't figured out what changed me. I had a ticket to pickle city and I blew it. I mean, Man, nobody hassled me or worked on my case out there. Every day it was the same routine. Whenever I'd get around to getting up, one of the Truth Center dudes who was kind of freaky looking himself would pull up in a beat-to-hell old Volkswagen minibus and we'd roll on downtown and score whatever I wanted and then head on back for another buzzy day. I had a lot of friends then, you know. As soon as the word was out that I had the magic loaf and could feed the masses, people started coming out of my past and claiming my future like bugs, Man. By late afternoon there were always ten or fifteen of us flopped out on the lawn, or sitting around listening to a dude strumming one string on a guitar, or running around trying to lick the butterflies, you know, Man. It was a crazy scene. I don't know why we didn't get busted, as open as we were about it. There was something really heavy about that place, though. I don't know whether they worked for the government of something, but the cops never bothered us. And, also, there was a kind of power about the place that seemed to keep the preachers at a distance—kind of like garlic and vampires. And the power, it seems like it was working on me, too. I mean, look at me, Man. I ain't no model citizen, but I'm no junky anymore either. After a couple of months out there they went down to the county jail and bailed out another doper and without even saying anything to me, I knew my time was over and somehow I was better off than I had been in years. I'll still smoke a little weed now and then, and I'll drink a few beers, and maybe I'm not the most substantial-like pillar of the community, you know; but, I've still got a few brain cells left and I'm not dead and I can still tell the difference between a sunset and a bottle of reds.

There was sure something weird about that place and it wasn't just me, either. There were others. They'd quit coming and I'd see them later and we'd wonder what happened. Some of those bastards actually amounted to something.

I never did figure out what they were working on—something about outer space, or death, or psychology, or something. I never did know, but I just kind of knew it wasn't important for me to find out. And, I'll tell you, we really did a hell of a job convincing anybody from the outside that the Willow City Truth Center was just another hangout for freaks. A hell of a job.

1 A Murderous Plot

The rifle cost over four-hundred dollars and the shells were long, cold, menacing cylinders—the stuff of death. I hated the rifle and the shells and their terrible roar as I spent hours target practicing against a secluded hillside. Sometimes as the slugs passed through the target beer cans they would sit there without moving an inch—the might and speed of the lead passing solidly through the thin metal sides of the cans and on into the loose sand and clay behind. Sometimes the cans would jump wildly into the air as if violently kicked. It made no difference to me. I could look through my powerful binoculars and tell which cans had been hit and which ones had survived my attack.

I was not a bad marksman when I started the drill. I was much better than average when one week had passed and a damned good shot by the end of two. Practice was not so much a matter of steadying the rifle or judging the distance and the sights, as it was a form of meditation. The mantra of a five-shell load and the reverberating report through the rocks and canyons swelled the tempest of my hatred and hardened my intent to an absolute. The fine details of my assassination plot are of little importance. Though Brother Earl was a very cautious man, his pride would make him a fairly easy target upon whom to level my sights. I was going to kill Brother Earl. I was going to shoot him through his evil head and make his blood flow onto the ground and make him dead like Lori. The final stage of the plan was to take place back in my old home territory. It seemed fitting that such an important event as the killing of a devil should take place just down the road from the original site of an innocent past. I was planning on hitting him only a few miles from the small apartment where Lori and I had begun establishing the patterns and rituals of mutual expectation and devotion which were to have made a long and fruitful marriage—just a short drive from the university and its never-turning hours, its dusty books, and its murky duck pond. It was my plan to blow Brother Earl away in the parking lot of Sassy Sally's Blue Bird Café and Lounge out on Skintz Bottom Road.

231

I was going to purchase myself a deluxe order of fried weasel "to go," perch myself up in the limbs of a huge old tree that grew in the parking lot, and get greasy eating while waiting for his arrival. It was deep in the heart of Brother Earl Country where the sinner's course was constantly cluttered by the outrage of the piously nosey. As reported earlier, Brother Earl had taken his first big step toward sanctimonious fame by converting most of the marooned and captive clientele of Sally's tavern during a flood. Though the bulk of his international operation had been moved to his Holy Headquarters on the campus of Brother Earl University in Texas, it had been easy to contrive a means of luring him back to Sassy Sally's. I had been a quiet adversary of his for years and Sassy Sally's was his old stomping ground. In a heated letter, I had just sent an irreverent challenge and knew that, once he had checked his computer files and found that my sister and brother-in-law, the scum, had placed me on his wanted list of incorrigible sinners, he would eventually show up. Besides, regardless of the extent to which his evil empire had grown, I assumed he would still be able to recall my name as a bit player in one of his earlier murders.

It would just be a matter of waiting, and hatred can foster a cold and persistent patience for revenge.

For a High Priest, one dedicated to the Mandate of Life, one who by his basic nature was bound to pacifism, it was surprisingly easy for me to seriously contemplate the destruction of a human being. I was superficially objective about the whole situation. And, when I tried to undermine my murderous will with thoughts of the horrendous implications of shooting any living creature, I knew that Brother Earl was the one exception I could make to my humane values. A part of me knew that even Glory Hallelujah would not totally disapprove of the action. Perhaps, in my killing Brother Earl there would be at least a symbolic touch of revenge for the slaying of Glory's young love.

Or, something like that. I was just rationalizing what was so obviously wrong about taking a life, whoever the victim may be. But it didn't matter. It seemed I would have to kill him regardless of what the ramifications might be to the state of my own soul. It wasn't just revenge for Lori, it was protection for Carrie.

So, I went to Sassy Sally's Blue Bird Café and Lounge.

As always, the jukebox was blasting away. It sang:

*I love your long slim legs and your flashing
eyes
and the feel of your body feelin' mine.
Your kisses and your touches are stronger than
my will—
you've got me cheating, though I ain't the
cheatin' kind.*

"Are these songs getting more explicit?"

"Oh, yes. Country music has definitely moved into the nastiness of its adolescence. All these moaning fools ever do is bleat out, in as much detail as current censorship will allow, the fantasies of one-night stands or their shameful magnetism for the wives or husbands of their best friends. The imperfection of the rhyme bothers me, too."

"'Mine' and 'kind'?"

"Yes. These songs a full of sloppy rhyming and atrocious grammar—sometimes it seems the whole English language is being weakened by these ignoramuses."

"Jeez, Dr. Fintin, you're the same old arrogant prick you always were."

"Well... "

We had been isolated at a table in a back corner of the room, but then others arrived and the conversation took a sudden turn to the twang.

"Heck, Blake, it's been a month a Sundays since I seen ya last. What's y'all been up to all these here years that have plum gone by?"

"Oh, just moseyin' around." And I whispered, "What was your name again, Dr. Fintin?"

"Hooker. Elmer Hooker," he replied in a harsh whisper.

"Yeah, Elmer, I've just been a-travelin', up to no dang good at-tall."

"Did y'all ever come up with any answers to those questions we talked about? You know, answers to the who-done-it mystery about your wife."

"Oh yes, Elmer, I remember that there mystery we done talked about. I ain't so much come up with an answer as I come up with a solution. I guess y'all know by now that you was right when you suspected those preachers a-doin' all that weirdo death to your lady-folks."

"Blake!" he whispered sharply. "Don't be so obvious. There are spies everywhere." And then speaking aloud, "Y'all don't say. Well yes, we do sort of suspicion that we-all might be on the right track there."

"Do you ever get together and shuffle the deck with those boys I met here that one time?"

"Heck yeah, Blake. We might even get a little game goin' tonight just for you."

"Wouldn't that be just dandy, Elmer. Just like old times again. Right?"

"Pretty much, except we don't meet down here anymore. Now we get together with some folks at a place a bit west of here and danged if we don't shuffle more cards than we ever done before."

"Sounds powerful good to me, Elmer."

"It's plum powerful, all right."

"Well, Old Buddy, what brings y'all down to this old splinter-stooled barroom if ya ain't meetin' here no more? I was right shocked to run up against ya here."

"Oh, a couple of us old boys got wind of that there 'solution' of yours and I thought I'd better get on over here and head ya off before ya got in a little over your head—if ya know what I'm a-getting' at."

Although I hadn't been totally unprepared for the prospect of encountering Dr. Fintin at the Blue Bird, it did seem a strong coincidence. "Are you tellin' me that y'all have been expectin' me?"

"That's right, Blake. We've on the lookout for you for days now."

"How'd you hear about my solution?"

"Oh, we got ways of knowin' what happens to our preacher friend down in Texas. Ya might say we got an earful of that little phone message you left him and an eyeful of that letter you sent."

"And how'd y'all know to show up at this bar this very afternoon?"

"Like I said, Blake. There are spies everywhere."

"Seems that-a-way."

"Well, I'd better mount up and head on out. I'll just see what I can get together for tonight. I know you're gonna be impressed."

"Will Mike be there?"

"Mike?"

"Come on, Elmer. You're shucking me now. Surely y'all remember that crusty devil with his sharp tongue and his burnin' eyes. You know, the feller who jumped under the table whenever it thundered."

"Of course, I do recall the person to whom you are referring. Unfortunately, he departed our company some time ago." And then realizing he had committed a communicative error due to his obvious nervousness at the mention of the name, he quickly added, "Y'all."

"I'm sorry to hear that, Elmer. I really liked that old boy. Well, anyway, it'll be good to see the rest of the group. But I'd better tell ya right up front. Ain't nothin' you can do or say that's gonna change my thinkin' about that there solution. I'm gonna do what I come here to do, if you know what I mean."

"Oh no, we ain't gonna try to stop you, Blake. We might slow ya down just a tad, maybe talk to you about a change in rodeo grounds so's to speak. Be we think your solution is just fine."

"You do?"

"You bet. It's just what we need. Our solution isn't quite ready yet so we're all tickled pink about yours. It couldn't have come along at a better time."

"Do you really know what my plan is?"

"Not exactly. We done read that letter you writ and we know how much ya hates that feller and we done put one and one together and come up with a notion that the OK Corral might just be this here parking lot."

"You ain't the fumblin' old school teacher you used to be anymore, are you, Elmer?"

"Shucks no."

"It sounds like you boys might just be playin' a little higher stakes poker than the last time I seen ya."

"You've got that right, Jackson."

"Well, let's get together tonight."

"I'll just scratch out the address here on my business card and y'all get out there sometime after dinner. About eight o'clock would be fine."

"Sure thing, Elmer," I said. "See ya then."

And, as I watched his silhouetted form walk out the front door into the glaring afternoon, I glanced down at the card and read the simple address he had written.

It read:

The Willow City Truth Center

2 Watching from the Tower

We talked quietly as we waited. After a tortuous week enduring the bullshit of Fintin and his fellows as a guest at the Willow City Truth Center, it was finally just me and some clean-cut guy with a haircut they had sent along to wait with me. I sat with the loaded rifle across my lap. The two of us had been waiting in the bell tower at the Willow City Truth Center for hours through the chilly night and then well into the morning.

"So, you're going to kill Brother Earl," he said in the early stages of our long vigil.

"Somebody's got to kill him."

"That sounds reasonable."

"Yes it does, doesn't it? Who are you, anyway? I know we've met and your name is Ted and you work with Dr. Fintin's little mob. But who the hell are you and what are you doing up here with me? You know I'm going to be killed after I shoot the son of a bitch. They'll probably kill you, too. You do know that, don't you? What are you doing here?"

"Just a job."

"What do you mean? Is Fintin afraid I'll skip out before I do what he and the merry professors are incapable of doing? Has he forgotten that it was I who instigated this plot? Has he overlooked the fact that it was he who escalated a simple assassination into becoming a conspiracy? I had even considered using the Truth Center before he butted into my plan. I met a former employee of the joint, a professional substance abuser who told me about the taunting of Brother Earl and the secret doings of the staff. I just couldn't figure out how to get in here so I decided on Sassy Sally's place as an alternative. I knew Brother Earl used to come here to confront the heathen hippies. I didn't need Fintin. I still don't. Brother Earl is coming today. The crowd is growing out front. As soon as enough of his zealots and media people gather he'll make his grand entrance and I'll blast his head off. So, what the hell are you really doing here?"

"Just a job."

"I suppose working at the Truth Center precludes the possibility of your telling a lie."

"Not necessarily," he laughed, "But I'll assure you I'm trying to tell the truth. I can tell you it seemed someone ought to keep an eye on you, and I got the job."

"'Just a job,' you say."

"One of my jobs."

"Are you here to protect me or guard me?"

"It's complicated, Mr. Blake. You'd have to talk to Dr. Fintin to really understand what's going on. I'm just doing what I was told."

"You're a fine young man. I'm sure your mother, God, and country are proud of you."

"I would hope so, sir."

"So, Fintin knows all the answers?"

"More than I do, yes sir."

"Well, Ted, I'll tell you I've had more than enough of Dr. Fintin and his Committee the past few days—my Truth Center captivity. I'd risk dying of suspense rather than enduring the boredom of another conversation. I've known that bastard for too long already. I mean, I met the original Committee when their cowboy suits were brand new. It takes someone young and naïve like you to find such an insuperable old asshole worthy of allegiance. Damned if I do. I don't hate him or even dislike him. It's just that he's every bit as worthless, he and his ever growing Committee of impotent grievers, as a decade ago."

"Surely you understand that there are procedures that must be followed in any matter as involved as the covert elimination of an enemy of the State."

"Procedures, my ass. It's the same indecisiveness that has made the pitiful bastards so impotent all these years. They think too much and do nothing."

"Perhaps they are trying to avoid repeating a mistake they made in the past."

"Fintin and The Committee. Are you kidding? They've never taken any action more radical than mass-ordering their cowboy suits that I know of."

"Perhaps so," he said thinly.

"Do you know something I don't know?"

"I'm just here to guard, I beg your pardon, escort you. I don't know anything."

"Cut the crap, Ted. I'll be dead in a few hours anyway."

"Yes, that's probably true. But I really don't know anything about the distant past—only the past few years."

"Look. This could all be over by now if it weren't for you people. Cold-blooded murder isn't one of my favorite pastimes. And the longer it simmers within me the more it corrodes—it hurts and I want to finish it quickly. Did you see the glee in their eyes when they were assured I was actually going to snuff the son of a bitch with my 30/30 Winchester rifle? Did you see how ecstatic I made them? What a bunch of wimpy jerks."

"They do talk a lot, don't they?"

"So you have noticed."

"I just do what I'm told."

"Like this suicide mission? Damn it, I'm the one who's going to be a murderer. I'm the one who'll probably be torn to shreds by that mob down there. And you, too. They'll kill you too, I'm sure of it. What the hell are you doing up here with me? I didn't invite you."

"Don't worry about me, Mr. Blake. I'll be long gone by time the mob shows up."

"Now, that's reassuring. So, who the hell are you, anyway? You can tell a dead man."

"Let's just say that I work for an organization that oversees Dr. Fintin's operation."

"I've got it! You're a government agent, aren't you?"

"I told you I was doing a job."

"And, for damned sure, you're not up here to stop me, are you? You guys are hardly newcomers to the world of assassination. You've probably popped a politico or two yourself."

"I'm not here to stop you, Mr. Blake. I'm here to help."

"I can pull this trigger all by myself."

"I'm sure you can, but one's resolve is never to be taken for granted in these matters."

"Now I've really got you figured out. Not only are you a G-man, you're a G-man assigned to Jackson Blake to give him amoral support in his time of need. Today I'm about to make inanimate the fluid, flowing, structure of a human form. With these trusty bullets I'm going to penetrate the frail flesh of a human being and let flow the hot red blood to turn it cold and thick and dark and make the eyes and the mind and the heart as dead as stone. And you're here to make damn sure I don't chicken out."

"There's nothing amoral about eradicating a rogue beast, Mr. Blake. If you were sitting up here waiting for Adolph Hitler to show up, wouldn't you be doing mankind a service by eliminating him? I think shooting Brother Earl is a very moral act. Don't you think you're getting overly emotional about wasting a deadly, hateful, incredibly dangerous bastard like Brother Earl?"

"If this is all so moral and good and beneficial to mankind, then why don't you shoot the bastard? You're likely at least as good a shot and less likely to lose any sleep over the deed."

"I would if I could."

"And how about Dr. Fintin or one of the other wonder brothers from the Truth Center? I know why I'm here and, regardless of my anxiety, my resolve is not the least bit weakened. I know I can kill the bloody demon. I've seen the Evil side of Death at its very best and I know Brother Earl throws it about with cruel and uncanny power. I am here to kill a murderer. But Fintin, and how many others down there, have existed with the same cause for hatred and revenge as I. Why haven't they been driven to this point of radical action? Why aren't they up here with me forming a long-range firing squad?"

"The answer is very simple," he said. "They're incapable of killing Brother Earl. At least until they perfect their techniques, neither as individuals nor as a group can they amass the power to destroy him. If hatred alone were a sufficient source to eliminate Brother Earl, I could kill him myself. I've seen some of his treatment of 'irreverent folk.' I've been there with the ashes and the twisted remains. I could do it morally and professionally but I don't think he would die."

"Why do you people lack these dark energies. What do I possess that you don't?

"I said it was simple. It probably isn't. The fact is, none of us has been to the face of Death and returned. We are not Priests, Jackson. We do not have the Powers of a Priest and, in case you've forgotten, you do."

3 The Rest of the Story

Ted told me about Dr. Fintin and the Truth Center and Brother Earl. Once I assured him I was going to be dead, he proved to be a wealth of information.

Similar to what Glory Hallelujah had theorized, the Truth Center people had determined death to be a phenomenon controlled by a wide and general system of natural causation with no specific or identifiable center. However, they too had discovered that there were in existence groups of death exploiters, ruled by super-inflated bureaucrats, fanatics, and various other individuals or clusters of individuals who had somehow achieved a degree of control over destructive natural phenomenon. It had been their observation that, without exception, the Power had been abused terribly—generally as a means of coercing subject populations into becoming fear-stricken cults of mindless followers. But then, how would one ever deal out death fairly?

For years the Truth Center people had been studying and experimenting with a vast array of ideas and methods gleaned from all the cultures and religions of the world in an attempt to assume a similar grasp upon a small aspect of death for their own use. It had been their intention to use whatever Powers they accrued to counteract the petty and cruel applications of Power across the world. Their plan was to neutralize evil with like Powers.

Years of study and observation had always brought them back to the same point in their understanding. From alchemists and gurus and mystics, sorcerers and witches, mountain hermits and spirit divines they had learned the methods but had produced no results. It wasn't until Brother Earl arrived upon the scene that the answer became clear.

It occurred during one of Brother Earl's regular visits to the Center to preach his interminable sermon against irreverence, particularly as practiced by the dopers who had been hired to give the place a front. The experimenters looked upon Brother Earl as a harmless crank who only served to heighten distraction from the actual nature of their undertaking.

241

It was not until one afternoon when a leader of the project was pinned down out on the front sidewalk and experienced a direct confrontation with the holy Brother that the final link was established. In the dark raging eyes of Brother Earl, the hapless scholar felt the energy of intense fury as it exploded into harmless babble. He knew then it was only with such intensity that the Dark Force of Death could ever be summoned. If one did not hate, if one did not rage irrationally against some great or imagined foe. If one did not pit one's whole violent self against a specific target—if one were not mad in the fixation of destruction—all the study and technique could have no effect.

For this reason, Brother Earl himself, the great crusader against evil and irreverent behavior, was taken into the innermost chambers of the Truth Center and indoctrinated with the most vital elements of the great body of knowledge accumulated there. He was the core of a very dangerous experiment. If the theory was correct, the secret would have been discovered. However, there would also be the pressing problem of a monster at large with frightening powers—a fire-and-brimstone man with his very own bolt of lightning.

The results were obvious. The experiment was a success but also its most dreaded consequence was realized.

"And, Ted," I asked. "Why is it that this particular faction seems to target only women, the wives of those with whom they have quarreled?"

"We've wondered about that too. The best explanation I know is that the way these vengeful fools justified their carnage was by considering their slaughter to be a means of instruction. The sinner himself had to survive to learn the lesson. Also, it seems in many of the "great" religions of the world, women are delegated to a lesser role than men—perhaps seen as being disposable.

"Yeah, I've read some of that thought. Women are procreativity useful, but basically they're a bunch of filthy whores."

"Well, I don't know if that's what they..."

"I do! These guys are all withered-dicked, hate-mongering perverts. They've been running the world with the distorted might of their own insecurity for so long they believe their own lies. Oh, yes, woman are dispensable. Just consider the fate of my wife. My lovely Lori."

This whole saga of the Willow City Truth Center had hit me

pretty hard and then, perhaps with a touch of well-placed insanity, I became madly amused at the irony of the situation. I could barely keep from bellowing laughter and endangering our clandestine roost in the bell tower at the idea that the well-meaning little scientists and philosophers of the Truth Center had created the archfiend, Brother Earl.

"You mean they created that son of a bitch right here? The same guys who are getting bubble headed over my plot to assassinate good ole Earl are the ones who armed him. I'm just here to cover their screw-up. Damn, Ted, I don't know which way to point this rifle now." Then, of course, I began laughing. A quiet muffled laugh, but a genuine laugh. (The best of laughter is usually spiced with a touch of insanity.)

He stared at me quizzically.

"It's funny, isn't it?" I asked.

"I don't think so."

"You'd have to have been there, Ted." I said giddily. "Tell me, how did Fintin and the boys ever get involved with such a group of mad scientists?"

"We all work for the same organization."

"So you guys have been in on the Truth Center business all along. You might know. When your plans to blow up Castro with a loaded cigar fizzled, you had to look elsewhere for nasty weaponry."

"No comment."

"Well, why did you connect Fintin and his coterie of fuddy-duds to the Truth Center?"

"Dr. Fintin was already associated with The Truth Center. And then, when he formed his Committee it seemed, in their own intellectual way, his group of widowers might collectively generate sufficient rage to counter the likes of Brother Earl and company."

"Then they're being used just like Brother Earl was. They've been brought to the Center as an energy source."

"Exactly."

"God help us all, you're going to create another monster. Don't you realize the first poor bastard who says 'ain't' around Fintin is going to get fried?"

"This isn't funny. Creating Brother Earl was a terrible step to take in the quest of knowledge—but it had to be done."

"And the others, the ones I heard about when I first met The

243

Committee. It was just like testing nuclear bombs, wasn't it? One **explosion wasn't** sufficient to test the energy. One Brother Earl wasn't enough, was he?"

"There were others, but they actually came before Brother Earl and weren't so powerful. They've been eliminated. It hasn't been pretty, I know. But it's been necessary to learn these secrets, regardless of the risks. Now the only way to counter a force like Brother Earl is to find a Priest like you—someone who has focused the powers necessary to confront his own.

"Do you know about my wife?"

"Yes."

"You wonder why I laugh at this atrocity. Perhaps I mock myself, but I can tell you what was truly funny. Everything my disposable wife and I knew together was funny, Ted. The world was a good deep laugh back in those days before this terrible experiment was perpetrated. Lori was such a young girl when your holy weapon killed her—only in her early twenties. You know, people aren't even real yet when they are in their early twenties. They are sensors—smelling, tasting, hearing, feeling, watching, and sending multitudes of happenings and near-happenings to a brain that is just beginning to recover from the shock of toilet training and puberty. People in their early twenties are touchers of real worlds, wandering about with senses open and memory flooding with sensations of what they have touched. Lori was just an embryo, in the early stages of a process that would have resulted in a magnificent real person if your creature had given her time to ingest the worlds she had only begun to encounter. I was as young, too, and I loved her for the delightful, mutually- naïve seeker of the Earth she was with me. Oh, how I love those memories we were storing together. I still have them and, even with the passing of these many years, I rarely can sort through them without bitterness muddling the joy they were intended to generate. You know, the worst thing that can happen to good memories is to have them bundled up with an overwhelmingly bad memory—it defeats their purpose. It loses them, it neutralizes them. I never had the opportunity to really know my Lori. I only knew the erratic, random parts of her that were gathering to build the person who never was to be. I only knew the touching. Never the being. Why did your Brother Earl kill my wife? I know you are too young to have been involved at

244

that early stage of the project, but do you know why?"

"No. I can't tell you."

"Damn! I was hoping you and the Truth Center death agents could explain it to me. You see, to this day I don't really know what I did to get on the deadly side of the bastard. I must have run into him just after the Truth Center had bestowed the great gift upon him. Perhaps he was just a bit frisky or trigger-happy—the sociopathic cowpoke who finds out he can out-draw anybody in town. As far as I can tell from eons of plowing through vague recollections, all I did was be an incorrigible window watcher. I worked in a large factory and when break time came I would rush the great distance to the nearest window and look out in order to see the day passing and, sometimes, to dwell for a moment on thoughts of better places. I didn't even know anyone noticed, much less, hated me for it. One day, Earl came over—he was just some part-time preacher/full-time spot welder back then—and he gave me some trouble about acting strange. All I did was react like any smart-assed kid is supposed to react. I wasn't afraid of him, but I wasn't terribly blasphemous either. How was I supposed to know that the sawed-off little son of a bitch could play God? One day I smart- off to a fat-assed Jesus freak and then suddenly I'm a widower. It never has made any sense to me. Lori was so pretty and, even if she was in her early twenties, she didn't have an ounce of smart-ass about her. Why her? I'll have to ask Brother Earl that before I take him down. I'll bet she was only a practice target—a human beer can to shoot his death beam at to see if it really worked. I'll bet that's what she was. Bang, and the beer can goes flying. I'll have to ask him about that."

"You're going to talk to him?"

"Oh, yes."

"How are you going to do that? Hey, what are you doing?" he asked in alarm as I began methodically removing the bullets one by one.

"So long, Secret Agent Man."

"Where are you going?"

"I'm going to talk to Brother Earl and then I'm going to destroy him. I just realized I won't need this rifle to do my dirty work. I am more powerful than that petty fool could ever be."

4 Capture

I sold the rifle to Dr. Fintin for five hundred dollars. He knew five hundred was too much to pay but felt some sense of obligation to make a concession to me for my bravery. Besides, the government was covering all of his expenses.

"Try not to shoot yourself, Fintin," I said and then I walked on past the gate and out into the holy mob and allowed the pious legions to capture me and take me away to Brother Earl University in Texas.

5 The Grand Tour

The people at the university gave me a tour of the facility. Apparently blinded by missionary zeal, the authorities at Brother Earl University believed I might be persuaded to join the forces of the good Brother in his war on irreverent behavior. It wasn't until I had spoken my frank opinion of several of the various activities and areas of scholarly pursuit that they gave up on me and decided what I needed was a good old-fashioned, Inquisition-style stake burning.

It started with the choir. It wasn't a pretty sight.

"You are fortunate, Mr. Blake," they had said to me as we reverently entered the huge chapel. "The choir is practicing." The large golden doors swung slowly closed behind us and the mammoth sanctuary gaped before our eyes. In whispered tones, one of my guides said, Brother Earl designed it himself."

"I would never have guessed," I said as I studied the fifty-foot high mural running the full length of one wall. It depicted Brother Earl and Jesus Christ standing on a hill overlooking a sea of at least ten thousand upraised faces, each individually painted and each with an adoring smile.

On the opposite wall was another mural of the same proportion. In vivid detail, this painting was a monstrous collage of grotesque death. It was of dismembered torsos, decapitated heads, smoldering piles of burnt flesh—all manner of twisted mutilation awash in blood and peopled with the tortured faces of slaughtered sinners. Above them, on a hill illuminated by a single column of sunlight breaking through a storming black sky, was a small group of men dressed in the costume of crusaders. The men were gathered proudly around their leader who sat upon a large white horse and glared mercilessly down upon the dead with squinting eyes. "Hey," I said, "that's Brother Earl up there on that horse, isn't it?"

"Why, yes it is—the victorious general in the war against the irreverent," said one of the smooth-faced young men.

"I see," I said. "Then am I to assume that the gory mass of

mangled bodies is all that will be left of the irreverent?"

"All sinners must be either converted or annihilated," said a pretty face with a crisp and cheerful voice.

I remember the remains of Glory's body and the mural took on a disquieting sense of realism.

"When will this holy war of yours begin?"

The small cluster of guides tittered in a momentary loss of self-control before one of them, smiling proudly said, "Oh, Mr. Blake, it has already begun."

"Already started, you say. Tell me, what's the body count today?"

A smiling soldier in a light blue blazer and a tie with a some kind of logo fashioned from a B and an E—the absolute antithesis of Sad Sack or GI Joe from other national massacres, said, "We won't know that for several more hours, will we, Mr. Blake?"

I was beginning to take all this rather personally. Just as I was about to say something profound like 'War is hell," a booming voice from down in front said, "Why, ladies and gentlemen, I declare I believe we have been blessed with a visitor."

Eighty songsters stood up from their seats in unison and in a perfectly harmonized shout said, "Praise the Lord, Praise Brother Earl!" and sat back down.

"Welcome, welcome," said the choir director in his powerful baritone voice. "Come on down and listen for a while and we'll praise the Lord and damn the irreverent in song for you."

"Amen!" said the young ladies and gentlemen leaping to their feet, and with a flash of a baton they began singing, with incredible exuberance, a song which rhythmically proclaimed the love and wrath of some distorted notion of a trinity consisting of Father, Son, and Brother Earl.

"It's amazing," I whispered as we stood in front of the altar with eighty, joyous, twenty-year-old faces singing their hearts out before us.

"Yes," said a lovely guide who pressed herself next to me in reaction to my comment, "aren't they wonderful, praise the Lord."

"It is truly amazing," I repeated. "All of them, boys and girls alike, every damn one of them looks just like Pat Boone."

For the remainder of the tour, I was treated as somewhat less of a visiting dignitary and more like a prisoner being given his last meal. "Brother Earl insists that we show sinners like you our university, Mr. Blake. He doesn't give up on a soul until every avenue of salvation has been exhausted. Though we try to live our lives just as purely, few of us have as much optimism in our missionary endeavors. Now, come along and we'll get this over with as quickly as possible."

Our next stop was the Brother Earl School of Mass Communication and Economics. The door opened immediately into a long hallway lined with glass-walled, simulated radio booths. In each booth was a young man or woman pouring forth dogma and praise and pleas for money into microphones which were connected to recorders. I was introduced to a tall young man with a deep clear voice and deep-set eyes. "This is Martin Trotter, Mr. Blake. He is one of our most promising students," said the Director of Diction and Donation Instruction.

"How do you do, Mr. Blake? I hope you are enjoying your tour of Brother Earl University. We are all quite proud of this facility, and it is an honor and privilege to attend. I trust that you will be much impressed by what you see here."

"I'll assure you, Martin," I said, "I am very much impressed already."

"Fine, fine, fine," he said as he stepped into a booth. The director flipped a switch and we heard Martin deliver a fifteen minute sermon of Biblical doom dosed with an artful pitch for listeners' "love" donations to support the battle against the irreverent and to cover the cost of getting Bibles to the spiritually deprived Tibetan monks. The change in Martin's voice from that which he used in our brief conversation to that which he used in the broadcast was striking. As he sat down behind the microphone a cast came over his face, and with a suspended cold smile, his natural, deep and resonant voice became higher pitched and nasal. The nature of his speech changed to emphasize the mispronunciation of certain words and to add syllables to others. There was a whining, sing-song quality to his voice which immediately aggravated me.

"You mean, you actually train people to sound like that?" I asked.

"Certainly we do, Mr. Blake. It is the voice of radio evangelism. Over the years we have taught people to associate this dialect with the harsh and beautiful truth of Bible-honest preaching. It's all very scientific. Research has shown us that by combining characteristics of dialects ranging from the nasal tonality of central Texas, to the aristocratic lilt of the Piedmont region of Virginia, to the soft rasping of southern Georgia, and with an occasional hint of a Bostonian syllable, we can touch the hearts and wills of a maximum number of listeners."

"Not to mention touching the pocketbooks of a maximum number of listeners," I added.

"Of course. The work of the Lord is not inexpensive."

"Then you're the guys who put the extra syllable in "Ja-ee-sus" and the 'aw' in the middle of God."

"Yes, indeed," he beamed.

We listened to Martin's closing appeal:

Brothers and sisters, today as you listen to this broadcast, I ask you to reach deep into your hearts and give with all of the love you've got for the Lord. I want you to give of your love with prayerful adoration for Him that loves you so. Reach deep, beloved, reach deep that through your love others might hear this message. Keep the love a-comin', dear ones, we've got a lotta savin' to do before we all sit down in heaven for the rest that lasts an eternity. Love the Lord with your nickels, your dimes, your hundred-dollar bills; love with your stocks, your bonds, your life insurance policies; love Him in your donations, beloved, that we can continue to share this radio message with you and with those who are yet the burden of the saved. Put us in your wills so that, when you go on to the waitin' place where the saved souls dwell until we've won this war, you'll know you've done your best to continue the struggle. God will be proud of you when those lawyers read your last testament saying, 'Hallelujah, she's given all her earthly worth to the Brother Earl Foundation. She won't be needin' her stock portfolio and her certificates of deposit now that she's waitin' with the Lord.' Keep your love a-comin', brothers and sisters, and, the Lord willin', I'll be talkin' to you again tomorrow. Amen.

"Amen," I said and we left for the Brother Earl School of Music and Psychological Warfare.

"Hush," said the guide as we entered a doorway labeled "Acapella Testimony." There was only one person in the large room. She was standing on a slightly raised platform with hands tightly clasped at her bosom, head tilted toward Heaven, and with eyes nearly closed as if in prayer and then suddenly springing so widely open that it seemed quite possible they might tumble on down her pretty little cheeks and dangle there at the ends of her optic nerves. Her face was so smooth, her features delicately sculptured, "Brother Earl must really be big among the Caesarean population," I whispered.

"Hush!"

The lovely girl, the vision of luminescent adoration, sang in sweet soprano tones:

> *I was lost on Desperation Highway,*
> *in the fast lane that leads on down to Hell.*
> *Through the Land of Temptation*
> *I was traveling,*
> *and by earthly standards*
> *living well.*
>
> *Oh, but my soul was empty*
> *in that life by Devil led,*
> *with stereos*
> *and fancy clothes*
> *and sinners in my bed.*
> *But then one day on the radio*
> *I heard the Brother speak,*
> *and with words of praise*
> *my heart did raise—*
> *now, the reverent life I seek.*

"Isn't it funny how Brother Earl creeps into everything you do around this place?"

"Quiet!" said several guides with eyes getting sterner as they began shuffling me out of the room. Just as I was nudged out the door I heard a final sweet verse of rhapsodic praise. With hands unclasped and spread wide and eyes upraised, and mouth in an angelic smile she sang:

251

With Brother Earl leading our legions,
a bludgeon I will bear.
And the flesh of evil about me
I will rip, and I will smash, and I will tear.

"Mr. Blake," said someone, "we would appreciate it if you could be more courteous. These students are very dedicated in their efforts and we don't wish them to be discouraged by your sarcasm."

"Oh, God forbid that I would discourage any of these delightful zealots of yours ' ... I will rip and I will smash and I will tear.' How loving."

"Perhaps I should remind you, Mr. Blake. It is your soul we are trying to save here."

"You don't offer a man many options, do you?"

"What do you mean?"

"Well," I said, "it seems I have the choice of either accepting Brother Earl's messianic bullshit or being ripped, smashed, and torn."

"I believe you're finally getting the picture, Mr. Blake."

"You'd be surprised how perceptive we sinners can be. Let's get on with this farce. I came to see Brother Earl and somehow I feel that this tour will have to be completed first."

"Follow me," said a guide as the others snorted and whispered to one another, "He actually thinks he's going to get to see Brother Earl."

After several more tedious and brutal exhibits, the tour was over and we were leaving the building. On the way down a back stairway I noticed a door labeled

REVERSE PSYCHOLOGY—KEEP OUT!

"What's behind that door?"

'Nothing you need to know about, Mr. Blake. Keep moving, please."

"No, I think I'll just go on in there."

Before the group could deter me, I forced my way through the door and came face-to-face with one of the strangest looking old men I had ever seen. He was a stark and dramatic contrast to the guides who had been smugly ushering me about the university. Where they stood straight, he was hunched over. Where their faces were soft and smooth, his was craggy and matted with a huge and wildly-strewn beard of various tones of gray and black and the color of whatever he had been eating over the previous few days. Where their teeth were perfect, polished rows of orthodontic pride, his were sparse and jagged as if filed to points. And, most importantly, where their eyes had the dull, veiled cast of the deeply brainwashed, absolute believer—his eyes were bright with life and rage and the clarity of outrageous vision.

Looking right past me, the old man said to guides who had immediately surrounded me, "What the hell do you goddamned posies want with me?"

With a virtual storm of tongue activated "tsk-ing" sounds and much rolling of the eyes, the group moved infinitesimally away from the still-opened door. I knew then that with all of their indignant affectation, truthfully, they were afraid of this twisted old man.

"Mr. Cable," began a female guide with impatient overtones, "we are attempting to conduct Mr. Blake on a tour of The University. Now, if you'll excuse us..."

"Excuse you, hell," said the old man as he took a step toward the young lady and the group. "The only way I'll excuse you, Missy, is to get a peek at that sweet young snatch of yours."

"Gasp," said the group, moving farther from the doorway.

"Yesseree, Missy, let Old Cable get his old whacker into that wazoo of yours and we'll see about excusin' you."

The retreat was on. With shoving and crushing, Earl's holy soldiers were fleeing from the crackling old man. "Let Old Cable suck those little nipples of yours right up his nose, Missy," he shouted down the hall at them. "Let him get a big sniff of your furry." And then, still shocking the air with a harsh, deep-felt, metallic laugh, he kicked the door shut.

"They'll be back fur ya with the guards, right quick now, boy. They'll probably shoot me this time, but it don't matter none anyway—it sure is fun stirrin' up the nut-less sum bitches and them proper little ladies. Don't you think?" he asked with another rush of laughter bordering on strangulation as he laboriously moved a heavy chair from his cluttered work table and wedged it under the doorknob.

After a moment to gain composure he asked, "I'll bet you're wonderin' what an old barb like me is doin' at Brother Earl University, aren't ya?"

"You do seem to be wonderfully out of place here."

"Well, I'll tell ya what I'm a-doin' here."

"You mean other than terrifying those decent young men and women?"

"Yeah. That's just a hobby. I've got a real job here, too,"

"Tell me about."

"I writes dirty songs fer Old Earl, I does."

"You what?" I asked, finding it hard to believe what I had heard.

"You heard me right, Boy."

"Dirty songs?"

"At's right, Boy. Nasty ones."

The old man stood there staring at me with his head at a slight angle and his mouth half opened in a grin emphasizing the jagged condition of his teeth, his eyes sparkling and crazed. "Ain't that somethin', Boy. I writes dirty songs for holy Old Earl. Guess why, Boy. Take a guess."

I had no fear of the old man. I knew that in the environment of Brother Earl University with its stifling predominance of self-righteous and goodly persons, this wild man was the closest I would possibly come to finding an ally. "It's my guess that once he has checked to see that all of his thousands of scholars and junior crusaders have said their little prayers and have been snugly tucked into their little Brother Earl cots, he listens to your songs and whips his willie."

The old man crackled and crackled, and sputtered, and hacked until he nearly turned blue. "You're probably right, Boy, but that ain't the only reason he has me writin' 'em—might be the best reason, but it ain't the only one.

Think about my door. What's my door say?"

"KEEP OUT!"

"No, not that. I put that sign up. What's the first part say?"

"Reverse Psychology, right?"

"You got it, kid. Reverse psychology. Now think about my dirty songs. They ain't little dirty songs, they're big-uns. You've heard most of 'em on the radio, I'm sure. I know you have. They're all about goin' down to a barroom and getting' drunk and screwin' your best friend's wife, or about how damn good it feels to slam the old whammer into a missy to the tune of 'Wildwood Flower.' You've heard 'em.   I know ya have. Let me think of the biggest ones. There was 'Love Is Like a Bucking Bronco' and 'She Was Just a Kissin' Cousin 'til Last Night,' and 'It Made My Poor Old Dead Mother Roll Over in Her Grave, But It Sure Felt Good' and..."

"I think I remember hearing that one."

"It was in all the bars and on all the country radio stations."

"Reverse psychology."

"Yep. And they're getting' worse and worse. I started out just hintin' about doin' the deed, but now I get to write about it like the ringside announcer at the Friday Night Fights—blow by blow."

"It sounds like you enjoy your work."

He crackled some more and said. "Oh, it's a livin'."

"So, you've been writing a contrived sequence of dirtier and dirtier songs."

"Ya could say that."

"And, the dirtier the songs get, the more the preachers have to preach about."

"Yep."

"And, eventually, you'll push it far enough so people will get disgusted."

"It's a known fact that average, standard, everyday human bein's can only tolerate so much filth and then they get religion. It's like with the dirty movies. They started out just showin' a little titty here, a little titty there, a quick glance at a fast movin' furry. Then they got better and better and did more nasty things and after a while it got to just being a world of God-fearin' church goers and those damned movie-goin' perverts.   Ya see what I mean? It really can draw the lines."

"True."

"Wait 'til ya hear my newest song. It's called 'When I Woke Up in My Sleepin' Sister's Arms, She was Whisperin' Our Dear Old Daddy's Name."

"It sounds like a masterpiece."

"Why, thank ya."

There was a loud knock on the door. "Open up, Cable. Open up or we'll kick the door down."

Cable grinned and said, "Hark, I believe I hear the guards."

I think you're right."

He picked up a pillow from his unmade cot and moved another chair over to the back wall of the room. Then, standing on the chair he pressed the pillow tightly over the intercom speaker which hung there. "Jackson," he said, "you are without a doubt one of the biggest dummies I have ever had the misfortune of running into. Don't you recognize me?"

I studied the grizzled, wan figure of the old man standing unsteadily upon the chair and traces of familiarity began to appear to me. "Who the hell are you?"

"Well, we could play a quick game of twenty questions, but I really don't think we have the time. I believe our first and only period of acquaintanceship began beneath a table in a bar out on Skintz Bottom Road."

"Mike?" I said in disbelief. "Is that really you, Mike?"

"Pretty decent disguise, don't you think?"

"You fooled me. Fintin wouldn't even talk about you—I thought you must be dead."

"He takes that CIA secrecy crap so seriously—he's an asshole but at least he's discreet. He wouldn't tell my own mother of my whereabouts."

"After getting a good look at you, I doubt if your own mother would want you back anyway."

"Just a compliment to the effectiveness of my disguise. As a matter of fact, there is only one disadvantage to the clever things I've done with myself to hide my identity. Once a fellow has filed his teeth to devilish points and has graveled his voice and allowed his hair and beard and mind to explode into crazed disarray, there is no returning. Once you're in this deep, it's pretty hard to ever go back. The fact is, not only am I now the absolute secret agent, I'm also a damned good dirty song writer."

"So it seems."

"So, Blake. What's your plan?

"I thought I'd just hang around until certain opportunities present themselves. I guess I'm a prisoner now."

"No, you're not. You're an assassin."

"I'm doing my best. How do you know about this?"

"I'm the inside guy. I know everything there is to know about this goddamned place. I've got wire taps, mailroom cameras, a cadre of stoolies—you name it, I've got it here."

"Mike, you're Fintin's inside man! You're the reason Fintin

and the boys knew about my plot to kill Brother Earl out at Sassy Sally's."

"Right on, Jackson. I've been keeping track of you ever since your sister ratted you out."

There was growing commotion in the hall—more shouting and obviously the massing of a sizable contingent of guards. "Open up or we'll break the door down!" they shouted.

"Not by the hair of my sagging old balls!" he shouted back at them.

"Isn't this going to get you in trouble?"

"It's all part of my disguise. No respectable secret agent would ever stir up as much attention as I do. Anyway, I know too much about Brother Earl. I'll never really be in trouble until the day they go ahead and murder me. They'll be coming through any minute now, Jackson. Good luck to you."

"Thanks, Mike, If I don't see you again, keep those secrets flowing."

"Oh, I'll do that, kid. It would break Fintin's old heart if he didn't have a spy to tell him secrets."

"Do you think any of this business with Fintin will ever amount to anything?"

"I doubt it. But, what the hell, if I hang around here long enough I might even get a shot at sticking it to old Brother Earl myself someday. And, besides, I sort of get a kick out of writing dirty songs and occasionally shocking the pants off of the prissy fools who inhabit this sorry place."

He removed the pillow from the wall speaker and began singing in a loud coarse voice.

> I put a hickey on the hiney of my dentist's dear loved wife,
> and that, my fellow angels, is how I lost my life.
> The jealous bastard slew me so quick I couldn't fight.
> He'd recognized my chewing
> by my goddamned overbite.
>
> With a tye-rye thumper bump
> I love my lady dear.
> I'll be cumin' night 'til morning
> 'til I'm cumin' out her ear.

"Would ya care to join me on the next chorus, Mr. Blake?" he asked between sheaves of laughter.

"I don't mind if I do," I replied in a shout over the sound of a heavy object bashing against the door.

> *I've screwed ewes in Yugoslavia*
> *and chickens in Peru,*
> *and now, my little darlin',*
> *I'll do the deed to you.*
> *So, lie on back and do your best*
> *and keep your mind at ease,*
> *with such a screwin' record,*
> *I'm immune to all disease.*

And together we sang as, with a great flourish of splinters and a rush of zealous strength, the crusaders burst through the wide-flung door:

> *With a tye-rye thumper bump*
> *I love my lady dear.*
> *I'll be cumin' night 'til morning*
> *'til I'm cumin' out her ear.*

And far down the stairway and along the hallway and until the outside doors had closed behind us, I could hear his laughter as they carried me away.

6 The Hearing

The meeting started out with a giant round of laughter. I had never realized what a comedian I was until, after searching the bland collection of upturned faces gathered for the Judgment Day, I asked, "Where's Brother Earl?"

After waiting several moments for the mirth of the situation to die down, a young lady with little laugh-tear streaks running down her face said, "Mr. Blake, Brother Earl is far too busy conducting the matters of his World Wide War Against Irreverence to take the time to sit in on such a low level hearing as this. He is a very important man."

"I see."

"Now may we get on with the procedure?"

"Sure," I said.

"Thank you," said the lady who was apparently in charge of the hearing. We were all sitting around a large table. There were probably twenty of them and, of course, just one of me. Outside the door of the meeting room there were several guards.

"Mr. Blake," she started, "we are gathered here to make final judgment upon the matter of your continued existence in this mortal world. Though my report states you have been rather uncooperative in your stay with us here, you must have perceived some indication of what our purpose is in dealing with people like yourself. It is written in The Revelations of Brother Earl that for the Legions of the Saved to make the final ascent into the Land of the Lord, all souls upon the face of the Earth must have accepted the Light of the Truth. Therefore, it is the task of those of us who are acting as agents of the Legions of the Saved to identify individuals who are contaminating the race of humanity; and, as we have done with you, offer them the means to their own salvation, or, as I'm sure you are aware, eliminate such individuals for the purity of the race. Do you understand?"

"I believe so. And I take it that Brother Earl himself is too busy to attend to my murder and it will have to be carried out by petty folk like yourselves in some conventional manner like hanging, or an electric chair, or a good blast of Brother Earl Sinner Gas. Is that correct?"

The chairperson briskly began shuffling through the stack of folders and envelopes before her on the table. "Let me see... Blake, Jackson Blake. Yes, here it is. Mr. Blake, I must object to your use of the word 'murder.' Our purpose in dealing with you is for the good of humanity. We are not murderers; we are aligned with the Will of the Lord."

She opened a large manila envelope and removed some papers. The brief statement by the prosecution consisted of references to my being reported by my sister and brother-in-law, the scum; the threat I had made to Brother Earl's life; and a description of my bad behavior during the days I had spent at the university. She concluded, "It is the unanimous opinion of the Judgment Staff that Jackson Blake is an incorrigible sinner and must be eliminated from the ranks of the Earth-bound race of human souls. Do you have anything to say in your defense, Mr. Jackson?"

I stood up. The guards at the door turned toward me. I took a deep breath, breathing the symbol of the air through the whole committee, the whole room, the whole university. "No, I don't have anything to say in my defense. I really don't feel the need to defend myself against this mob of gutless wimps you call an army. I don't feel the need to justify my actions to such a mass of piety-dazed fools as yourselves. I will, however, for the sake of a good argument, tell you that Brother Earl is a fiend. I'll tell you that Brother Earl is a murderer—he murdered my wife for target practice with a bolt of lightning and now the dumb son of a bitch thinks that he's going to murder me using misguided schoolchildren. What else do you have in that lumpy 'Jackson Blake' envelope of yours, Miss? Let me see it." I walked around the table to where the prosecutor stood in stunned rage. I grabbed the envelope from her hands and spilled its contents out on the table. "Look, here are my hundred-dollar bills," I said as I gathered them and crammed them into my pockets. "I think I might be needing them more than you. And look what else," I said. "I've been wondering what happened to this since you folks incarcerated me." I picked up the ankh of Glory Hallelujah and placed it around my neck. And then I laughed fiendishly and strode toward the door.

Stopping suddenly, I turned to face the group. "You tell that bastard Earl I'll be waiting for him out there at the center of his goddamned university. And tell any young ladies who come near me they're likely to get leered at, and any of the soldier boys that they'll likely get their tiny little nuts kicked off if they get too close."

And, laughing with a most honest curl of insanity, I parted the guards, brushing them aside like cheap drapes, and left.

7 Arming for War

Even before the darkening of the sun I sensed the coming of the evil clouds by the electricity in the air. The heart of Brother Earl University was a huge green. The center of the great square lawn gently rose to a knoll upon which I was sure Brother Earl must have often stood to bless and harass his flock.

I had been sitting there for some time before I began feeling Brother Earl's wicked presence in the area. I knew he was out there somewhere conjuring up a fresh batch of hot new lightning for my sinning flesh. It could have been a very solemn occasion—the final showdown between the irreverent and the reverent; the shoot-out between poetry and piety; the confrontation of a lifetime. But, of course, always true to character, I was Jackson Blake and thus incapable of maintaining the proper seriousness of the moment. There must have been thousands of them gathered about me. They sat there cross-legged upon the grass silently praying, or reading Brother Earl books, or simply staring blankly at some invisible point of reference several feet above my head.

For myself, I was sitting upon a large blue ice chest packed full of Budweiser beer and playing a banjo. While strewing the empty cans down the slope of the rise, I strummed and sang such ditties as my favorite cowboy song, "Charlotte, the Harlot," and wondered if Pete Seeger or Woodie Guthrie had ever encountered such a non-receptive audience in their folk singing careers. And, naturally, at intermittent intervals I had to interrupt my musical vigil to make my way, picking the banjo and dancing in foot-flung circles cutting swaths through the crowd, to the Brother Earl Facilities to relieve the recurrent pressure of the beer upon my bladder. The walls of the men's room were covered with neatly-lettered Christian graffiti.

It was so inspiring I scribed a little verse myself:

> Here I sit in reverent rest,
> for Brother Earl I'll do my best;
> with holy writ upon my lap,
> I'm raisin' praises while I crap.

It was a real good banjo—the best I'd ever owned, a much finer instrument than the one I played when I was with the "Bulge River Boys Bluegrass Band." Between the cost of it and the expense of the huge, blue ice chest and more Budweiser beers than a mortal could ever have consumed in the most drunken of afternoons, I had spent the last of Glory's stack of hundred-dollar bills. There was a certain feeling of accomplishment in spending those final hundreds—as if, at last, something was to be truly resolved. I was completely broke and as prepared as any soldier in history had ever been to do battle.

I had led quite a parade after leaving the Judgment Room to the shouts of my inquisitors. They cried, "Guards, guards! Stop that sinner." And I had passed through them like a bullet through a beer can—some of them stood motionless—stunned at my encroachment. Others flew like they had been kicked.

With a gathering mass of jeering zealots trailing my stormy exit from the campus, I walked briskly across a boulevard bordering it and sat down upon a bench at a bus stop. There was a small old lady sitting there waiting for a bus. I smiled and said, "Excuse me, does a bus stop here that will take me downtown?"

By then there were hundreds of students lining the edge of the university across the street from us shouting pithy mass slogans like, "Burn the filthy devil, burn him."

The old lady looked at me rather strangely and then, after glancing at the ugly face of the raging mob, she said, "Yes, it will be here in about ten minutes if it's on time and it usually is."

"Thank you."

"That's all right, young man," she said. "You seem to have caused quite a commotion over at the college."

And the chanting crowd said, "Rip his evil flesh in half, stomp him into the ground."

"Yes, ma'am, I do believe I have upset the boys and girls a bit. But, don't worry, they're young—they'll eventually get over it."

Then her curious smile turned wry and she said, "To be honest, young man, I don't care if they get over it or not. I wouldn't mind if they all choked on their own spit."

The mob said, "Smite the demon, make him bleed, crack his head."

"Do I detect a touch of anger in your view of the youthful

263

scholars of Brother Earl University?"

"You're darn tootin' you do, Son. I'd like to take my cane and whack the smugness out of a few of them, that's for sure." And then she laughed and said, "You've really got them going, don't you?"

"They do seem a trifle miffed at me."

And the holy children cried, "Call Brother Earl! Call Brother Earl—he'll kill the devil! He'll kill the devil!"

"Tell me," I asked, "what causes you to have such animosity toward the decent boys and girls of the university?"

"Don't get me wrong," she began, "I'm a God-fearin' Christian and I have been all of my life. My mama and daddy taught me about Jesus and His Christian love and took me to church every Sunday I can remember as a child. And I still go to church every Sunday morning that my hip isn't too stiff, or that it's not raining too hard— I have to take the bus. I know Jesus understands."

"I'm sure He does," I said.

"Well, these Brother Earl people might call themselves Christians but, I'll tell you right now, they aren't. They might carry around crosses and pray all of the time but that doesn't make Christians out of them."

The mob sang, "We're going to burn you, Blake! We're going to burn you, Blake!"

"He sends them into town in groups and they stand around with their stupid looking smiles and tell folks they're going to burn in Hell if they don't listen to Jesus and Brother Earl—and what they mean is just listen to Brother Earl. That Brother Earl is just a sawed-off, fat-faced devil, I'll tell you. I know he is."

"Did they ever do anything to you?"

"Don't misunderstand this, Young Man. I'm not a drunk. But I do enjoy going down to the Beacon Lounge around three o'clock in the afternoon and having a couple of bourbon and cokes and cooling off a bit with my friends. We've been getting together like that for years—you know, a bunch of old fogies having a few drinks and kind of forgetting about our aches and pains for a little while before we go back to our empty apartments or to the tiny bedrooms our children stick us in when we have to live with them."

"It sounds like a good time."

"Well, it is and it doesn't hurt anybody. I'm sure the Lord doesn't get too upset about it either. Then one day I got down to the

Beacon and all of my friends were just standing out on the sidewalk—mad as the dickens and fit to be tied. I asked what was the matter and they said to go on inside and I'd see for myself. I said, 'Okay,' and went on in. After standing in the entryway for a minute for my eyes to get used to the dim light, I saw what was wrong. Every table, every booth, every single barstool in the place was filled with Brother Earl people just sitting there looking holy and drinking Nehi sodas."

"Every chair in the bar?"

"There wasn't a seat left in the house, and, not only are most of us too old and broken down to stand up and drink it's also illegal in this county. You have to be sitting down before they'll serve you. Those brats had no right to stick their big noses into our business. They sat there all cocky and self-righteous while old folks were standing outside in the heat of the day nearly fainting."

"Was there anything you could do about it?"

"You bet there was. We might be old but we're not helpless. I went over to the bar and said to one of them, 'Pardon me, young man, will you give an old lady a seat, please?' And, of course, he just faced me and said, 'Praise the Lord,' and then turned back around to his bottle of orange pop on the bar. So, I got into a real fury and I bopped him one on the arm with my cane and I said to him, 'Young man, you are disrespectful, you are impudent and rude.' And then I started really hollering, 'You lousy, no good so and so, and then I just spun around a time or two and flopped right down on the floor as if I'd died.

"Well, that got them stirring off their holy duffs. My friends outside heard the commotion and came rushing in yelling about how they'd killed an innocent old lady and all the Brother Earl missionaries jumped up and were running around scared they'd really killed me and as soon as they got up it didn't take my friends long to sit down. Then my friend Charlie who had saved me a stool just calmly said, 'It's okay now, Sadie. You can get up.'"

While the students were chanting something about decapitation, Sadie and I sat there on the bus stop bench having a real good laugh.

The bus came, we got on, and she showed me where to get off downtown. I found a music store and bought the banjo and a beer store where I bought the cooler. I just told the clerk to give me my change in Budweiser and then caught a bus back to the university.

On the way downtown I had asked Sadie if she knew why the students hadn't crossed the street and tried to tear me to shreds while we were waiting. She answered that she wasn't sure of the reason but thought it had something to do with needing a pass before they were allowed to leave the campus.

8 War

"Think it might rain, Earl?"

"Sure is gettin' powerful dark, praise the Lord, isn't it, Blake?"

"I'd better warn you about something, Earl. You can't kill me. I might step out into the street and be squashed by a bus, or have a belch backfire and choke to death on a popcorn husk, but, Earl, you just aren't holy enough to kill me."

"I do the Lord's work. No mortal can stand in His path, hallelujah. No mortal can resist His might."

"Bullshit. You do Brother Earl's work, that's all. And looking around us here, it seems like it must pay a pretty fair salary—a lot more than a man might make running a spot welder, don't you think, Earl?"

"The Lord shall smite the sinner," he shouted with arms raised to the swirling sky.

"You're making a big mistake, Earl,"

The sky was black with clouds and the air was a yellow-green. The wind tore through the crowd of praying and cheering students and wrapped its dire torrents about me. I felt the hairs upon my head rising toward the energy of the sky. I said to myself, "I sure hope I don't blow this and end up diving under the ruffles of some Sister Earl's petticoat."

I breathed the Power from the symbol of the air. I breathed deeply, mightily.

Earl stood there in an opening made for him in the multitude below me—his chubby face illuminated by the eerie light and the cold passion of his evil eyes glaring at me with the full force of the storm he had created. "And the Lord shall smite the sinner," he shouted as in a rush the roaring, rumbling might of the elements bore down upon me to the screaming voice of the mob saying, "Praise Brother Earl, Praise Brother Earl."

And from the depths of the darkest cloud a mighty bolt of lightning ripped from the heavens to the Earth and with a terrible explosion cracked through the roof of a nearby dormitory and was gone.

The air smelled of ozone. The crowd became silent. Brother Earl stood stunned as smoke rose from the smoldering roof. I pitched another empty can of Budweiser on the lawn and, as I carefully leaned my banjo against the ice chest, with an extreme effort at maintaining a semblance of self-control, I said, "Hell of a shot, Earl."

Earl started to raise his arms again but must have realized the sky was clearing and dropped them limply to his sides.

"Now, just tell me a couple of things, Earl, and don't try any of your bullshit on me. You've got to tell me right now. Why did you kill my wife? I've got to know. Were you just throwing your power around or was there some deep, dark reason you had for what you did? You've got to tell me."

"The Lord will... "

"Earl!" I shouted, only then realizing how forcefully emotion was beginning to thoroughly dominate the regions of thought and reason within my mind. "Why did you kill her, Earl? She was sweet and kind and pretty and you burnt her to a crisp, Earl. Tell me why?"

He knew he had to answer.

"You had to be taught. You were being irreverent at the factory. I could tell it. You didn't have any decent respect about you. You had to be taught."

"You killed her to teach me respect?" I said with a hysterical shaking in my voice. "That's it? That's the entire reason?"

Building in me I could feel the same mad rage that must drive the fiends.

Brother Earl feared me.

"Tell it all," I said as I slowly walked down the hill to where he stood.

"There was more," he said. As I approached him the students backed farther away. He was alone.

"It was a kind of experiment." He spoke nakedly, flatly. Even his dialect was abandoning him.

"An experiment," I said with terrible, quiet rage in my voice.

"Yeah. I had learned some Powers from some folks and it was time to try them out."

And the blackness rose up inside of me and colored me and swelled huge within me. With great strides I stepped down the hill to get directly into the face of Brother Earl. I commanded all manner of elements as cruelly as any devil of Hell. He was doomed.

"Damn your wretched soul!" I roared and with the wrath of a mighty Priest, I punched the pathetic bastard right in his fat ugly nose.

No bolt of lightning could have been half so effective.

With a trickle of blood running down his upper lip he sat sprawled upon the grass. The throng that had been his following began dispersing from the field to find other charismatic insanity. Brother Earl and his evil powers were finished.

Wiping his bloody nose and nearly sobbing he replied, "It was that uppity professor that told me. I swear it was. He said for me to use my powers for the good of mankind and then when I attacked the irreverent he called me a Frankenstein. Said I was a monster. Just doin' the Lord's work and he talked to me that way. It ain't right."

"Professor. Did you say 'professor'?"

"Holy Christ," came the voice from behind me. It was crazy Mike with the jagged teeth and the wildman eyes. It was Mike who had spoken. "That bastard Fintin was in on it from the start."

9 How It Ended

It was going to be very simple back at the Willow City Truth Center. We would talk a bit, then I would strangle him.

I cornered him in his study and demanded, "Why!"

"Because they killed my wife. I told you about that—they dropped a bloody tree right on her lap."

"Earl killed your wife?"

"No. No, Blake. It was the early ones. The prototypes—Dr. Hazzard and the rest. They had to be destroyed and I honestly thought Earl might do the job."

"So, he was to be your weapon against the murderers of your wife."

"Yes, you could say that."

Fintin was frightened of me but not really surprised by my arrival. He knew if I defeated Earl I would eventually find my way back to him. I think he might have been relieved by this confrontation so long in the coming.

"But why my Lori? Why did you have Earl kill Lori?"

"I never meant it to happen that way. It had been my intention that Brother Earl become a champion of the right causes. But, as you of all people well know, it totally backfired on me and, God forgive me, on your wife. I told him to go out and flex his new muscles, so to speak—try out the Powers we had channeled through him. I honestly believed he would just give a Sunday, fire-and-brimstone sermon replete with some special effects. You know, some pyrotechnics to get the attention of his flock. He misunderstood my intent and went out to 'do right' by picking a fight with you. I didn't realize what he had done until too late. Once he realized the power he commanded he was out of my control. I didn't even realize who his victim was until we talked at graduation."

"So, you might say," I said with rapid breath and lightness in my burning skull, "there was a little breakdown in communication between you and your student. Now there's some irony, isn't it. Dr. Byron Fintin, Professor of English. Dr. Fintin, the great communicator."

"Ironic. Perhaps. Look, Blake, I moved too fast, that's what happened. I was so blinded by hate and remorse I didn't think it all through and then it was too late."

"I see. Now, what's this ridiculous Committee of yours about?"

"Oh, The Committee is no joking matter. It's a genuine effort to combat the evil of such vermin as Brother Earl. I knew we had to get rid of Brother Earl and I knew I couldn't do it on my own for fear of creating another monster. I needed The Committee."

"Why?"

"So I could take carefully-measured action to correct the threat I had created without further endangering innocent people such as your wife. Until you gathered your forces and were willing to take on Earl, it was the hope I had. And it was exceedingly safe."

"What do you mean?"

"Jackson, there is nothing in this world slower moving, or more deliberate than a committee of academics."

I stepped toward him and in my mind I could see his gaunt face turning black, his body limp, his erudite voice crushed to pleading rasps. And then, just short of actually grabbing his bony throat, I let go of the wicked vision, shrugged my shoulders, and walked away thinking of how much like a duck was the learned professor.

And then it was very late, or early, I suppose, and the High Priest of Hallelujah sat shivering upon the cold steel of the railroad track that ran behind an abandoned structure that once had been Izzy's Highway Hamburger Haven, and, strumming his banjo, waited for the 2:17 westbound train.

271

10 At Last

"Are you sure this is the way you want it to end?" asked a familiar voice.

"Where have you been all this time? I could have used some help."

"I've been watching."

"Not a bad show, was it?"

"I do not think I could have improved upon it myself, Jackson. I might not have been quite so haphazard in my methods, but, I don't believe I could have gotten any better results. You have pretty well taken care of business for this lifetime."

"It hasn't been easy. And, as you can see by the fact I'm sitting here on a railroad track, it has taken its toll on my sensibilities."

"I never told you it was going to be easy."

"It's all over, Glory."

"Not really."

"I know. But I can't believe it's safe, even now."

"You have confronted your enemy and you have emerged victorious. Just don't pick any more fights with supernatural thugs and you will do fine. Now, you don't really want to sit there and let a train run over you, do you?"

"I'm not sure. It all seems so poetic this way. Such a perfect circle. Over there in the grass is where Lori and I first made love right after the terrible roar of this damned 2:17 train had revealed the immense passion that was in our hearts. This train began it. Why shouldn't it also end it?"

"Poetic perhaps. But it's going to be so messy. Is it absolutely necessary? Are you sure you're completely finished with this turn of your world?"

"You think it's going to be okay now?"

"Safe enough—at least until we stir it up again. Now, have I ever misled you?"

"No. You've scared the hell out of me a time or two, but you haven't led me wrong yet."

"Then trust me. You and whomever you might allow to come into your life are as safe as any mortals on the planet—no more; no less."

"That safe, huh?"

"Yes."

"Well, in that case, there is a matter of a hundred-dollar debt I owe a mutual friend of ours back in Arizona."

"An honest man should pay his debts."

"But, damn, it's too late anyway."

"Irrevocable fate?"

"No. Nothing so profound."

"Then what's the problem?"

"I think my ass is frozen to the track."

And as he helped me up we laughed, for there shall always be laughter where there is the human spirit.

"Thanks, my friend," I said. "Now tell me, how are things in Heaven? I heard of a fellow named Milton Larbletter who could bake potatoes with God's invisible rays beaming down from an ambient force field. Was he right about Heaven or was he just another wild-eyed guesser like all the *ism*-builders?"

"I couldn't tell you. I didn't learn any more about the absolute nature of the Universe from Heaven's lofty perspective than I did from the dusty floor of the desert. I just knew the Absolute, I didn't dissect it. I don't have answers, I have experiences."

"Kind of like in life, right?"

"Yes, Jackson. Just like in life: no answers, only the times we live and the feelings we share. It seems like we get into the biggest trouble when we start answering the questions."

"Brother Earl and company."

"Exactly. And I'll tell you, when in Heaven, the best part is that there aren't any questions. An Absolute is not an effect, it can't be. Perhaps we scientists and mystics and poets have missed the point all along by seeking dimensions of understanding that do not exist. Maybe, Jackson... maybe there are no questions in Heaven because, in fact, there are only answers."

"And the answers, Glory. Was it worth the climb to get to the answers?"

"Indeed, it was worth the climb."

"Glory, tell me about music in Heaven."

"How it sings, Jackson. Like no sound upon the Earth."

"... and the light."

"Such a glow, such spectra, My Friend."

"... and, Glory. How about the women?"

"Get your mind out of the gutter, Jackson."

"I was just wondering."

"I know what you wonder. I can tell you this much. All that we sense of love in its emotional and physical aspects upon this earthly plane is but a single dimension, a single color of a kaleidoscopic array beyond means of comparison."

"How could you stand it?"

"It was a challenge, but..."

"So, what are you doing down here in mortal world of tin-eared tunes and so-so sex?"

"I've got a few matters I need to take care of."

"Yes?"

"Well, first of all, obviously, I needed to save you from a poetic squashing beneath the wheels of the 2:17."

"Why?"

"Jackson, now that you've survived the Darkness, it is time for you to go into this world and share the Light."

"Okay, that makes sense. I can do that. But how about you? Are you going to head back up to Heaven for another feathery orgy?"

"Not just right now."

"Why not?"

"It turns out that Heaven is the pure form of what is adulterated by mortality and called life."

"Is it too perfect? Are you bored?"

With a gentle laugh he replied, "No, Jackson. I'm not bored, just enlightened. I think I'll roam this humble planet with you for a lifetime or two more and see what we can do to save it from self-destruction before I retire to infinite bliss."

"So, you've only been gone for a short time and already you miss the old aches and pains and miseries of the world."

"I don't miss anything. I realize that Heaven and Earth are but greater and lesser degrees of awareness of the same thing. It means that evil and good, Brother Earl and Lori Blake, sand storms and swirling seas, you and me, Kitty and Carrie out in Arizona, and the choirs of Heaven above—we are all facets of the same magnificent Diamond."

I looked at Glory and realized he had not left Heaven. Rather, Heaven was with him. He and Heaven and all the Celestial Wonders were always as close as any of us would let them be. I had been hearing the Songs in the sound of Lori's sweet and subtle laughter resounding through all of those years.

There was a powerful rumble roaring our way from the east.

"Come on, Jackson, grab that banjo. Let's catch this westbound freight of yours and get on with our work."

"But, it will be flying through here."

"What's the matter, Kemo Sabe? You scared of a train.?"

"Did you say, 'Kemo Sabe'? I've heard that before, and not just on Saturday morning cowboy shows."

Glory stepped closer. He wore a single feather. He was as old as all my histories and as ageless as the spirit that forever dwells within me.

"I am your Spirit Guide and a genuine transmigrated Angel of Heaven. And you, Jackson, are the High Priest of Hallelujah. Don't you think with such credentials we can catch a fast-moving train?"

"Yes, My Friend. I think we can."

Other Works by Robert Nichols

Most of these titles are currently published as e-Books available through all the major distributors—Kindle, Nook, etc. Also, printed editions are in process through Amazon Books. Gradually, I will get them out—hey, it's a lot of work.

Books etc.

The Kristin Book (1987)

Story of the first fifteen years of the life of my daughter who was born with Down Syndrome.
This book, reissued with an update, is now available in eBook format as *The Kristin Book: Update 2013*

Take the Aspen Train (1988)

Co-authored with Edward Larsh. Coffee table, Colorado history / social philosophy / train book. *(No longer available.)*

Adventures in the High Wind (1990)

Collection of my poems, stories, and essays.
    eBook edition, 2013.
    Paperback edition 2017

Leadville, U.S.A (1993)

Co-authored with Edward Larsh. Oral history of Leadville, Colorado. *(No longer available.)*

The High Priest of Hallelujah (1999)

Niche-less novel of poetic vision, humor, and satire.
eBook edition, 2015.

Summer Words, 2000 (2001)

Collection of short essays about laughter, God, knife throwing and much more.
e-Book edition, 2014.

The Booklets (2001 and...)

12-14 page booklets of poetry, short stories, essays—you know: literature. Currently there are five of these little gems published with more to come. Some day…

The Five Great Truths of Uncle Bob (2002)

A culminating work of philosophy, religion, and practical wisdom (and all on one side of a sheet of paper).

God of the Poets (2003)

It took me twenty years to get this one right. When I finished the first version in '83 I didn't know enough to write my own novel. Perhaps now I do. I was pretty much just a stenographer for the real author, God. This isn't traditional stuff. It's a story of art, love, humanity and... *the purpose of life.*
e-Book edition, 2014.

Albatross: The Curse of Honesty (2013)

The first novel I wrote, and re-wrote, and finally published. It's a funny and touching tale of a fellow whose life is nearly destoyed by the curse of absolute honesty.

The Great Book of Bob (2009)
***The Great Book of Bob* eBook edition** (2014)

    A unified collection of humorous, soul-wrenching, and harshly honest tales and thoughts gleaned from a lifelong love story—stories of a poet's love of sunrises, poetic epiphanies, laughter, and for the soulmate of his life. And the best part about it, it's not some icky-sticky, lovey-poo bunch of hearts and flowers. It's hard-edged wonder and real reason for all of us to be glad to be alive. I tell *my* stories that we may each realize the significance of our own.

Uncle Bob's Big Book of Happy (2017)

I should make this clear from the start. None of this is easy. The first chapter of this work starts out saying exactly that: This will not be easy. I tell some hard truths. Don't be misled by the mirthful lilt of my title. Uncle Bob here will do his best to help you be happy, but none of this means diddly-squat if you can't face harsher aspects of our everyday journey. I write this book in hopes that my stories, theories, blathering bilge and sublime prayers may be of help to you in avoiding the burden, the curse of bitterness. It's no fun living in a world of bitchy whiners, angry jerks, and cranky bastards. You know what I mean.

THE FOOTLOCKER SERIES

This is a series of eBooks gleaned from fifty years of writing excavated from Robert Nichols' old footlocker of notebooks and scraps of papers—the repository of a life of art.

For information contact Robert Nichols at Mtmuse44@aol.com.

Titles:

about Time
about Mountain Living
about Seasons
about Paths

about Time: Poems and Other Stories (2015)

The first in the series—poetry, stories, and photography about ancient time, the time of children, the time of young adults, and the time of growing old. It's really not about time at all. This is a book about life.

about Mountain Living: Finding a Way (2015)

A journey told in story and poem. A life trek from discontent and restlessness to commitment and discovery. This work tells of a succession of habitats and lifestyles progressing farther and farther from the city and further into a better destiny—from apartment to cabin to tipi to hilltop shrine of art, nature, and spirit. A journey from complacent certainty to out-on-the-edge primal survival. Perhaps my story will encourage yours. And, beyond the tale I tell, just read the poems and stories as the art they are intended to be. You will laugh and weep and contemplate—you will be changed.

about Seasons: the Wind and Weather of Our Days (2016)

Poems of the seasons—not just some cliché sweetness about leaves and blossoms either. This is the core stuff of being. Seasons, wind, and weather—the fierce and beautiful power of Nature that can keep us humble and exhilarated throughout our lives. It is the very "life and death" intensity of these metamorphic cycles that excites the turning of our years with risk and wonder. Time takes away our days, storms wash away our safety, seasons etch our flesh with danger. Old Spirits out on the plains once told me, "Earth shall never be tame... celebrate your fear and feel you are alive!" Yes!

about Paths: Journeys Through Wonder, Danger, and Self (2017)

The fourth in the Footlocker Series of books published by Robert Nichols, *about Paths* is another collection of beautiful and moving poetry and thought-provoking essays. Robert artfully takes you with him as he recounts youthful journeys hitchhiking the country, expresses vignette word-sketches of people and places along the way throughout the years, and gives a sense of purpose to the paths all of us take.

Read these works and you will know the harsh and enlightening truths of the road, you will contemplate the ugly realities of American racism, you will observe the humor and pathos of the passing scene—you will travel the path of an open-hearted poet.

Robert Nichols—former school teacher, carpenter,
truck driver, factory worker, Maytag Man, etc.—
is a poet, novelist, essayist, etc. who writes, carves, sings,
and loves life with his family in Oregon.

www.ingramcontent.com/pod-product-compliance
Lightning Source LLC
Chambersburg PA
CBHW071301170626
46809CB00001B/315